(In)Human

by

Britt Field

This is a work of fiction. Names, characters, places, and incidents are either the product of the author's imagination or are used fictitiously, and any resemblance to actual persons living or dead, business establishments, events, or locales, is entirely coincidental.

(In)Human

COPYRIGHT © 2021 by Britt Field

Cover Art by *The Wild Rose Press, Inc.*

The Wild Rose Press, Inc.
PO Box 708
Adams Basin, NY 14410-0708
Visit us at www.thewildrosepress.com

Publishing History
First Edition, 2021
Trade Paperback ISBN 978-1-5092-3811-8
Digital ISBN 978-1-5092-3812-5

Published in the United States of America

"Be ye angyal or be ye daemon?" Melek asked his question again as though it were a choice, as if we could select which path to walk, or fly—once my wings grew in anyway—lest my daemon genes proved more dominant, keeping my fleshy appendages dormant and buried within my scapulae. Currently, the single thing I was sure was growing between my shoulder blades was a puddle of flop sweat. The room's temperature seemed to have risen in the seconds I sat there.

I shouldn't have been frightened by the query posed to every hybrid, yet I was. Answering whether I'd follow the Word of Gabriel or the teachings in the Book of the Morning Star wouldn't merely affect me or my list of universities. It wouldn't be a mere designation on my identification card next to sixty-four inches tall, auburn hair, etcetera. It would affect everyone in my life, including my family, friends, my beau, and how society might view me.

Judging by the disgusted tone at the latter part of his sentence it was obvious how the vice principal wanted me to respond. Behind him hung a gigantic oil painting of a long-dead officer in a disbanded angyal army. General Dumah was famous for allegedly decapitating daemons and showcasing their heads on pikes with their severed tails jammed into their mouths. This occurred days after they'd been nailed to a crossbar affixed to a post and succumbed to asphyxia. Melek maintained he displayed the portrait for posterity.

Dedication

For my brother.

Chapter 1

"Be ye angyal or be ye daemon?"

A bulging dread surged up my core. It tugged at my chin until my gaze plunged to the floor. I gulped. Angyal or daemon? The question thrummed through my blanking mind and drowned out all other noise. I no longer heard the opening and closing of metal lockers in the hallway, nor the ticking clock on the wall, or my feet shifting nervously below my seat. My sandals tapped against the wooden chair leg in rhythm with the thrumming. The preliminary interview prior to The Fateful Inquiry—I wasn't expecting it today.

"Miss Zephon," the words were slightly muffled, "it's disrespectful not to face someone speaking to you."

I peeked upward to see Vice Principal Melek still sitting at his desk and sternly peering at me over his steep nasal hump. Each exhale comedically fluttered his lengthy nose hairs and a lone bristle sprouting from one of his many moles. They clustered everywhere, garnishing his ears, mug, and neck in brownish nuggets. He couldn't carry one more unless he held it in his hand, and I couldn't resist playing connect the dots.

"Amitiel, has thy hearing gone?"

My hearing? Is that what this was, a trial by judge? Because my aural faculties were fine. "Sorry?" I abhorred the feeling I always had to apologize, like I'd done something inexplicably wrong. It was a conditioned response to be remorseful, sorrowful, or despicable ingrained in a curriculum they titled the Values of Femininity. A caveat to graduating secondary school was taking four years of classes in Hospitality and Politeness—be obliging and never complain, Etiquette—say please and thanks in an octave higher than normal, and a contradictory course in Modesty and Advanced Cosmetology—I'm pretty. Don't look at me! Bonus points for those who signed up for the online newsletter touting the virtues in compliance and docility.

"Be ye angyal or be ye daemon?" Melek asked his question again as though it were a choice, as if we could select which path to walk or fly—once my wings grew in anyway—lest my daemon genes proved more dominant, keeping my fleshy appendages dormant and buried within my scapulae. Currently, the single thing I was sure was growing between my shoulder blades was a puddle of flop sweat. The room's temperature seemed to have risen in the seconds I sat there.

I shouldn't have been frightened by the query posed to every hybrid, yet I was. Answering whether I'd follow the Word of Gabriel or the teachings in the Book of the Morning Star wouldn't merely affect me or my list of universities. It wouldn't be a mere designation on my identification card next to sixty-four inches tall, auburn hair, etcetera. It would affect everyone in my life, including my family, friends, my beau, and how society might view me.

Judging by the disgusted tone at the latter part of his sentence, it was obvious how the vice principal wanted me to respond. Behind him hung a gigantic oil painting of a long-dead officer in a disbanded angyal army. General Dumah was famous for allegedly decapitating daemons and showcasing their heads on pikes with their severed tails jammed into their mouths. This would occur days after they were nailed to a crossbar affixed to a post and succumbed to asphyxia. Melek maintained he displayed the portrait for posterity, heritage, and history—not hate, all the while proudly wearing a crossbar pendant tie clip.

"I am, uh…" Anxiety tightened my larynx, like Melek's very glare was choking me, starving me of oxygen. I envisioned bounding through the awning window to sprint seventy miles down the asphalt road, dodging cars and cyclists crossing the West River Bridge before scaling the perimeter wall that encircled our realm, separating us from the tornado-plagued Barren.

Would the sentries plead for me to halt as much as my aching lungs would beg me to? The furlongs of barricades were meant to keep creatures out, not in. Would the guards bother stopping me? Surely they'd lower their crosshairs, realizing I'd be one less consumer sucking limited resources. They'd likely open the pylon, saying to themselves, "That lunatic must've drunk mercury milkshakes for breakfast. Good riddance!" I'd clamber over and land in a desolate eroding wasteland teeming with remnants of a forgotten, battle-scarred world. But I'd be free.

"Well?" Melek's sharp nostrils practically threatened to cut me if I didn't reply.

"Um…" *Who am I, or who do I want to be?* Why did I have to choose? And why did I only have two options? My mother was born of angyals, my father of

3

an angyal and a daemon. As a mixed-blood, I was drawn to each kindred. What does it even mean to be one or the other?

Some archaic tomes stated we all die, travel into an alternate universe called Empyreus, and either become reincarnated in human form or suffer for our sins in the inferno of Avern. The scripture's failure to expound on its vague doctrine molded my skepticism like clay and baked it in an Atheist brand kiln at three hundred and twenty-five degrees. The pottery vases of doubt and disbelief sat on an imaginary shelf collecting dust. Religion was a social construct devised to deny one's culpability in his or her actions and often used to defend indefensible acts.

I dared not ask the vice principal his opinion nor disclose my agnosticism. "I am," I coughed to clear the gravel from my throat before blurting, "I'm neither, and I'm both."

He rolled his beady eyeballs. "Despite your emotions, the answer will evince itself soon. We'll have a second meeting in the future with the other board members."

"Great." I forced a smile. From the frying pan to the firepit.

He consulted a sticky note atop his desk. "Ah, before that, you need to schedule a physical exam and provide the medical record proving you're healthy and received all your vaccinations."

I shivered at the thought of butt-baring hospital gowns and new medical technicians practicing on me with a hypodermic needle. "I already had my booster shots."

"These are different. Just make the appointment."

He crumpled the paper and tossed it into his trashcan. "If you need guidance, I can give you my private number."

Gag a maggot. I bet the ole coot's digits weren't the only private thing he intended to bestow. "Appropriate personal reflection time is all that's needed."

He jotted a notation into a folder and waved me away as if I were an annoying fly.

I snatched up my book bag and hustled out of his office, hoping my mane was long enough to cloak the damp patch that had formed on my blouse.

"Hey, hey, whoa." Mrs. Gadreel, the school receptionist, waggled a pen and card at me. She was riding the tail end of an angry bout of conjunctivitis. "Sign for your hall pass."

"Uhhhh…" and risk getting a goopy virus?

Pinkeye was very contagious and prevalent among children. Her *WORLD'S BEST NANA* coffee tumbler provided a hint to how she contracted it. She scratched at her crusty red lids with a crinkly tissue. "Come on, missy, take it." She leaned toward me.

I blanched as my lymph nodes linked arms to tow me away. "Nahhhh…"

"Sign it so I can stamp it for you."

The three twenty-five bell dinged. *Hallelujah!* I had five minutes to get to class. "I won't need it." I thanked her and departed the main office.

My friends, all wearing concerned furrowed brows, greeted me outside. They were a blend of angyals, daemons, and hybrids, so they yearned to know what side I'd pick. Since I was the oldest, almost eighteen, my choice would set a precedent for our group. I loathed the uneasiness it brought.

Hardly a decade had elapsed following the latest heir to the Gold administration assuming the governorship and desegregating public schools. The Golds were a political dynasty having served on a gamut of prominent positions: city comptrollers, mayors, governors, military officers, classic backslappers, and butt-kissers. They claimed they could trace their lineage to before the common era. Presently, they campaigned on a progressive platform to promote tranquility without enacting specific laws defining discrimination. The Establishment believed it was unnecessary because, they professed, "Prejudice doesn't exist." The unwritten rule stated exposing intolerance equals promoting it, so deprive it of attention, and it'll die. Their priority was assimilation and harmony, not gender equity or inclusivity.

Governor Sachiel Gold was too preoccupied with the legal case against his spouse to govern. His wife, Nanael, struck and killed four pedestrians with her rental car during a driving tour in East Realm. She absconded from the scene and repudiated extradition. Easterners demanded justice, saying they were sick of western politicians abusing diplomatic immunity to escape prosecution for crimes. The Golds' joint refusal to accept the repercussions endangered the delicate state of our peaceful diplomacy and trade accords.

More than a half-century prior, our progenitors had paid the price for a racially charged civil war. Those ruthless battles, combined with Earth's catastrophic weather phenomena, decimated sections of the country and large chunks of the population who dwelled there. Their petrochemical bombs enkindled bushfires, generating so much heat they created their own weather systems. Refugees already fleeing a war had to dodge dry lightning storms and fire cyclones raining down from pyro cumulonimbus clouds. Most areas were left unrestored and uninhabited, except for the landlocked East and West realms—each containing about twenty thousand square miles—and the vast highway connecting them.

Gossip circulated about a colony branching off the two realms and vanishing into the northern tundra. The story's versions changed depending on the teller. Was it a scavenger party, researchers, anarchists, criminals who'd been excommunicated, or citizens driven out by hatred?

Regardless of the truth, search parties weren't dispatched, and from then on, inter-realm travelers and supply trucks required armored transport with a motorcade of escorts to shuttle them to and fro. The bulletproof transport shuttle, fitted with grappling claws, could anchor itself in the ground to withstand winds produced by sporadic twisters blowing along the Tempest Belt. Passengers experienced a tense three-hour trip. On seldom occasions, they didn't survive the journey, although their convoy did. Shredded communication lines and ruptured highway lanes devoid of any trace sent the bereaved scrabbling for clues.

WHAT BEFELL THE MISSING? was spray-painted on the wall's concrete blocks because law enforcement kept removing the posters staked into the ground. So many signposts had accumulated it resembled a picket fence. The government's hushed explanations on the unsolved incidents proved their apathy in peace-keeping. They furnished no clear plan on improved security or protection within our walls from bigotry they declined to acknowledge.

Even if they had, our region was averse to change and slower than a tortoise runs regarding implementation. Leaders wouldn't decide how to proceed, stating, "Disagreements are normal. Behaviors perceived or misperceived as micro-aggressions are not worth starting a war. We've received your complaints and shall discuss methods to improve our environment." Those discussions fell short of ever reaching a decision.

How was I, a notoriously indecisive damsel, going to bear such a similar responsibility deciding what identity to adopt, especially if it meant I might have to leave my realm? I disliked leaving my sector to visit the other three, and they were all within West Realm. For teens such as me, the scary unknown beyond the barricades meant death. I was uncertain what to tell the four curious faces gawking at me.

"We've been waitin' forever out here." Vasiariah, the most outspoken angyal, broke the silence first. Slender and statuesque, she had beauty pageant good looks and beauty pageant wins thanks in part to her dramatic monologues embellished with windmill-mimicking arm gestures. They were as prominent as her rouged cheekbones. She was *extra* to the max. "Is something wrong? We're on pins and needles." She proceeded to use those pins to needle me for information. "Are you in trouble?" she poked. "What happened in there? Were you dress-coded?"

Our school had a policy book on dress code, largely targeting females. Staff members could accost us on the basis we were breaching the rules and distracting male pupils. Their presumption was our guilty verdict. We were scapegoats for males to shirk accountability for their thoughts and deeds. Our semi-bare shoulders or kneecaps, apparently capable of sending observers spiraling into unbridled carnal fits, could get us suspended.

"You *are* looking hot today. Did Holy Moly try his private number trick?" Mahlen's mischievous grin twinkled. "I know I would have."

Mahlen had been my beau since we started high school. We met in the library. I was reading about mythology when a silverfish squirmed from a dusty book jacket and startled me. I shrieked, stumbled out of the bookcase aisles and into Mahlen's thewy biceps. "Head over heels for me, eh?" He'd asked as if he'd memorized the line from a rom-com script.

We remained inseparable since that day. He was cute, athletic, and drizzling charisma. Ninety-eight percent of his peers had crushes on him at some duration. I was the luckiest creature on the planet when he cast his baby blues upon me. I could blissfully get lost in his stare and forget I was different.

"Rein it in, captain hormones." Heat had done me no favors today. I peeled my blouse from the clammy spot on my back. "But yes, he did try it."

"We know what happened," Eleleth, a hybrid, interjected, "and it's not about tank tops." She was my best friend and had been since she introduced herself to me with a gentle peck on my nose in the daycare center her mother owned. She was a social butterfly in every sense of the phrase. Even the sable freckles on her septum coupled with the unique, curvy shape of her alae resembled a mini Monarch. "Give her a break. She'll tell us when she's ready."

Everybody grudgingly nodded.

Phew, thank goodness for Eleleth.

"So," she continued, "did Melek make you choose?"

Crap.

"What did you say?" Agares' almond eyes rounded. His combative temperament was stoked. He was a passionately political daemon who advocated for equal rights for all, and recently created a club called the Young Independents. He scheduled a meeting immediately after hearing the school receptionist call my name over the public address system. "Your birthday is months away. Why is he pressuring you?"

"He wasn't exactly pressuring me." It was more akin to an intimidating suggestion. "It was about colleges …"

"That would appeal to you if you declare yourself an angyal?" Agares possessed an adorably irritating knack for finishing my sentences.

I grumbled. In my peripheral, I saw Mr. Crocell swagger up to us in his skinny slacks. He kept those pant seams working overtime. He was too attractive to be a civics teacher, and he knew it. He also didn't seem old enough to have an education degree.

"Mahlen Forneus, you aren't bothering these lovely maidens, are you?" He inserted himself into our circle, lacking compunction about invading one's space.

"No, sir."

He patted Agares' sinewy tricep. "I swear, Mr. Gamigin, you grow half an inch every week. Doesn't he, gals?" He bumped his shoulder against Vasiariah's, which bumped her into Eleleth. He was too attentive to certain high schoolers. Moreover, he missed the irony of fraternizing with pupils when he taught lessons on workplace impropriety. "I miss having you scholars in my class this semester."

They blushed. Their conditioning to be demure kicked in. They were under the flirtatious spell cast by Crocell's squared jaw and hooded eyelids that gave him an air of mystery and made them feel special. The flattery had worn thin for me.

He strutted away. I felt as uncomfortable as his bum crack looked, overstuffed with trouser fabric. He probably triple-washed his underwear to clean the skid marks.

"Somebody give Vasi a handkerchief," Eleleth said. "She's drooling."

"Look who's talking. Your eyeballs are bugging far enough outta your skull."

Rivaling for a male's notice to increase their self-worth—another eye-rolling *Value of Femininity*. It could pit best pals against one another.

"No need to bicker. I'm positive he'd have a grossly inappropriate affair with both of you," Agares assured them.

They stopped bickering to counter his mocking remark. "Shut up!

"Yeah," Eleleth agreed. "Suck a fart!

"A wet one."

"Okay, okay, truce. I was teasing." He ran a hand through his dark hair. "Besides, I'm the one he was pawing at."

"Only because he knows I'm out of his league and in a relationship." Mahlen slung his arm around me.

I laughed at his joke, whether or not he was kidding. "Let's go before we get a tardy slip." I headed to my next class, and they followed. I was thankful Crocell, and his infamous pants, had interrupted my interrogation. I was ready to forget about the preliminary interview.

"Did Melek persuade you to pick angyal?" Mahlen asked.

Dang it. "I don't have to decide yet. It's not time. Besides, he said facts will evince themselves. Whatever that means." I shrugged. I didn't understand what he meant. He made it sound like I didn't truly have a choice at all. I, however, wasn't about to admit that to my pals.

"It means ole Rumpled Foreskin has a trick up his sleeve." Agares pivoted into his chemistry class.

Eleleth and Vasiariah entered the stairwell to their classroom, reciting the nickname and giggling.

"Don't fret, gorgeous. No matter what you pick, I'll support you."

"Oh really." I playfully squinted at Mahlen.

"What if I said my spirit animal is a wolf; therefore, I'm a wolf?"

"Then we'd howl at the moon together." He planted his warm lips on my cheek. I sensed how much he loved me and how much he longed for me to embrace my angyalic side due to his being an angyal. His body pressing firmly against mine made a good argument. He gave me a reassuring squeeze before letting go and announcing his presence into our classroom with a quick, "A woo!"

His teammates in the class howled back and milled around doing their silly secret handshakes. I was hailed with a bevy of hellos. I endeavored to answer them all.

"Hey, Daevah. Cute purse." It had a drawstring top and decorative rainbow beads.

"Thanks." Her eye shadow layers matched the colors on her beads and the clips pinning up her fawn tresses. "I saw yours and loved it."

I realized her bag was identical to mine except in the hue and bead placement. "Well, you've got great taste."

"Don't we." She hung the strap on her desk chair.

My concern hopscotched to the student with a teensy bandage on his neck. "Cass, what happened? You get bitten by a vampire?" I kidded. "Or a werewolf?"

"Close." He touched the square gauze patch, "Is it bleeding again? My sister's cat clawed me."

"Trying to rut it, perv?" Succu driveled from her desk nearest the door. Her tear ducts watered under the opaque, indigo liner slathered around her lids. She constantly appeared a bit unwell, like she was in an incessant feud with a sinus infection. Whatever she had, nobody else wanted. My grandpa would say the variation in her family's gene pool was too small. Others called her inbred.

"Ain't nobody talking to you, bee-otch," Cass riposted. "Bestiality is your thing."

"Humph!" She swiftly readjusted her sights. "Mahlen, hey." Her kinky hair cascaded down like sewer sludge. She wound a greasy strand of it around her chubby middle digit. "Mahlen!" Undeterred by his irrefutable disregard, she continued pestering. She was the sort of angyal with a reputation for flashing her winglet holes to anyone who unwittingly ventured into the grungy mobile home park where she resided, and she tended to fixate on those in relationships. "Hello! Mahlen!" She engaged in mild stalking and major lurking. "Oy, Mahlen, nithe jeanz." Her "s" sounds lisped amid her skewed yellow teeth.

"Uh-huh." He scuttled past her to converse with his buddy in the last row. "Hey, Turail, you see the game last night?"

I sauntered by Succu. Her rapacious, lipstick-smudged grin evaporated, leaving cracks in her cakey foundation. "Amitiel."

"Succu," I replied in a monotone. I refused to allot her the satisfaction of knowing her conduct irked me or the false impression she was competition. She was a plain, pitiable wretch from an indigent clan full of delinquents and offspring who didn't know who their fathers were. I'd felt sorry for her once. Howbeit, her infinite duplicity erased any sympathy her circumstances conjured. She rebuffed kindness and retaliated with belligerent rancor.

Unable to domineer her way into popularity, she seemed to seethe with envy at females she deemed a threat and sought notoriety by becoming their nemesis. Her unrelenting obsessions kept her from making real friends. She banded with insecure associates who harbored collective jealousies. Their shared sniggers, taunts, and whispers secreted in hisses from the overlooked corners where they skulked.

Even though they were categorized as poor trailer trash, they acted entitled, as if they were owed something because they were born angyals. They were wicked shrews known to incite physical altercations, either with their continual passive-aggressive comments or blatant gibes. Up to this time, they'd each gotten a well-deserved baseball glove, drink, fist, or foot thrown in their ugly mugs. The police would get called and scatter the roaches, but they wouldn't intercede.

One of the petulant cronies, Kalahzo, had been suspended from school after vandalizing a teacher's car and ordered to attend anger management therapy. She remained a ticking time bomb but worked harder at managing not to get caught. Succu's sister, Jahckristani, was less subdued. She was expelled once parents threatened to sue the school board for not protecting students from her menacing and erratic antics, like pulling out her super-sized and used sanitary pad and chucking it across the cafeteria.

Another bottom feeder buddy, Taiybethna, quit school due to an embarrassing episode during a fundraiser kickball practice. She kept finger-pointing, making bizarre threats, and angrily yowling, "Why won't you be my friend? I'll make *you* my friend! This must stop! Be my friend!"

Picturing her aberrant idea of friendship—being chained to a pipe underneath her mobile home next to mangled dolls with patchy scalps and plucked out eyeballs—heightened my fight or flight response. Aspiring to ease the tension, I invited my beau to accompany me on a walk. Taiybethna then brazenly stalked us around the venue like a rabid stray dog. She conveyed no intent to desist even after Mahlen barked at her, "Get lost, ya in-heat bitch!"

Her salivating mouth retreated from her bucked incisors as she kept iterating, "Whatcha gonna do 'bout it?"

The Phys. Ed. teachers didn't reprimand her, nor

bother the teens canoodling below the bleachers. They were preoccupied in their attempts to tongue-lash the student coaches of our grade. They hoped to hinder another loss to them.

Mahlen gestured to Mr. Charpston breathing down the napes of female students. "I guess teachers are just onlookers now, jizzing their jeans instead of doing their actual job."

I was twenty minutes past agitated, plus I needed to show I wasn't vulnerable prey. I threw my clipboard of team rosters onto the ground, clenched my fists, and hollered at Taiybethna to stay away from me and go home, or I'd kick her fat butt up between her shoulder blades. Thanks to my grandpa's boxing tutorials, I believed I could. She must've too, because she ran off with her tail between her legs. I still spent subsequent weeks guarding my six, anticipating her tossing a net over me and dragging me to her dismembered doll dungeon.

"Dang, you're frothing like a bloated cow, Succubus." Vehuel was a self-proclaimed class clown. He liked to holler "Stampede!" at Succu and her herd during the jogging portion of their Phys. Ed. class.

I was reminded of the story, *The Cow Bully*. My mother used to read it to me at bedtime. It was about a troubled bovine compelled to bully her classmates and who, after experiencing their wrath, amended her attitude and apologized.

"Thut up!" Succu whipped herself around to the front of the room, jiggling her biscuit dough body in the process. She'd spend the rest of class sneaking slack-jawed glimpses.

"Should we put down a *WET FLOOR* sign?"

Vehuel pretended to inspect the tile squares as he stroked his mahogany sideburns. They were larger than the facial hair guidelines in a subsection of the dress code, but males were never cited for breaking those rules. "You didn't slip in the sneaky liar's slobber pool, did you, Am?" His grudge stemmed from a rumor Succu disseminated which led to his and Eleleth's break-up when they were ninth graders. She claimed Eleleth had a furtive make-out session at a party. When Vehuel interrogated Eleleth about it, she was so furious at his insinuation she would fool around on him, and for believing a known liar like Succu, she ended their courtship.

"Shh." I put my forefinger to my lips. "Let's not dignify her actions with a response." Her inner turmoil was enough punishment. She lived a tortuous dichotomy, hating what she coveted simply because she could never have it and would never be it.

"You're too noble. It's another reason that malicious wench is so obsessed with you and Eleleth."

"And Tannin." I sat in the adjacent empty desk. "Hasn't she been driving by his house and honking the horn repeatedly?" She even sneaked into the wedding venue of Tannin's older brother, alleging she was invited and then had the outrageous gall to say *he* was stalking *her*.

Succu was a loose cannon. I didn't know if she was born fully crazy or her desperation to find a mate nurtured her craziness into full bloom. In a culture that assigned a currency to attractiveness and youth, and being young was all you had, you didn't have time for patience or rationale. And Tannin had no time for her bullcrap. He detested her, chiefly because she disrespected Caim, his high school sweetheart.

"Yeah, but I think her goal is more to irritate you and Caim than it is to get Tannin or Mahlen's fleeting acknowledgment."

"Double fail for her."

"That's right, babe." Mahlen sat beside me. "And the same for that psycho's crotch-scratching pals: Rat Face, Cellar Dweller, and Buck Teeth. You just know she's gnawed on a corn cob through a picket fence."

We all snickered.

"Now onto a better subject," Vehuel said. "Does Eleleth have a date for the dance? I'm thinking about asking her. Should I?"

"Uhhh." I didn't think I should speak for her, mainly because she was more interested in someone else.

Mahlen, observing me flounder for an answer, jabbered, "You should call her, bro. You can't make a shot you won't take."

"Settle down, class, and find your seats," the teacher said, her adorable pregnant tummy still conspicuous behind the lectern. She marked our names on her attendance roll. She double-checked the vacant desk in the fourth row.

Kamael Erlik had been absent since Wednesday, citing trauma from a midnight burglary at his house. The story aired on the local news. The robbers hadn't been apprehended. Poetic justice, really. Kamael was a thief himself, plus he used to say females weren't as smart as males because God hollowed out a section of their brains to make room for their 'verginers.'

"Open your history books to page one fifty-seven. We're discussing the Malleus Human Trials of

Antiquity."

A hand raised. "Ms. Hashmal."

"Yes?"

"Humans don't exist. Why do we have to study about them?"

She sighed with frustration from being questioned weekly about why history was a subject. She removed her humongous glasses, exposing the indentations they left in her ebony cheekbones. "It's a piece of our past, an ugly piece which must be recognized. It's a stain on our democracy. Dozens of innocent angyals and a few daemons were branded humans and executed. Those who don't learn from history are doomed to repeat it." She returned her spectacles to her face. "Plus, this will be on your quiz."

A second hand raised. "Was the unanimous animosity toward humans what brought angyals and daemons together?"

"Aye. The hypothetical human symbolized a step in our evolutionary chain some didn't want to accept."

"What prompted the investigators to think they were neither daemons nor angyals?"

"Upon examination, they had no tails nor wings, just scars near their shoulder blades or base of the spinal column where the apertures should've been." Ms. Hashmal spun and pointed to those spots on her lower dorsum and around her scapula. "The victims said their winglets had grown in so painfully deformed they were sliced off. They were disbelieved in the era, with their accusers alleging they'd mutilated themselves to shield their detection and that they'd used supernatural wizardry to alter their bodies. But we know now the atypical condition they suffered from is," she scribbled on the dry erase board, "*Amniotic Band Syndrome*. It occurs when bands develop from the inner lining of the amnion, attach to other parts of the anatomy, and constrict them, causing agonizing pain. The sole cure is amputation."

Ouch! I thought. *How horrible for them.* If guardian humans existed, they sure didn't help those poor angyals. I was nearly a grown-up, and I could see how silly that notion was. How did so many adults fall into mass hysteria over humans?

When I was little and terrified at night by phantasmal monsters underneath my bed, my grandmother, Marduza, attempted to pacify me by saying my guardian human was watching over me.

"You can't see them, yet they're there," she'd say. "They reside in the ethereal, and their prayers protect good little children."

"Protect me from everything?"

"Yes, dear." She'd tucked the quilt around me. "Unless you're very naughty." Her angular features, in my overactive imagination, would sharpen beneath the shadows into a sinister raven's beak. "Then Rawhide and Bloody Bones will get you."

"No, they won't." Mom traipsed past my bedroom door.

"They will." Grandma peck, peck, pecked with her beak, undermining my mother. They were nothing alike, not in personality nor physical traits. My mom was amiable and stunning with lustrous strawberry blonde hair and high cheekbones, whereas Grandma was as jagged as the cut of her jib and pricklier than her unplucked chin whiskers. "Best not risk it."

Rawhide and Bloody Bones. Their grisly monikers,

more descriptions than names, triggered a visceral reaction. I pictured a creature skinned alive, oozing blood and puss and hungering for vengeance; the other, a resurrected fiend in the form of a bleeding skeleton. They were urban legends told to make children behave. They also broke up monotonous fairytales about villainous females. An evil stepmother, cruel stepsisters, wicked witches, or tyrannical queens were always mistreating a helpless wannabe princess until she is rescued by a wealthy fellow who thinks she's pretty enough to marry.

Rawhide and his crime partner, Bloody Bones, lacked an origin story, and my lack of superstition didn't let me believe they were real. I also never believed humans were real because nobody had any proof. I read about them in comics and fantasy books.

Some said our creator fashioned invisible benevolent beings to console us in moments of woe. I figured my grandmother said it because it helped *her* feel better. She said tons of things that didn't make sense, namely outlandish guff rooted in fables or religion. Numerous odd ideas branched off her knowledge tree. But spirits help you if you attempted to bring up science in her mothball-scented house. That sickly-sweet odor permeated, too dense in the air for humans to move through it, despite how microscopic homunculi purportedly were.

Before Grandma Marduza moved into the old folk's home, and after she began gobbling medications like candy, she compelled me to attend church twice a month. The first day, I'd hear the declaimed word of Supreme Seraphim Gabriel at the patriarchal Gabrielites Church. The preachers changed, but the sermons ran on a loop. My only takeaway was females were cursed with a menstrual cycle and had to be subservient to return to God's good graces. Clearly, primitive barbarians had concocted these tales to explain events in nature, like thunder was a coughing deity. LOL. Yet Gabrielite males dug in their spurs and rode their magical unicorns to the finish line of power, leaving hoof marks on the backs of their sororal counterparts.

I had to bite my tongue to prevent my telling them to go screw themselves while simultaneously evading ole Molester Mastema. He tried to corner you, palms oozing prayer oil, and insist on praying for your soul. I rescued a young lad from him more than once. His deacon title kept him above reproach.

For the second day of church, it was the same meal cooked by a different chef—one more matriarchal. I'd listen to a Celestian service at the Morning Star Cathedral to learn about faith-based natural science prophesized by the astrology goddess, Celestia. One of her gospels explained God cursed the listless angyals with pale alabaster skin so they couldn't laze about enjoying the beauty of nature without enduring painful sunburns.

I didn't conform to the beliefs of either sect, who exhorted their congregations to forgo paying their bills in order to donate tithes to the church. I avoided the cultish atmospheres where sheep were led to bankruptcy slaughter. Both faiths condemned questions, scrutiny, and non-conformity.

I did enjoy learning about constellations, though. There was even one named for a human, Kushim. He appeared to be tied to a huge stake, presumably awaiting his execution by bonfire.

Eons ago, those suspected of being human, whether good or bad, were put on trial, scourged, and killed because their existence, particularly in physical form, was feared by angyal and daemon alike. They also seemed to resent the men and women. Nowadays, they pop up as helpful sprites in fairytales or in the minds of hardcore believers. They're pretty much only recalled as bedtime stories or used as a racial slur against somebody who's disliked, and only in a hushed timbre.

Slurs were hurled a lot after desegregation when angyals and daemons were permitted to attend school together. In my secondary school, Cherub High, some angyals still belittled daemons, calling them fag-enders; and those daemons ricocheted insults, like fowl-fornicators, right back at the angyals. If the traditionalist principalities and archangyals had their druthers, the law wouldn't have passed, and none of us would ever sit in the same classrooms. Those who experienced bullying from classmates and maltreatment from teachers were inclined to agree.

Bullied kids had no lifeline except to figure out what made their harassers tick. One second they were nice; another, they were mean and fearful. Their fixations were perplexing until, upon closer inspection, the bullies' own transparent actions betrayed them. They'd mock someone's outfit, then come to school days or weeks later in nearly identical clothing, albeit from cheaper brands.

They wrestled with envy or were frustrated with lovey-dovey inclinations the Establishment forbade them to have. They couldn't reconcile their attraction and sexuality, which mutated into resentment, jeering the very things they admired, such as how someone laughed, or their slim hips, or their attire. I was targeted by a few pugnacious broads because I wouldn't be their inamorata. I caught them once in the locker room during P.E., rifling through my clothes, fondling and sniffing them, checking the brand names and size. It was violating and puzzling.

"They want to capture your essence," my mother told me. "You're a light others gravitate toward like moths to flame, but the jealous ones, tormented by poverty, self-hatred, and overall ugliness, will aim to blot out your beautiful light. They'll kill themselves trying to tarnish your luster."

Mom was right. The bullies' infatuation-fueled hassling backfired, leaving them ashamed and garnering me more friends and sympathizers. I was elected class representative that semester and the spurned hasslers quit school, transferred, or faded into obscurity. Whatever inner demons they battled, it didn't grant them the authority to hurt others.

I learned to overcome adversity, harassment, and mass ignorance. Bullies learned they wouldn't win. My world would be less rich without the varied experiences, the conflicts, the triumphs, and creatures I'd befriended along the way.

Segregation seemed so bleak. I tried imagining the different life I'd live—one fraught with stifling loneliness and divided by color. I'd struggle to take a breath, and somebody would warn, "No ma'am, not in here. Not you, jade eyes!" Irises could determine one's nature. Colored contact lenses were deemed 'impersonation paraphernalia' and banned.

Every place would be segregated, separate but coequal, to each their own. Angyals would cluster in varying shades of azure. Daemons would congregate in earthy umber hues. Hybrids would be relegated to the virescent-colored section.

I'd be haunted by signs reading *NO CROSSBREEDS ALLOWED*. I would've never had the opportunity to meet my friends or fall in love and have my first kiss with Mahlen behind the simulated waterfall at the spring formal. Recollecting it sent goosepimples dancing along my spine.

The final bell rang and awoke me from my daydream. I'd been blindly gawping at the cinderblocks for an hour.

"You zoned out for a bit." Mahlen patted me. "I'll see you after basketball practice, okay?"

"Mmm, hmm." We parted at the doorway.

A jovial Vasiariah passed me in the hall. Her long flaxen ponytail seemingly waved at me. "See ya later," she said en route to her play rehearsals.

I maneuvered amid the fleeing students to meet Agares, Eleleth, and the dozen other free thinkers at the Young Independents meeting in the parking lot. Most were mixed-bloods. A few were pure-bloods there to support their hybrid chums or somebody in their family. We exchanged pleasantries before Agares called the meeting to order.

He stood in the center, a full head taller than the rest, a folder tucked neatly underneath his armpit. His coppery complexion was aglow in the lone sunray burning through the overcast sky. "Rumors are swirling about Vice Principal Melek, along with other faculty members, pressuring hybrid students to declare a solitary path of heritage, and due to most of the higher-ups being archangyals, you can predict what direction they're pointing."

Murmurs undulated across the audience. Agares glanced at me standing by his pickup. Perhaps he speculated whether I'd correct the record and remind him I specifically said I wasn't pressured, or lose my cool and spit sparks faster than the unstable lithium battery did in his truck last month. I crossed my forearms over my chest, opting not to undermine him in front of his followers, but he'd get an earful later.

He nodded. "Yup, not to live their true selves. *Our* true selves. This goes against our civil rights." He surveyed the assembly. "I see the majority of us are seniors who'll be faced with this decision in a few months. It shouldn't be lightly considered, nor should it be forced on us." He opened his folder and passed out the papers inside. "Go home and read this info. Some call it hearsay; however, what these pages recount are stories of survivors who were brainwashed and forcibly coerced into choosing a race without knowing the painful consequences."

He held up two photographs. One showed irregular black and white patches on a figure's back, leading to a bloody incision at the base of the tailbone. The other displayed staples resembling a miniature railroad track following the curves around a pair of bruised and swollen shoulder blades. "Those who opted to be angyals had their flesh bleached and their tails amputated while daemons had their wings clipped!"

An audible gasp resonated from the circle. I couldn't believe what I was seeing. There had to be an additional explanation. He must've mistakenly received photographs from sufferers of botched cosmetic surgery who were looking to get their doctor's medical license revoked.

He exhibited a third picture showing a shaved scalp with puncture wounds. "Daemons also had syringes stabbed into their skulls!" Gasps yielded to winces. "These poor souls were injected with massive doses of the hormone, melanocortin. It's derived from the pituitary gland at the base of the brain that accelerates the production of melanin to darken skin pigment."

Disgruntled mumbles grew louder.

"Is that real?" I heard myself ask. If declaring equaled self-mutilation, I'd maintain my hybrid status.

"He knows how to rally his troops, eh." Eleleth elbowed me. She was Agares' first devoted disciple and, unbeknownst to him, he was her first love. She carried a torch for him the entire time she dated Vehuel. "He'll be a superb class president."

Why not? I thought. He'd outgrown being the nerdy bookworm who used to pull our pigtails at recess. He was the toughest alpha in our school. *Don't mess with Agares* was a common phrase. I'd seen him knock out a bully in a single punch. He was smart and handsome enough. He was also an excellent public orator, replete with drama and spellbinding intrigue spoken in a deep, commanding baritone. "Remember these images," he said. "Read the stories. Share them with your trusted friends and relatives and convince them to join our ranks. We'll reconvene in a week."

The attendees, including numerous groupies, said their farewells and dwindled elsewhere. One devotee lingered. "You promised we'd see a movie next weekend."

Eleleth's jealousy radar pinged. "Does she even go to our school?" she muttered to me.

"No clue." Apparently, his reputation got around.

"I'll see you Saturday?" She poked her boobs up and out, awaiting Agares' reply.

"Looking forward to it," he said.

"Call me." She slipped a note into his shirt pocket and moseyed to her car.

He turned to us. Eleleth instantly smoothed her curly tresses. I didn't care if the wind blew my hair into my face; my arms remained defiantly crossed.

"I know you said you weren't pressured," Agares began, "but what happened still wasn't right, and other students are saying they're being pressured. I speak for them. Hybrids are underrepresented in everything." He counted on his fingers. "PTA, the school staff, city council, our legislature."

He was right. This issue was bigger than me. My mood softened. Agares grinned and tickled my ribs until I surrendered in reflexive chortles. "Okay, okay." I swiped at his hand. "I'm not mad."

"Then let's all go to the Café to celebrate the turnout."

"Great idea!" Eleleth interjected before swiftly composing herself. This wasn't a newly proposed notion. We concluded our Fridays at the eatery every week. "I mean, sure, I guess we could go." She motioned past us. "Look, there's Poyel. Let's invite her."

"Hey, Poyel," we yelled in unison and beckoned to her. She and her family had lived on Sycamore, my street, since fourth grade and hosted a potluck every summer. I wondered if they planned to throw a big bash for graduation.

I loudly called her name again, "Poyel Harut!"

She unlocked her car door, and her tawny head made a minor twitch indicating she'd heard me.

"Is she snubbing us?" I asked.

"She could be bulimic again. She got really standoffish sophomore year trying to hide it."

"Eleleth." I cut my eyes in Agares' direction and back to her.

"What? If she didn't want anyone knowing, she wouldn't have constantly been barfing in the school restrooms."

I'd told her that in confidence after catching Poyel outside the stall. We'd returned from summer vacation, and I hadn't seen her in three months. She rinsed her hands in the sink before bringing a palmful of water to her mouth. She froze, drinking in the silent skeleton coldly glaring at her from the mirror. She swore to me at that moment she'd get help for her eating disorder. I was elated when I noticed her gaining weight.

"You two didn't hear, huh." Agares packed the leftover paperwork into his truck's console. "I'm in fifth period with her twin, Peth. He said she's back with her prick ex-beau, Daggon."

"The wanker flasher?" I detested Daggon Yarhibol since first grade when, sans provocation or warning, he tugged down the elastic waistband on his shorts and bared his wee wiener to Eleleth and me. Our teacher penalized *us*, the victims, by revoking our recess. She even phoned our parents. Eleleth's mom berated her daughter as though she was a seven-year-old slut who should've gouged out her own eyes. My mother angrily hung up the telephone mid-conversation and assured me I wasn't at fault. "The one who bragged about cheating on her at Caim Moroni's party?"

"He's a lying prick," Eleleth said. "I was at that party, the one when you and Poyel were at dance camp."

"Oh, yeah." Jazz and tap had been devouring my leisure time exponentially since age seven. Aside from Physical Education, our school didn't offer competitive sports for my gender, and I yearned to play, not pretend to play like actors in drama class. I was uninterested in singing, baking, or knitting competitions. My mom's solution was enrolling me in dance classes at various studios. By thirteen, I'd volunteered to help coach younger pupils. Eventually, it became a paying gig, and I sacrificed fun things like parties with my peers.

"Succu showed up uninvited wearing a pop-out-your-tits top and proffered Daggon a hand job if he'd persuade the host to let her stay. He mooed and said everything about Succu made him limp. She attested he couldn't get it up, so right in front of her, he tried to get gropey with Caim and me, proclaiming to the whole party, 'If only you were pretty like these hotties.' Everyone laughed. Caim punted him right in his twig and berries." Eleleth kicked the air. "He almost threw up. It was straight magical!"

We both chuckled.

"That explains why Succu resents you." The story affirmed Vehuel's accusation that a spiteful Succu manufactured a lie to hurt Eleleth by ruining her romance with him and striving to mar her pristine reputation. "And why Daggon doesn't want Poyel talking to you."

"That's not all." Agares climbed from his vehicle and shut the door. "Peth said Daggon's manipulating her. In fact, she declared early. She's a soon-to-be

Gabrielite now, so she won't acknowledge anyone who isn't an angyal."

This surprised me for several reasons. First, I didn't know how the summer could begin without the Haruts' customary backyard barbeque. Second, usually a formal announcement was made like the birth or marriage notices in the paper. At minimum, a social media post would go out on the cyber network. I grabbed my cellular phone and scrolled through the state-run bulletin board feeds. "I'm not seeing a ceremony announced. How did she declare?"

He shook his head. "It's not an official declaration 'til the ceremony. More of a preemptive strike. She couldn't wait to cut off contact with her mom after her parents finalized their divorce. Peth's worried about her."

"What?" Eleleth's chartreuse eyes widened. "She cut off contact with her own mother?"

"It's kind of an implicit requirement when one declares. Her mom's a quarter daemon, I think." His tone lowered, "Peth's a Young Independent, but don't mention it because he doesn't want his sister excising him from her life too."

"Her loss if she does," Eleleth said. "She's missing out on some yummy burgers and fries today."

"I'm craving a grilled cheese sandwich and tomato soup."

Agares crinkled his nose. "You eat like my widowed granddad."

Eleleth's exaggerated cackle flew around my ears.

"Hardy-har-har." I smirked at them both. "Let's go. Mahlen and Vasi will be there later."

Chapter 2

The Café's brick building stood less than a mile from Cherub High. We strolled there when the weather was nice. Nice meant a respite from knuckle-sized hail, blow-your-skirt-off gales, and torrential rain that stung like sewing needles piercing your flesh. Our realm was situated at the peripheral of the superstorms scourging the Barren.

"Crap! I forgot to tell you." Eleleth wedged herself between us on the sidewalk. "A crazy slap-fight broke out in choir class today between two guys. They chucked music stands at one another screaming about their solos." She giggled. "It was a riot."

"Who were they?" I asked.

"You don't know them. They're sophomores. One's an angyal, and one's a daemon. They squabble daily over who's the better tenor."

"Oh, I thought it might be the same two Mahlen said were brawling in the locker room last week."

"I bet it's nothing compared to whatever *they* were disagreeing about." Agares pointed to the newspaper vending machine. The cover photo showed bloodstained pavement below the headline *KNIFE FIGHT KILLS TWO IN POWER & LIGHT DISTRICT*. It was a rough part of town. The bars and billiard halls had given up installing surveillance equipment due to patrons destroying the cameras and demanding privacy.

Rumors about illegal gambling and what they called queer encounters of the furtive kind spread like mold. Agares dropped a few coins in the slot, liberated a paper, and scanned the article.

Eleleth and I tugged on his wrists to bring the paper lower. "What does it say?"

"It says cops are investigating the incident and searching for whoever may have witnessed the fatal stabbing of two daemons outside Club Pinion. They're saying it's an isolated occurrence resulting from a disagreement between the two victims." His pupils galloped over the paragraph. "Acting Mayor Danjal Jinn said the possibility of a hate crime hasn't been eliminated, but sometimes the obvious conclusion is the right one."

I'd seen the bar's cartoonish advertisements: *Club Pinion ~ Fly in for a drink ~ Wings required.* "Isn't that an angyal hang-out?"

"Yeah, it is," Eleleth said. "My cousin on my dad's side goes there."

"Someone wants to ensure it stays an angyal only hang-out." Agares balled up the paper. "That *someone* may get their way considering the article regarding Bune Town's problem with police corruption and their inability to solve a string of burglaries throughout the sector."

A nauseous storm churned in my gut. The three of us had daemon blood. What if we had targets on our backs? First, it was a locker room brawl, then a fight in choir class, and now two daemons were found murdered. "You should notify the Young Independents. I've got a bad feeling."

"On it." He hurled the paper into the recycle bin

and retrieved his phone from his trouser pocket. While he walked, toes pointed slightly outward, he composed a mass text. He had connections to group leaders in other high schools. A year prior, their instantaneous communications thwarted an attempted mass shooting by a Dominion High student gunning for our school. The Dominion Diamondbacks and the Cherub Chimaeras maintained an intense rivalry. The aspiring sniper's yearbook photo blasted out in a message to hundreds of phones until a witness spotted him and dialed the police. Their collaboration saved countless lives that day. Agares requested the leaders alert him if they noticed an escalation of aggressive episodes among their student body. He added, *mainly toward daemons*, but deleted that portion before sending.

Eleleth's freckled visage puckered like she sniffed something rancid. She rested a palm on her abdomen. "Has anybody else lost their appetite?"

"Aye." The bloody pavement image was reminiscent of the disgusting snapshots from earlier. They kept flashing in my mind. Who were the victims, and were they authentic photographs? He had a relative on the police force. "Agares, where did you get those gross pictures of the mutilated angyal and daemon?"

"I can't divulge my sources. What kind of future investigative journalist would I be?"

Journalist? When did his plan to join the elite fossil fuel crew and explore the Barren change? He must've been kidding. "This is getting serious." I could hear my pitch rising. "The name-calling and snide remarks can be ignored, but the brutality directed at our kind cannot."

"I totally agree, which is why I'm protecting my

sources."

"So, you believe one hundred percent the photos weren't faked?"

"I do. I also believe victims are injected with hormones and chemicals to stimulate their growth." He screwed up his face. "Wait, do you think I'd actually use phony pictures and preach lies to gain members or something?"

"No, but there's a chance you were fooled by some jerk who thought it'd be funny." I regretted saying anything. It sounded like I was either accusing him of lying or suggesting he was stupid. "I'm not implying you're a fool or a liar."

He raised an eyebrow. "Uh, huh."

I felt my cheeks begin to flush. "Today has really been messing with me!"

Eleleth laid her hand on my shoulder, and her pouty lips stretched into a smile. "It'll be okay, Am. We're in this together."

I halted to draw her in for a much-needed hug. "Thank you," I said low into her ear.

She whispered back, "You're welcome."

"Don't leave me out." Agares wrapped his long arms around us both. "Making me look like an ass."

We all laughed. I secretly held in tears. I cherished my friends, and it horrified me to think anything dire could happen to them.

A horn honked. "What are you weirdoes doing?" Mahlen steered his car toward us, head out the window, wind batting his wavy blond locks.

Vasiariah sat grinning in the passenger seat. "Ya'll startin' a drum circle or somethin'? Dibs on the bongo."

They sped off and wheeled into the restaurant's

congested parking area. A grilled meat aroma lured us to the entrance. Caim and her stocky beau, Tannin, trotted out with a to-go bag. "Hey, Agares," he said, "sorry we missed the meeting."

They shared a handshake that concluded with a fist bump. "No worries, buddy."

"We'll fill you in at game night," I said. We usually had a friend's game night no less than once per month, alternating who would host unless we met at the bowling alley or the paintball range. We played board games, gambled for a few bucks at poker, and shared gossip or ghost stories. Humans, supernatural villains, Rawhide, and/or Bloody Bones were often key characters.

"Awesome." Caim guided her sunglasses up to rest atop her multi-braided crown before peering around. "We're avoiding you-know-who."

"She'll be changing her flat tire for a spell. Somebody bought you some time," Eleleth said with a wink.

"Thanks, sugar bear. My parents are burping bullets since I got a three-day suspension for hitting Succu in the head with my Physics book. They didn't buy my explanation she needed a lesson on energy transference." They must've also been as flabbergasted as we were to hear their usually introverted daughter had acted out. Succu had crept behind her and snapped a pencil in half. When it cracked, so did Caim. "If I get arrested for battery, they're going on trial for filicide." She glided her shades downward to rest them on her nose. "Catch ya later, mass debaters."

We giggled at her colorful vernacular. "Cheers." We entered the bustling Café, each hitting one pump from a sanitizing gel dispenser. The orchestra of clinking knives and forks played us to a corner booth.

The gum-smacking waitress had our order memorized. "One chicken sandwich. One loaded veggie burger. Baked potato chips for the table. One birch beer soda. One caramel milkshake. Two waters and a chamomile tea?"

"You forgot a bison patty melt," Agares reminded her.

She thumbed at a small sign by the menu board. "It's unavailable for the next two months. Our substitute's the soybean or venison burger." Throughout the year, bison meat would be temporarily rationed until enough calves reached maturity to breed and replace the adults shipped to slaughter. Health regulations were recently passed to ensure ranchers provided better conditions for their animals and to help replenish their numbers after one rancher lost a fourth of his herd to bovine flu.

He reluctantly accepted the venison swap.

Fetching a pen and notepad from her apron pouch, she scrawled the order. "Anything else?"

My dicey stomach cautioned me against the sandwich and soup. "No, thanks."

"I'll have it out shortly." She blew a bubble and popped it en route to the kitchen. She was an efficient waitress, even ensuring our stalkers were seated on the other side of the diner.

"Babe." Mahlen fondled my waist. "You've got to start eating more than tea. A swift breeze could come along and blow you away."

I swatted his hand. "I'll eat plenty after the Serelia gala. I already bought my gown, and I don't plan on having to get it resized." That excuse was better than admitting I saw and read some vile stuff earlier and hoped not to puke in his lap.

"You're going to look amazing." He traced an hourglass in the air. He scooched nearer and spoke nigh to my ear, "I'm excited to see you in that dress." His sultry breaths nuzzled my earlobe. I returned the gesture by snuggling into him.

"Is the theme 'Under the Stars'?" Eleleth kept shooting hungry glances at an oblivious Agares playing a crossword game on his phone. "Or did they settle on 'Twilight in Paradise'?"

"It's a masquerade ball. 'Secret Admirer.'" I winked at her. "We can shop tomorrow morning for masks. I need a mauve one to match my gown."

"Speakin' of admirers." Vasiariah stirred her splayed fingers over the table in her typical grand gesticulations. "Guess who asked me this fine afternoon?" She gandered at our puzzled faces, pausing for effect. She'd acquired the method in drama class. "Peth Harut."

"We were just talking about him." I pondered how coincidental that was. If his twin sister was shunning our entire mixed-blooded group, why would he intentionally ask to escort our friend who he knows will accompany us to the gala, which means her date will too?

"And his sister," Eleleth added.

It was Vasiariah's turn to look puzzled. "What about her?"

"She unofficially declared herself angyal and is renouncing anyone who isn't an angyal, like one hundred percent."

"Daggon was boasting during Sci-Tech class that he's dating her again." Mahlen pretended to gag himself with a twisted napkin.

"What?" I could see Vasiariah's invisible happiness balloon deflating. "But if I cancel, it's goin' to be awkward during Biology—he's my lab partner, and we've been pretty flirty." She wilted backward in her seat. "I told him I'd been crushing on him for a while. Do ya'll think he's expecting me to go with him, his sister, and her prick beau and not with you guys?"

"He can screw off if he thinks that." Mahlen skipped his napkin across the table. "We've gone together every year. It's tradition. He's welcome to come with us, but you shouldn't be boxed into a corner."

"Unless he's spying for her and Daggon." Eleleth's premise garnered Agares' notice.

"Peth's not a spy."

"Because you're a shrewd judge of character?" She scoffed, alluding to the fact everybody except Agares knew she fancied him. "You can't guarantee you know his intentions."

"Ohh-kay," he muttered. "Whatever."

Vasiariah shuffled through her purse. "I'll text him we're all meetin' at my house." She glimpsed up. "Which we are, by the way, so we can ride together to the dance. I'll see what he says." Within seconds of hitting send, her phone dinged. She read the message aloud, "'Okay, see you all then. Can't wait!'" She beamed. "Well, that was a big deal over nothin'."

"Yeah, we're going to have so much fun." I decided to expel the past unpleasant notions from my psyche and focus on the present. I put my palm on the table's center to recite our mantra from a slumber party when we were in junior high. "Fancy."

"Funny." Eleleth placed hers atop my hand.

Vasiariah dropped hers atop Eleleth's and shook her hair. "Foxy."

"Fit." I slapped on my other hand.

Eleleth followed suit, "Friends."

"Forever," Vasiariah concluded.

Had Caim not already left, she would've spouted a catalog of random adjectives starting with F. Flatulent and frugal were the least offensive.

"Okay, triplets, break it up," Agares joked. "We can't spare the table space."

Our food arrived, and the next several minutes were filled with loud chewing, slurping, and wiping. Mahlen's hands dripped burger grease while he shoveled in potato chips. Although they were for everyone, he'd pulled the basket next to his entrée. "Amitiel, babe." He shifted his dorsum toward me. "Scratch my upper back, quick."

"Where?" I set my tea atop the table. "Here?" I dragged my nails in circles over his clinging T-shirt, still moist with perspiration from practice.

"Higher." He sank downward. "My shoulder blades. I think my apertures are forming."

"Really?" I scratched around his scapulae for any trace of knots, welts, or separations, which enabled an entry and exit for wings. "I don't feel anything." My fingertips trailed across his stout trapezius muscles. Those robust fibrous bands could easily support a magnificent pair of wings as easily as a ship's spar carried huge sails to harness the wind. I imagined how his pinions would appear. He'd jerk his shoulders forward, allowing a pleated cape of thin, pale pink flesh to erupt and outstretch wide over hollow bones extended beyond his sides, ready to soar.

Our culture frowned upon displaying them in public unless it was an emergency or you were in flight, and sky travel was government regulated. Our wings were only suitable for short-distance flying anyhow, the way chickens and turkeys fly over low fences or up a tree to roost. Hence the derogatory term connoting fowl intercourse. The originator must've thought the play on homophones was cute—*foul* as immoral and *fowl* like a bird—though angyal pinions didn't have feathers and were more akin to those of bats.

Exhibiting one's daemon tail was also restricted. Showing either extremity resulted in binding; shackles were clamped around the base of their respective appendage and impeded their ability to retract.

Artsy black and white photographs and museums depicting artists' paintings of wings or tails were safer and easier to view. Pornographic magazines stashed in somebody's basement also provided a rendering, albeit quite distorted. They were an enigma, branded as art and adjudged as obscene; be proud to have them, but don't dare show them. I opined they were beautifully crafted extensions of our vertebrate.

I could only see Mahlen's in private if we were intimate, much more than brief over the clothes stuff, and I wasn't ready to take that leap. I'd certainly fantasized about it, touching the soft, smooth webbing while it cocooned our bodies together in a torrid embrace. The vision, and the sensations it conjured, remained on my mind the way his succulent kisses lingered on my mouth.

I couldn't wait for him to drive me home so we could kiss goodbye. "One more," I said, releasing the car's door handle to grab him and taste his balmy lips again. His hands entangled themselves in my hair. Excited goosebumps raced from my scalp to my toes. His fingertips delicately massaged my neck, and I shivered.

"Are you cold?"

"Far from it." I leaned in, spurred by my unsatiated desire.

He recoiled. "I almost forgot!" He opened his glove compartment and presented me with a petite velvet box. "I was waiting 'til our anniversary to give you this, but today was such a drag; I hope it'll cheer you up."

"You're so sweet." I opened the gift. An exquisite green baguette cradled in a silver band sparkled at me. "My birthstone?"

"Yes! I mean, it's not a genuine emerald. It's malachite, but it's pretty, and it made me think of you."

"It's beautiful." I glided it onto my right hand's fourth digit. It fit snugly and complimented my periwinkle nail polish. "I absolutely love it!"

"So does that mean you'll accept it as a promise ring?"

"Like as a promise it'll ultimately become an engagement ring?" Engagement rings led to wedding rings. I was astonished. We were seventeen. I hadn't cogitated marriage amongst everything else on my plate. In May, I'd be graduating from high school, having a birthday, deciding what university to enroll in, and facing the biggest decision of all: daemon or angyal.

"Exactly! Marriage, kids, the whole deal!" His teeth shone like an ivory wall.

My thumb twiddled the band. I had to be honest, although it meant leveling that wall.

He mistook my hesitance for something else. "I'll ask your grandad's permission first, of course."

His antiquated concept on proposing wasn't my biggest worriment. "What if I don't declare myself angyal?"

"What do you mean...of course you're picking angyal." His grin crumbled. "Aren't you?"

"Well," I dithered. "Ya...you heard what happened with Poyel. She won't talk to daemons or hybrids anymore."

"Poyel is pissed at her mom and acting out. Nobody is forcing her to shun anyone."

"You can't be sure."

"I can be sure I love you, so if I were declaring, it'd be whatever you are!" He smacked the steering wheel. He'd already earned a basketball scholarship to a Gabrielite university in the East Realm, not that his family couldn't afford tuition. His parents were both doctors, sort of. His father was a pediatrician, and his mother was almost a physician. She was an obstetrician's assistant. She had to quit graduate school once she started having children, and she only worked part time since her full-time job was raising Mahlen and his two younger siblings. She'd often emphasized how she wanted her oldest son to graduate college. I didn't know if she said it to make conversation with me or she thought I'd try to hinder him.

His dad thought I was dense or forgetful because he constantly reminded me I was a hybrid and Mahlen was an angyal. He'd say in a lagging timbre, "You two are sooo different. How dooo you make it work? I hear interracial relationships, particularly looong-distance ones, are verrry challenging."

Not coincidentally, he and his wife scheduled a tour for a distant college and anticipated their son's major to be pre-med. Mahlen's destiny was set for him, and he acted as if he were powerless to alter it. "I can give you a great life, you know. College would be for fun. Being a wife and mother is what's fulfilling. My mom says it all the time."

"I know." And that was part of the dilemma. Naturally, he assumed our lives would mimic his parents', and his career's financial gains would dwarf mine. His thinking was, *why work when your husband earns a ton?*

"You won't ever go without anything. I'll be able to take care of you."

"I know."

He threw his hands in the air. "Then what's the problem?"

"It's not your job to take care of me. I want a career for myself too."

"Is this a test, or are you searching for some way to break up because the promise ring freaked you out?"

"No. I love you. I do." I gripped his hand. "I'm sorry I can't give you a definite answer other than I want to be with you." I couldn't confess I did have apprehensions about our future should I refuse to disavow my hybrid nature, and he took the angyal oath.

"It's only jewelry." His pale visage was stoic. "Wear it when you're ready or don't."

"I'll wear it tomorrow night on our date." I tried to

sound upbeat, hoping to coax his dimpled smile to the surface.

"I'm working, remember? The country club has an event for Serelia week." He reached over my lap and opened the passenger door. "We'll talk later."

He ushered me out. "Are you mad?"

"I'm tired, Amitiel." His round face grew long, and his expression chilled to an icy blue glower. "I'm tired of contemplating when we're going to be in the same place in this relationship, and I'm coming to terms with the possibility maybe we never will." He pecked my temple. "Goodnight."

In a daze, I egressed the car, expecting the ground to swallow me. Mahlen had been a constant in my world for nearly four years, and it felt like it ended in a second. A terse goodbye punctuated by fading taillights in my driveway. I scrambled for my phone, typing, — *Please, don't do this. I don't want to break up!*— SEND.

His tires screeched to a halt, and his engine slammed into reverse. He parked and leaped out. "I'm not breaking up with you!"

"You're not supposed to read texts while you drive." I ran and vaulted into his arms. "I'm sorry."

"No, I overreacted. I'm sorry." He pressed his forehead into mine. "Forgive me?"

"That ninety-second break-up was agonizing."

He flourished his dimples, and I savored his delectable mouth for the final time that evening. The blinking bulb above the attached garage indicated our date was over. "Oops, Grandpa spotted us."

"Tell him I say hi." He saluted the house. "I'll try to get off early tomorrow to meet you and the gang at the carnival."

"Okay, babe." I retreated to my front door. "Drive safe."

"Of course. We can't spend our lives together if I don't." Mahlen rolled out of my driveway and shouted through his open window, "Bye, Mrs. Forneus!"

I waved farewell. Rays from the setting sun glinted off my ring. Was I ready to trade my selfhood for a bauble? I'd lose me and become a mother, cook, maid, laundress, child-rearer, tutor, chauffeur, and babysitter while my husband lived his life outside of the home. He'd work his own hours at his office, and then he'd have lunch with colleagues, play golf with buddies, and go for a workout at the gym. I'd complain, and he'd reply, just as his father did to his mother, "Darling, get a nanny or a maid."

Or would he be the groom who, ten or twelve years post-nuptials, goes out for a pack of smokes and never returns like my dad? Mom was so livid she'd resumed using her pre-married surname and legally changed mine to match. The gem promising me to Mahlen suddenly weighed hefty as I swiveled the doorknob.

"Amitiel, that you?" My maternal grandfather called from his puffy recliner in the parlor. His bottom lip protruded with a wad of chewing tobacco. I heard it in his altered pronunciations, plus the flickering television illumined his pallid countenance. He spent the bulk of his weekdays gardening to sell produce at the bimonthly farmer's market and the remainder watching programming from the local stations or, periodically, a station from the East Realm Network.

"It's me, Papa." I shut the door, locked it, and kicked my sandals onto the linoleum ingress. Three steps later, my bare feet sank into the cushiony beige carpet on their trek to his chair.

"Mahlen gone home?"

"Yep." He was having a lucid day. His age-related memory loss seemed at times to be edging more into mild cognitive impairment. His older memories were intact. However, stress could make recording newer data too burdensome on his hippocampus. The likelihood of embarrassing him wasn't worth correcting minor misremembrances. His condition was getting more difficult to conceal, just as his thinning comb-over couldn't hide the two liver spots atop his scalp. I bent and plonked a smooch between them. "Did you have a nice day?"

"I did, Erem—er, uh, sweetie." He caught himself mid-syllable before addressing me by my mom's name. Eremiel. She always said his boxing days would return to haunt him. And there were lots of those days in his younger years.

The shelves in his bedroom sagged from trophies and medals engraved with the same phrase, *Aur'ell Zephon—Prizefighting Champ*. My toddler gaze would marvel at the gleaming rows. He'd curl his gnarled joints around a set of brass gloves and regale me with tales of the bouts. "You see that name, sweetness? It's your Papa's name, Aur-ell," he over-enunciated the phonetics. I thought his name was actually the letters R.L. Mom would snap a picture and add it to our family photo album. They were some of my favorites. Heaps of pics with Grandpa were by his trophy case or the tv.

"Except every commercial interrupting my sports and my stories is a political ad," he said. "That one racist fella who's always running for something is a certifiable kook who looks like a clown and sounds like a carnival barker. I mean, I *never*. Here." He clicked the channel button on the tv remote using an arthritic knuckle. "See for yourself."

A reporter on the nightly news held a microphone toward an orange-haired male named Ebel Drumpf. His wispy strands looked like a threaded wig borrowed from a longhaired tabby cat. I expected it to hop up, meowing and scamper off. "Ha! Your Ginger Tom got reincarnated."

He adjusted his horn-rimmed glasses. "Nah, Ginger's fur was much nicer than his dollar store wig."

The screen's image warped momentarily. "You need me to jiggle the cable?"

"I've jiggled it all day. It doesn't help. Now hush." He mashed the up-volume arrow.

"We need to raise tariffs on the East Realm imports." Drumpf's dentures clacked as he spoke on the screen. "They're selling us crappy products from a daemon-owned company. I'm the only creature who can fix the economic mess the Bune Town, Leyak, and Nyettzach mayors have put us in. They're running a Deep Sta—"

"Lunacy." Grandpa pressed the power button. "And you 'member hearing last month about the Omunkar fella who inhaled exhaust fumes to kill himself?"

I nodded. It was a sad case. The depression abyss had swallowed the guy for good. Still, he couldn't get professional help for his mental illness because his Gabrielite parents believed sinister gremlins possessed him and he needed an exorcism.

"Cops done arrested his fiancée for indirect

slaughter. Said she was to blame for his actions and should've prevented his suicide."

"What did she do, knock him out, lock him in the garage, and tie him to the muffler?"

"Nope. She wasn't even in the same city." He spat onto the paper towel lining his tin spittoon. "They argued over the phone. He threatened to hurt her and kill himself, and she called his bluff."

"That's ludicrous. I didn't think Omunkar could outdo itself after convicting that new mom of indecency after she was seen inside her own house wearing a nursing bra." I was perplexed why females continued to live in the angyal-controlled city. Waitresses would get fired if they set a plate down in front of a female patron before setting one in front of her male acquaintance.

Maternity and postnatal care were a crapshoot. My aunt's infant daughter died in Omunkar General's newborn unit. It was a rare but operable condition, fetus in fetu—its parasitic twin was developing inside it. However, surgeons declined to excise the embryonic tumor, citing fear of being jailed in a municipality that outlawed anything falling under its extremely broad definition of abortion—including early labor induction. There were no exceptions for preserving the mother's life, extremely young age, rape, incest, disease, viability, or a physical or genetic defect. Innumerable companion plots for preteen female corpses and their unviable, inbred fetuses filled a cemetery quadrant.

The sounds of shovel scoops digging another grave resonated in the obstetrician's foreboding sighs. Every minute of inaction dug a foot deeper. My aunt slipped into a coma while her husband was out in the Barren working with the fossil fuel crew, so nobody else was permitted to legally take the baby to a different hospital and save its life. My aunt awoke only to plummet instantly into postpartum depression and grief. She wouldn't eat or drink. She died from dehydration ninety-six hours later.

"That's a fanatical religion." He held up his left fist. "On one hand, they say females are troglodytes unable to make difficult decisions or form abstract thoughts." He held up his right fist. "On the other, they say they're evil geniuses who've mastered mind control to corrupt others, yet, for undetermined reasons, choose to be subjugated by their inferior gender." He punched his fists together. "These two things are mutually exclusive. How was your day?"

"The vice principal sprung the preliminary interview on me this morning."

His cloudy cobalt orbs focused on me. "You didn't declare, did you? You can't trust the government."

"It's the school, Gramps, not the government."

"Once you're in the system, that's it." His distrust, which motivated my mother to forgo a hospital for a home birth, had grown over the years into paranoia.

"I know, and vaccinations have mind-control drugs, but don't let the microwave hear you saying that."

"I may be old," he wiped his chin dribble, "but I'm familiar with mockery."

"And that's one more reason I love you." He'd been a surrogate dad when my biological one abandoned my mom and me. Grandpa made sure I didn't feel deprived of a father figure. He let me shadow him everywhere, whether he tinkered on a car, an appliance, or completed home repairs. He taught me how to camp, fish, and shoot at wild quarry. He coached me on how to throw jabs and crosses. My grandmother cautioned him the exercises would broaden my already broad shoulders and I should be in the kitchen cooking. In protest, he further instructed me on uppercuts and hooks right outside the kitchen window. I loved it.

Our spar sessions were postponed after surgery to repair tendons in his thumb and pinky, but my life lessons continued. He had me remove the sutures, then paid his physical therapist a few bucks to teach me first aid skills, saying a creature had to be well-rounded to survive in the world.

"Love you too, kiddo. Your ma will be home late, but there's bologna, sour kraut, and bread for sandwiches." He was in a perpetual state of waiting for my mother.

"I'm not hungry." I'd filled up on baked potato chips at the café. Besides, a bologna and kraut sandwich sounded repellent.

"More for Josa then. She loved it." Josa was a seventy-five-pound tricolored rescue hound Mom adopted from a kill shelter two years ago. She gifted her to Grandpa after his ancient, three-legged feline pussyfooted itself to the great beyond, and he needed a pet. The dog had been trained on the canine task force but nipped one of her handlers, and they deemed her unfit, according to the employee at the pound. She'd written on the adoption paperwork: *Josa's trainer said she bit him, yet he didn't have a mark on him. His problem seemed to be with females, even canine ones, as he requested a male worker assist him. Josa is smart, affectionate, has shown no aggression, and will make a great companion.* "Isn't that right, Josa?"

She trotted in from the kitchen, licking her chops, and bopped her tan noggin against me for pets.

I rubbed around her pointy ears. "You eat all you want."

Seeming to comprehend, she wagged her tail back into the kitchen.

"I'm going to shower, study for my history test, and hit the sheets." We traded goodnights.

I ambled into my bedroom and to the jewelry box atop my dresser. I placed my new ring between the cushioned rolls and closed the twirling ballerina lid. I didn't want to think about it anymore.

I redirected my thoughts, performing the stamps, scuffs, and ball changes I'd choreographed for the Tiny Tappers at their last recital. They did a fantastic job. I tap-danced the routine into my bathroom, shedding clothes and brush-stepping on the tile, gleefully reminiscing.

I checked my scapulae in the mirror to see the raised prodromal welts. There were three feasible outcomes: One, my wings could grow in sans any brouhaha; two, the three-inch welts could heal without becoming winglet apertures; three, they could burst and develop an infection. I took care to clean and disinfect them while in the tub.

After showering, dressing, and a cursory scan over my notes on the Malleus Human Trials, I decided to look over my math equations. No matter how long I studied and knew I understood the material, I'd second guess myself on the quizzes and mark the incorrect answer.

I closed my notebook and clicked off my bedside

lamp, accidentally knocking over the framed snapshot of Mom and me lounging at the community pool. We had goofy looks on our mugs because Grandpa snapped the picture after somebody shrieked, "There's a turd in the pool! There's a turd!" Creatures behind us were fleeing from the water, save for a few who seemed oblivious to the exclamations.

I'd memorized Mom's funny inscription on the backside. *When life's giant cesspool overflows, threatening to drown us, we have two choices: The strongest of us, regardless of the tiring distance or risk of dying, will swim for the safety of the bank with hope of rescuing ourselves; the others will swallow enough shite to keep their toes on the ground and their noses just above the surface. They're still smelling the shitty truth; they've simply chosen to ignore it.*

I straightened the photo, clicked on my radio for white noise, and nestled below my weighted blanket. A calming numbness slinked over my body. Raindrops pitter-pattering on the roof quieted my chattering neurons and relaxed me. My brain slowly cycled through the day's events, easing me into suspended phases of consciousness. I drifted to sleep, hoping pleasant dreams would bring me clarity.

I felt anesthetized and somehow cognizant yet locked in a drowsy stage of slumber hanging in a dark berth, a prisoner between dimensions. The infinite medium starved my senses, yielding a lonesome echoing stillness. Occasional sparks, like shooting stars, zipped by my face. I wondered if they, too, were souls inhabiting this surreal world. Attempting to ask, I realized I possessed no voice, or if I did, I couldn't hear it. I pinched myself. My quiescent nerve endings didn't register any pressure.

A haze lifted, and nighttime morphed into day. My vision gradually adjusted to see a shapeless gray space occupied by vital creatures in my life. I mouthed their names. My vocal cords wouldn't emit sound. One by one, my friends and relatives were sucked away from me in different directions.

Panicked, I reached for them, stretching and lunging, going nowhere. My translucent hands wildly pawed the air as I aimed to propel myself forward and failed. No longer governed by gravity, I buoyed in the same spot, my feet not grazing the floor. I flailed and kicked in place, hoping to advance. I gained more ground, sailing across half the area. I was an arm's length away in the midst of an invisible, stationary swim treading against the current.

And then I hovered into a hospital room. "Rather young for an aneurysm." The physician read through pages on a clipboard.

"Appreciate the compliment." My mother's sallow flesh sagged from her bones. After suffering from migraines, profuse retching, and dizziness, her general practitioner ordered a brain scan and found multiple bulging vessels. "Amitiel." She summoned me beside her. "You are my greatest joy."

"That's the brain bubbles talking, Mom."

"You're loved and valued. Swear you won't ever let anyone treat you as less than."

I experienced a tug as if a noose jerked me backward. Mom's image shrank as my tether to reality reeled me out of my dreamscape. Rapping at my windowpanes further woke me.

I listened. The rain had ceased. The raps persisted.

Prior to opening the drapes, I knew Agares would be on the other side of the glass, his face and knuckles marred by a fight. On the alternate Fridays his father got paid, Mr. Gamigin's whiskey habit frequently exploded into violence. He'd attack his wife, and Agares would break it up. His mom would then order her son out of the house. It was a straight line lit by moonlight through a row of backyards and barking dogs to reach my home. This was the routine for the last year.

I padded to the window and verified it wasn't a burglar. Agares had smooshed his nose into the pane, so his nostrils were like a pig's snout. "Dork." I unlocked the clasps and hoisted the sash.

He poked in his head. His thin bottom lip was busted in the center. We exchanged the usual knowing look, his imbued with anguish and mine with compassion, but we didn't talk about it, not anymore. He didn't like to. He said rehashing the ordeal made him feel weak. Our hypermasculine culture didn't permit males to show weakness or sensitivity, so I wept for him, which he also hated. He wasn't here for my commiseration. He derided pity.

I quelled my tears and the urge to hug or question him. It was a harrowing secret he kept, a personal shame that impelled him to quit wrestling and only play baseball for the summer league because he worried his dad would attend a game during the school term and humiliate him. He preferred we treat *it*—the abuse he wouldn't name—as just something that occurred, like leaves changing color in the fall. He crawled inside, bringing a few soggy brown ones on the sole of his slippers and a thorny seedpod from the sweetgum tree. I kept old sales papers beneath the window to keep my carpet clean. The pages crinkled under his weight as he wiped his feet.

I lowered the sash, muffling the trilling insects. Agares found his pillow and two folded quilts I stored in the bottom drawer of my nightstand. He lay on his makeshift pallet on the big fluffy rug beside my bed, and we said our goodnights. He'd be gone before dawn.

Chapter 3

Saturday mornings meant Papa's pancake breakfasts. The aromas of scrambled eggs, fried bacon, and flapjacks drizzled in syrup coaxed me out of bed. I yawned and stretched my way down the hall. Grandpa was at the kitchen stove, whisking together milk and yolks to make the fluffiest eggs. Josa was lapping at her bowl. Grandpa rarely fed her regular dog food. She'd beg at him with her big, sad onyx eyes, and he'd toss her morsels from his dish.

"Smells tasty, Pop." I fetched a plate of food and poured myself a glass of milk.

"Thanks. Did you sleep well?"

"I did." I stuffed a big bite of syrupy pancake into my mouth. It was buttery and sweet, and I'd probably collapse from a sugar crash in thirty minutes.

"The quarrel you had with Mahlen didn't keep you awake?"

The flapjack fluttered in my throat. Grandpa's forgetfulness never happened when I preferred not to recollect something. "You saw?"

"I did." He dumped golden clumps into his bowl. "And I saw the ring which I hope doesn't mean anything serious."

I munched slowly, crafting my response. "It's an anniversary gift."

"Huh." He offered his one-eyed squint of disbelief.

"So, what were you quarreling about?"

I didn't want to lie. I kept it vague. "A misunderstanding. We worked it out."

"That's grand." He added salt and pepper to his eggs. "I hoped you weren't putting up with ill-treatment from him because he's an angyal, and you think you can't do better 'cause your scumbag father has you believing daemons or hybrids like him are worse choices."

"I'm one-fourth daemon, Pops, and the other three quarters supply more than enough conceit to remind me how good I can do." He'd oft reminded me how creatures confused the words bridal and bridle; one was meant to govern a workhorse.

"Okay." He sampled his eggs and talked amid chews. "Don't make the same mistake I did, marrying the first creature I dated more than a few weeks and learning too late she was crazier than an outhouse rat." All the chatting chews worked his large spectacles down his nose. He pushed them back up. "Don't get me wrong, I'm grateful she gave me your mama, but your grandmother got hooked on religion, and it poisoned her mind, saying crud like 'a female can get somewhere farther and faster on her back than on her feet.'" He topped off his coffee cup. "She was such a battle axe, interfering with your ma's love life, insisting she not continue dating the beau she liked because he had no angyal pedigree and then pushed her into marrying the first guy who proposed."

Had he not done the math, or did he think I wasn't aware Mom got married because, as she put it, she was harboring a uterine stowaway? I was born five months after their wedding. Grandma Marduza babysat me while Mom finished college. "Don't fret. I won't." I changed the subject. "Don't you have a rummy game tonight?" He and three chums played Saturday nights.

He stirred cream into his beverage. "I was thinking about visiting your mother this weekend."

"That's nice. Bring her flowers."

"You could come too if you don't have plans."

"I'm booked up. Eleleth asked me to shop with her for a gala dress." I insisted on shopping with her for an ensemble to wear to the annual dance at Cherub High. I had to persuade her not to buy a sheer dress so revealing you could see everything but her future. "I also promised Vasi I'd go to her play before meeting Mahlen at the fair this evening. Then there's the parade Sunday, plus I'm scheduled to coach the Tiny Tappers."

"No church, where intellect goes to die?" he teased. Grandpa considered himself a mere spiritual creature, and intelligence was an antidote to religion.

I crossed my eyes. "I have none to spare."

"Sounds as though your calendar will be overbooked through the Serelia season."

"It always is." The festival's activities—a carnival, a craft fair, fundraisers, sporting events, and a parade—occurred in the first weeks of October. Originally, it was to commemorate the equinox harvest. We enjoyed the revelry, mostly the preparation to enjoy it—whose house we'd meet at, what games we'd play, and what we'd wear to the dance to either win best-dressed couple or make a statement by challenging tradition and donning pantsuits or risqué gowns.

"Enjoy it while you can. If that warmongering politician gets elected, our four sectors will become so sequestered, nobody'll be celebrating until ordered to do so by an autocratic monarchy."

"Voters who choose a buffoon to represent them get what they ask for. You can't think the populace is that stupid?"

"They have yet to disappoint, and I've lived a long life." He sipped his coffee. "You should pencil in a visit with your mom sooner than later."

"I will." I scarfed my plate clean.

"Slow down, or else you'll get the hiccups."

A few respiratory spasms were worth hurrying out of the kitchen before our chat became his laments on quality family time. "Eleleth is expecting me to be ready when she gets here." I placed my dishes in the sink and went to my room. As I dressed and finished applying concealer to my chin blemish, my cell phone chimed a text alert.

From Eleleth: —*Going to be late. Tied up with chores.*—

She was habitually late, usually delayed by her mother. Mrs. Gremory was vain, self-centered, and emotionally absent from her child's life. She treated her more like an indentured servant than a daughter, and no matter how hard she worked, she couldn't earn her mom's approval.

I studied the sunny day beaming through my window and observed a tiny flock of cardinals eating at our birdfeeder. I touched the windowpane. The temperature was mellow enough to substitute long sleeves for a coat.

I typed a reply to Eleleth: —*I'll walk to your house. See you in a couple minutes.*—

Autumn's cool climate tiptoeing in behind the waning summer offered ideal weather to stroll a block over to her house. "Hello." I knocked on the side door. It was slightly ajar, and I could see Eleleth in the kitchen removing a dish from the oven.

"Come in. I cooked brunch." She set the baked egg omelet on the stovetop.

"It smells good, but I already ate. We need to leave." I stood on the doorsill. "We're supposed to be going shopping and then to Vasi's play."

"We are. The quiche isn't for us. Mom's having acquaintances over."

Of course. Mrs. Gremory couldn't be troubled to cook her acquaintants brunch or at least notify Eleleth in ample time so it wouldn't affect her plans.

"Amitiel," Mrs. Gremory irrupted, slicking a loose curly strand into her bun. "How're you?"

Don't reply. She doesn't care. "Oh, I'm doing g—"

"Elly, the omelet's edges are too crusty."

Why didn't I heed my own advice? Unless your presence served her purposes, you were casually dismissed.

"I ain't a chef, Mother." Eleleth tucked the potholders into a drawer and snapped it shut.

"Tone, young lass, or I'll take your scooter keys. And no, you *are not*," she corrected her grammar. She scrutinized the tidy room, clicking her perfectly manicured nails on the counter. She was awful.

I once overheard Mr. Gremory say he was so unhappy in his marriage he'd kill himself if he wasn't sure his wife would somehow come after him.

"Did you finish cleaning?"

"Yes, ma'am. Can I go now?"

"Where were you going again?"

"Shopping for a dre—"

"Yes, yes, go." She couldn't be bothered awaiting the ends of others' sentences. She had zero interest in anything not directly concerning her.

I'd never seen her have a real dialogue with her daughter. It made me appreciate my mother so much more. I granted her the compliment Mom would've paid me. "You've been hiding how well you can cook, huh?"

She half grinned and passed me her spare helmet. "Yep."

We mounted her three-wheeled scooter and rode to the outdoor mall. The quiet, electric motor topped out at thirty miles per hour. It could really blow your hair back going downhill. There was an exhilarating freedom in that little sidecar shaped like a silver bullet. We'd top hills at full throttle and lose our stomachs on the descent.

Mrs. Gremory's attitude was promptly overshadowed by the thrill of our ride and our delight in dress-shopping. We relished the fabrics, colors, textures, trying on various outfits, and pretending to be royalty. Perhaps it was the nostalgia in reliving our childhood games or practice for the wedding gowns and bridesmaid dresses we'd someday be buying.

"He gave me a promise ring." I held out my adorned digit. I was wearing multiple costume jewelry pieces, including rings, and she hadn't spotted the glaring secret on my fourth finger.

"Ahhh!" Eleleth ogled the stone. "It's gorgeous! Engaged to be engaged. I'm happy for you two." She sifted the racks at Boutique Ball Gowns, sliding hangers along their bars. "I wish Agares liked me even an eighth of the amount Mahlen loves you."

"He does like you. Aren't you going with him to the dance?"

"Because I asked him, and it was strongly implied we're going as friends in a group, not as a couple on a date."

"Why don't you tell him how you feel? The theme *is* about secret admirers."

"Right." She skimmed the tags trawling for her size. "And have him reject me and spend the year awkwardly evading each other? No thanks."

That was an additional aspect I wrestled with. Had I declined Mahlen's promise ring based on personal apprehensions, our relationship would've changed and inevitably ended because I wasn't ready this nanosecond for marriage and kids. "I kind of, temporarily, rejected Mahlen last night."

"What? Why?" Her jaw nearly plopped to the linoleum.

"Ahem!" The frowning apparel attendant butted in, startling both of us. She favored an anemic wraith. She observed our trunk jolts and didn't apologize. "Are you lost?"

My pulse thumped. Lost? Likely a year off my lifespan from that scare, I thought. "Uh, we're looking for a mid-length dress for the Serelia dance or a suit."

The collection of wrinkles serving as her lip generated a snarl, and she motioned at the exit. "Perchance, you'll find what you seek at a different store."

My gaze bobbed around the interior at the fancy attire. "Don't you carry formalwear?"

"Not what you two are seeking."

Judging from her elderly age and lengthy dress, I

assumed she was a hardcore traditionalist who bristled at the concept of trousers on females during formal events.

"Excuse me?" Eleleth scowled.

I envisioned her brain's gears clicking. A spasm of trepidation oscillated in the pit of my stomach. Discord made me super anxious, and nothing—from Ashwagandha to Magnesium to Zinc—calmed my nerves. I sampled every natural remedy from A to Z to cure the fickle and relentless anxiety beast. It beleaguered the current last quarter of my life with negativity, criticism, and gnawing worry. I distracted myself by multitasking to outrun the irrational phobia that chased me, but it was a dogged foe lurking forevermore.

She dragged her rude expression over us. "Our shop cannot accustom…your kind."

Click. Click. "Did you say, 'Our *kind*'?" Eleleth simmered with anger. Boutique Ball Gowns had gotten poor ratings for less than accommodating treatment, i.e., not having alterations finished when guaranteed or selling a dress reserved by another customer.

"If there's fixing to be a problem, I can call the police." She pulled an encased cell phone from her pocket. "We reserve the right to refuse service to troublemakers."

"Troublemakers!" *Click. Click. Click.* Eleleth had been testing herself for years, building up her bravery. She used to step one foot onto a stranger's lawn just to tell herself she was courageous enough to trespass. She pissed off one homeowner and was justifiably sprayed with a water hose. We had to alter our route to and from school. I was relieved because the peculiar twosome residing there, a conjoined at the hip adult son and his middle-aged mother, whom we dubbed a "susband and mife," gave me a prescription-worthy case of the heebie-jeebies. Plus, their bizarre two-week cellar excavation destroyed pipes and left our block without running water for nearly three solid days.

The attendant opened her phone's rubber casing.

"You think you're close enough to the tower to get a signal?" Eleleth let the dress she held fall to the floor. "You think responders will get here before I smash your ugly mug and send you back to haunting whatever cemetery you crawled out of?"

The attendant's shaky digit began to dial.

"Come on, let's go." I grasped Eleleth's wrist before she ruptured a head gasket. "This senile racist isn't worth going to jail."

Eleleth swung open the door causing the alert bell to tinkle to the ground in a melodious crash. "I'm so ready to leave Bune Town for good!"

"Leave?" Bune was a municipality where all races intermingled in everyday life. Our realm, formerly demarcated into three sectors—one each for angyals, daemons, and hybrids—had been redrawn to add a fourth to permit the gradual integration. "Where're you going to move?"

"I'm getting out of here." She trudged along the sidewalk. "I'm gonna tour the Political Science college in East Realm."

I was astounded. "What?" My initial prediction was she was going to Nyettzach City, the sector nicknamed Hybrid Hamlet, where we could easily shop without being hassled. I couldn't fathom her leaving our home entirely. I hurried after her. "Are you saying this because you're mad, or are you serious?" This also hinted she was considering declaring herself angyal. "Are you disconnecting from your daemon heritage?"

"As long as angyals outnumber both daemons and hybrids, they'll retain better privileges. I'd be stupid to remain in the minority."

"What about Agares?"

She shrugged. "What about him? He's busy trying to change the world. I'm nothing more than a groupie to him. I can't stay here worshipping a guy who's never gonna have feelings for me."

Yet she was majoring in Political Science when she didn't care diddly-squat for politics until Agares created the Young Independents Club. "Okay, then what about us, our friendship?"

She paused. Her scowl dissolved. "We'll be best buds forever. Aren't you already going to East Realm with Mahlen?"

"That's what I tried to tell you earlier with the," I held up my two index and middle digits to make quotation signs, "'engaged to be engaged' promise ring argument. He's practically planning our wedding, but I don't want to uproot my life, move two hundred trillion miles away, and then realize he and I aren't working out."

"I thought you two were in love."

"We are, I think. It's just..." I grappled for the accurate words. "He's not listening to me. When I say I need time, he hears we need time apart and gets angry."

"I can't believe you aren't coming with us."

"I didn't say that." I couldn't believe the nightmare I had where my pals deserted me seemed to be coming true. "I just prefer the decision be mine, what's best for me, not because I'm afraid or peer-pressured into it." A greater terror lay in leaving more than staying. I wasn't prepared to abandon my identity. The old, mixed-blooded Amitiel Zephon had to die for the future angyalic Mrs. Mahlen Forneus to be born.

Her posture slumped. "I honestly thought you'd already chosen to go angyal and accompany Mahlen to East Realm. Maybe I hoped you'd choose it because I want out of this quadrant, and we'd be together over there." She clasped my hands. "But in case it's not destined to happen, that's okay too. It won't affect our friendship." She smiled like we were those two little tots in daycare again. "We can call and visit a lot."

I contemplated how long before the visits and calls tapered off, and she made new friends. "Or I could consider studying history and philosophy at Thelema University."

"Yes, you could!" She hopped up and down. "Will you come on the tour with us?"

"The one six weeks from now?" I hopped with her.

"They moved it up, something about beating tornado season. It's tentatively set for the day after the Serelia gala, for seven to ten days depending on the weather forecast and whenever the convoy gets the all-clear."

I mulled over the dates and ceased hopping. "I'm helping coach the wee ones at tap camp then. It's for their recital. I can't cancel." They relied on me. With few dance schools, children who couldn't enroll in the better options had to go to Rebilka's Bountiful Boogie. It was a subpar studio with a lousy owner on Independence Street who had a loosey-goosey relationship with honest business practices. One stellar review stated, *Wanna dance studio you regret taking your child to more than you regret running a marathon braless, walking barefoot over flaming coals, or petting a rabid cat? Bountiful Boogie is for you!* The pupils desperately needed an adept instructor. I wouldn't work in the studio due to the congested hallways being a fire hazard, so I taught at the community center-sponsored camp.

"Darn! We can't reschedule." She shook her head. "Both our parents are adamant about it."

"I don't want you to delay it on my account." I wasn't too disappointed in the scheduling conflict. "I'll catch the next orientation. Maybe you can show me around campus."

"It's a deal." She gestured toward the local drug store. "Come on. I need to get my mom and dad a commemoration card before I forget."

"Oh, and you know what else?" Drugs and Such pharmacy stocked a plethora of small items. "We should also get Vasi some flowers for after her play this afternoon."

She was no longer the understudy since Caim got sick. Some speculated stage fright held her hostage. She was shy outside of our group and had joined the drama club, hoping to conquer her fear. Most of us surmised she couldn't cope with the anniversary of her elder sister's disappearance. Balam was presumed dead after cops found her vacant car partially submerged in a flooded creek. It devastated Caim. With only eleven months between them, the siblings were very close.

Her parents, Levi and Uriel, clung to the chance their rebellious older daughter had stowed away on a motorcade to East Realm, so rather than the finality of a funeral, they opted for a candlelight vigil on the Luna Bridge. Their grieving process worsened when a stocker at the hardware store blabbed about seeing Balam's dad going on expensive shopping sprees, which included buying gloves and a shovel, days before she vanished. The town's pot-stirring busybodies alleged his vegetable garden was a grave. He quit renting a booth at the farmer's market after overhearing a shopper berating another for buying homemade dog treats and produce "fertilized by Levi's murdered daughter" and saying she couldn't look at his lettuce heads without seeing Balam's face.

"She's not dead!" he'd shrieked.

His outburst cost him clients at his veterinary clinic. Not us. We continued bringing Josa to see him.

"That's right." She snapped her fingers. "You get a bouquet, I'll get a card for my parents and a get-well card for Caim, and we'll meet at the register."

The store wasn't big. It was a glorified apothecary composed of four rows: cosmetics, toiletries, nonprescription medicines, and the gift shop section. Browsing the latter, we heard a disagreement filtering from the pharmacy counter. We keeked around the aisle.

A pharmacist's assistant quarreled with a female customer. "Why don't you come back with your husband, and he can help you decide what medicines to buy, or better yet, go home and pray away the pain, you Gabrielite!"

"Just when you're fed up with racism, fate tosses in some misogyny to sweeten the pot," I said.

The patron lobbed a bottle of liquid cough suppressant at the employee. It burst, soaking him and his white coat in a reddish fluid.

"Ha! Ha!" Eleleth cheered. "Good for her."

The furious angyal stormed out. The clause, "You're banned," nipped at her heels.

We purchased our wares from a snickering cashier. Her face contorted, striving to conceal her amusement. "Sorry about that."

"Don't mention it. The cloudy day is getting brighter." In a happier mood after observing a chauvinist get doused and determined to buy herself a flashy suit for the dance, Eleleth drove us to Dandy's Duds in Hybrid Hamlet.

We passed the signposts *NOW LEAVING BUNE TOWN and WELCOME TO NYETTZACH CITY.* The municipalities were comparable in size and design. Identical one and a half or two-story houses with lush, grassy lawns comprised the suburbs; small businesses, restaurants, and entertainment venues constituted the town; apartments, duplexes, and cheap rental properties divided the town from the smog-belching factories in the industrial area.

Many of our clique's parents worked at the factories. Agares' worked at the timber mill. His dad lost part of a digit to a skill saw. His mom was an assistant manager in the gum rubber department overseeing sappy latex removal from trees and shrubs. Caim's mother worked at the paper recycling plant and her father at the natural gas refinery until he got his veterinarian license. Eleleth's dad managed a solar panel factory. Mine supervised a department at the automotive plant prior to his transfer to the East Realm Company and subsequent resignation from our nuclear family when I was twelve.

In his final letter, which he signed Anzu—not Dad, he wrote, *Fatherhood ain't for me.* Neither was paying child support. We were no more than a wrecked automobile on his assembly queue, and he'd scrapped us. I didn't know nor care whether he was alive or dead. I avoided the East Realm because he was probably there with a new wife wrangling about which house they'd buy or what car they'd own and contemplating having a baby. I inherited my indecisiveness from him, but not his cruelty. He didn't just leave Mom and me; he left us during her recovery from a hysterectomy. She'd developed a uterine infection after her water broke at four months pregnant with what they hoped, or rather she hoped, was my younger brother. She left the hospital without a husband, a baby, or the ability to have any more.

Beyond Nyettzach's industrial parks were the ranches and agriculture zones adjacent to the windmill farm and the perilous swampland in the Restricted Acres. If you smelled spoiled eggs, you were too close. The odorous methane gases produced by the bogs often spontaneously combusted, and the smoldering flames below the surface created quagmires that sucked down things. I sometimes felt like I was stuck there in a bog and being sucked down while my friends were leaving.

I mused on incentives to entice Eleleth to stay in West Realm. I drew blanks. I foundered in providing a rationale for myself. We'd come to a fork in the road of our lives. One lane diverged east; the other swerved into a familiar dizzying roundabout that would ultimately spit us out at a dead end in the West. I was a programmed robot going through the motions. It hardly registered Eleleth was trying on an outfit.

She burst from the dressing room. "Do you like it?" She twirled in a fuchsia and white pinstriped pantsuit. The bell bottoms swept the floor.

"I do! You look taller." I checked the hems on her pant leg. "Are you wearing heels?"

"Nah, it's the elongating effect of the vertical stripes."

"I saw a striped mask that will match perfectly."

"I'm hoping to make a bold statement." She unbuttoned her jacket and let it drift off her shoulders to reveal a midriff-baring, racer-back halter top.

"Oh, now I love it."

"You think I'd get arrested if my wings popped out?"

"Eleleth!" She was a practical joker. I wasn't sure if she was kidding, if she had winglets yet, or even the beginning apertures. "You wouldn't."

"Just the tips." She winked.

"Indecent exposure is a crime. Besides, they'll kick us out of the dance."

"Pfft." She yanked her jacket back in place. "Males can unbutton their shirts down to their cummerbunds."

"Because they've made the laws for centuries, and it's easier to call females indecent than take responsibility for their actions against us. This data isn't new."

"Maybe I'll trade these pants for the skirt and let my tail accidentally creep out."

I shook my head. "That joke could get you in a lot of trouble." A clock on the wall chimed the noon hour. "We don't have time for nonsense. We can get everything here and have enough time for lunch before Vasi's play at two o'clock in Bune."

"I hope it's not three hours long," she said from within the dressing stall. "I wanna get to the carnival before all the good parking spots are taken."

"Well, I'm starving. Let's go to the sandwich shop. It's on the way to the theater."

"Sounds great." She enthusiastically chirped on about the articles she purchased and how the dance would go, saying she planned on it being a grand last hurrah.

The last hurrah. The final act. The end. I feigned excitement because the finality of it depressed me. I again went on autopilot, smiling, nodding, agreeing, pretending to relish my sandwich that lost its flavor. Inside, I was two-box-of-tissues sad. This would be our last Serelia gala. We'd graduate, and everything would change. I wasn't ready. I was petrified. I couldn't see the opportunities around the corner that Eleleth saw during our zoom through the city. I envied her optimism.

"We're here." She swapped our helmets for the flowers in the storage compartment.

The school's billboard displayed the message, *Matinee Play: Mistakenly Yours. Tickets available at the booth.* Vasiariah rehearsed for weeks to portray the heroine in the darkly romantic comedy. I helped her run a few lines, and the play sounded hilarious. This new material allowed her to showcase her talent and not be trapped in the chorus. She had a future in acting.

We meandered by a nice automobile parked underneath the billboard. Its two taillights were smashed. "Is that Vasi's mom's car?" I asked. She owned a popular model with flared fenders. I could've counted seven others in the lot.

"Whosever it is, some butt wipe rear-ended it. Come on."

Friends, relatives, and school faculty packed into the theater. Eleleth and I, lilac daisies in hand, located empty aisle seats in the third row next to Vasiariah's mother. Her distinct bouffant puffed out like lemon cotton candy. "Hi, dolls. I saved your seats." She removed her shawl and purse from the chairs.

"Thanks, Mrs. Beliel," we said.

"Y'all brought flowers too?"

Too? She wasn't holding flowers. I didn't see her husband. To whom was she referring?

From the other side of her, a smiling Peth with a bouquet in his lap leaned forward and waved. We returned his greeting. His presence indicated he liked Vasiariah for more than a one-time date to the dance.

"Hey, Peth," Eleleth said. "I didn't know you'd be here."

"I couldn't miss Vasi's debut." He gripped the playbill prominently listing her name in the cast. "I'm on deferment from training during Serelia week." For the last eight months, Peth had been training to become a realm sentry under advice from his father, a Guard Sergeant who supervised squads patrolling the wall. Peth aspired to earn his certification and be permitted to join the sentries once he graduated high school. He'd rapidly completed the academy courses, including first aid, driver education, and weapons qualifications.

His job sounded exciting, but I'd never know for sure since females weren't allowed to work in the guard services or the police force other than in a clerical capacity. The groupthink level of cohesiveness was also a real turn-off. Many cadets we knew who didn't drop out due to hazing and psychological harassment became so insulated within the organizations they no longer associated with outsiders.

"Are you coming to the carnival afterward?" I asked.

"Yep, there's an escape room I've heard is amazing."

The dimming lights shushed the audience, and we watched the curtains open. The scene was set in a fancy restaurant where the tabletops were the size of teensy supper plates. A waiter toting a tray approached the lead duo at their itty-bitty table in the middle. He handed them breadsticks and water, which they had no choice but to hold due to an outrageous floral centerpiece covering the limited dining space. "Here are your menus." He tapped their throats until they pinned the menus down with their chins. Spectators chuckled. "Would you like an appetizer to start?"

Freeing a hand to clasp their menus, the diners stuck the bread into their mouths like giant cigars.

An overhead spotlight groaned and crashed onto the stage. It scarcely missed the actors who screamed and shielded themselves from the shattered glass and shrapnel ping-ponging through the air. The waiter endured some scrapes. Blood trickled down his forehead.

It was clear this wasn't part of the show when the actors bolted into the wings, and the director bellowed, "Close the curtains!"

Stunned viewers scrutinized the lighting units affixed to the catwalk above the stage to deduce the calamity's cause. Was the entire structure about to collapse? Was it an isolated freak accident, a prank, or sabotage? Mrs. Beliel, Peth, Eleleth, and I rushed to the wings to ensure Vasiariah was unharmed. We rammed ourselves through the narrow hallway amid the various props and bypassed the throng of other actors in theatrical makeup. The chaos transformed our daisies into decorative stems.

Vasiariah, her milky white visage paled from shock, braced herself against a wall.

"Vasi!" we exclaimed.

Her unfocused eyes resembled sapphire saucers encircled in bold black liner. "Hmm?"

"Are you okay?" We inspected her for wounds. "Are you hurt?" We didn't find any visible injuries.

"You think it's safe to stay here?" Eleleth kept her aim partly on the ceiling. "If a raccoon family busts through those drop-down tiles, I may crap my pants."

A nervous chortle escaped me. I didn't know what culprit may have been responsible for the incident. "We shouldn't tarry in here much longer."

"Vasi, dear?"

"Mom?" Color returned to her face. "It's a cosmic joke." She tousled the glass shards from her costume. "The playbill described this as, 'A comedy of mistakes, misunderstandings, and a near-fatal mishap.' A little too on the nose for me."

"It was a close call, yeah." Peth tenderly petted her hair.

"You think that creepy janitor had something to do with it?" I asked. He loitered around, mumbling to himself. He sometimes manifested like a ghost, squealed, "Boo," and horrified students in the restroom. His albinism made it worse. He looked bizarre as if a chalk stick came alive and leered at you with blazing pink irises.

"You mean Frag Russelifeld?" Mrs. Beliel asked. "He's in jail for elder abuse, fraud, and theft. I reported him when I did a welfare check on his ailing older brother who was a recent widower." She was a vocational nurse whose duties often involved supervising home health care assistants. "He'd stolen any and everything that wasn't nailed down."

Peth scrunched his tawny brows. "Elder abuse?"

"Yes, against his own sibling. Adopted or not, that troll should've felt some kind of familial connection." She draped her shawl over her shoulders. "And I don't mean how he acted like *he* was the spouse who was supposed to inherit everything rather than it going to his brother's children and grandchildren. The rightful heirs."

"No, I mean, I always got a child predator vibe."

"Right! He had a weird, whiny baby voice," Eleleth imitated his childish timbre.

"Heck of a coincidence," I said. "Vasiariah's mom gets a scumbag who used to work at her daughter's school arrested, and then her daughter is almost seriously injured at school, from equipment he was likely responsible for cleaning."

Mrs. Beliel nodded. "It is an odd fluke." An odd fluke was one way to describe Russelifeld. "However, Caim would've been the one on stage had she not gotten sick this morning."

Interesting point. "You think Caim was the target?"

"I'm not saying anyone was targeted. It was probably shoddy construction. Coincidences happen. I know a female who stole from an elderly grandpa on his deathbed—money meant for his grandchildren—

and, well, the thief herself later died and was buried on her victim's granddaughter's birthday."

"Is that a coincidence, or was it—"

"Natural causes," she interrupted. "She wasn't murdered."

The PA system screeched. "Sorry folks, we're canceling today's performance due to safety issues. Refunds are available in the lobby. Have a Merry Serelia."

"I guess we're hitting the games early today and shattering some targets, eh?" Eleleth grimaced, "Nope, sorry. I shouldn't have said hit or shatter. Let's just enjoy the rides."

"Speaking of rides," Peth said, "we can all fit in my dad's UCV. He let me borrow it. I need to clock more hours to move up a tier on my license." He took Vasiariah's hand. "You feel up to being my navigator?"

"Of course. Gimme five minutes to change outta this costume."

Chapter 4

To circumvent the crowds in the auditorium, we egressed through the untidy dressing room's rear exit. A startling gust whipped at our faces. Mrs. Beliel tied a sateen scarf around her bouffant to preserve its meticulous shape. We said goodbye to her and hello to Agares, who met us outside by Peth's borrowed Utility Cargo Vehicle. "Can I drive this?" he asked. The UCV looked akin to a sand monster wearing a silly triangular hat. It had amber headlights for eyes and a chrome grill for teeth locked in a permanent growl.

"Not a chance." Peth typed in a code to unlock the doors. They were all steel, several inches thick with teeny, quadruple-paned windows. "You get cut from the fuel crew?"

"Nah. Seismologist said his graph was picking up tremors in the zone of the Barren where we were slated to scout. The boss rescheduled the fracking." Agares squeezed between Eleleth and me on the second-row bench seat. We apprised him of the freak accident during the play. He suggested it may not have been accidental. "Didn't a maintenance worker get sacked recently because of something Vasi's mom said?"

"Yep, Frag Russelifeld," I confirmed. "When his keys rattled, everyone said it was orphan teeth in his pocket."

"That's the creep who followed my mom around

the grocery store one time."

"He's in jail now," Peth said. "I think we should all say it was an accident around Vasi. She's pretty shook right now."

We concurred. The motor roared to life, and we drove near the theater's exit to pick her up. She hopped into the front seat, and we began a bumpy ride to the fairgrounds. The armored automobile, although immense on the exterior, had a cramped interior littered with buttons, knobs, gauges, and levers, and none of them switched on the shock absorbers. I sent garbled texts to Mahlen about the stage accident. *Falling play's light fixture nearly split actor's head open* became *Calling Fay might mix near shit factor shed open.*

His reply: *"What? Who's Fay, and why is her shed open? You need me to call her?"*

My battery was dying. I didn't waste any power correcting the text.

"Sorry about the turbulence," Peth's voice vibrated. "It's an older model, built for combat, not for comfort."

"Can you turn on the fan? It's suffocating in here." I couldn't find a button to open the window, and Agares' physique radiated like hot oven elements in the wheeled metal box we rode inside.

"Sure." He mashed a series of controls until the vents exuded a whirring noise and crisp air circulated.

We arrived at the strip mall parking lot where the fair was in full swing. Blaring music and whirling machine noises bombarded our ears.

Peth adjusted his rear-view mirror. "Does that slob Succu and her rat-faced herpes-horde really think we don't know they're following us, or do they want us to know?" We all turned to see them prowling behind a row of cars. They did resemble subterranean rodents scurrying from the revealing light. The emaciated one looked like she'd gnawed through a bag of dope. A protuberant pair of denim-covered buttocks divulged their hiding place. "Succu's nasty fat butt is her worst enemy."

"Bargain bin bitches." Vasiariah fiddled with her door's handle. "Let's get the lead out and lose 'em in the crowd before Eleleth smacks 'em around and causes a scene."

"That was sixth grade, Miss Prissy, and the twats deserved it." Eleleth reached from the backseat to help open the passenger door. She waggled a knob. Nothing happened.

"I tried that one already," Vasiariah said.

"Then it's this one." She yanked on a lever, and the knob sprang up. "Dang it."

"Yeah, I tried that one too."

She smashed on some buttons, and the window rolled down and up. "For Celestia's sake, get us out of here, Peth!"

"Gimme a sec. You jammed it." He typed on the screen in his dash, and the four doors unlocked.

"Thank you!" We were all grateful to flee the UCV's claustrophobic interior.

There was a sense of urgency from the day's beginning, and I hadn't had a chance to catch my breath; the abandonment dream, the reality my friends *were* leaving me, rushing to Vasiariah's aid after the accident, hurrying to outrun our stalkers, and striving to pack fun into every minute while avoiding the two colossal questions in my life: Am I going to marry

Mahlen and am I angyal or daemon?

We paid the entry fee at the gate and zigzagged through the craft booths toward the food vendors' section. Peth and Vasiariah waited in a long queue for fried cornbread sausages.

"Too greasy for me," Eleleth said.

"Or," I suggested, "is it because you prefer not to be in public deep-throating a breaded wiener?"

"Ha!" She snorted, and a string of mucus blew out of her nostril. We chortled harder, and she covered her nose.

"Let's get those cream cheese puffs before they run out." Agares hot-footed it toward where he thought was the pastry stand.

"It's this way, near the sharpshooter game with the rubber ducks," I said. It was at the same spot every year.

"Oh, that's my favorite one." Eleleth grabbed my arm. "Come on!"

"Hold on." Agares was deterred by a commotion amid the ring toss and coin pitch booths. The operators griped that potential players wouldn't stop at their games due to the rented kiosk situated between the two booths, or rather the tall, paunchy, and slightly hunchbacked angyal looming there.

A white banner with glittery golden letters read *Ebel Drumpf Ministries*. I recognized him from local television commercials, billboards, and his ads on bus stop benches. His droopy jowls looked as though they might drip off his jawbone and puddle onto the bench's seat. He and his walleyed minions, flanked by two armed and husky bodyguards, held up donation pails while relaying propaganda literature that normalized bigotry.

Agares picked up a discarded leaflet from the ground and read the slogan aloud with an upward inflection, "'A Gabrielite is eternally right.'"

"If that's a question, the answer is no." Eleleth plucked it from his hand. "'Don't let the Celestian temptress lead you astray.' Ha! Lucky for Limp Dick Drumpf he's not capable of being tempted."

"Well, maybe to eat the corn outta your crap."

"Yuck!" She thwacked Agares. "You're crude."

"You love it."

Her poorly hidden simper proved his case. Whether sincere or harmlessly toying with her affections, his flirtation could bore a hole through her tough exterior. She was wise to want to leave him behind after graduation. High school and romantic mystery novels taught me about unrequited love. From any source, whether withheld by one's mom or a prospective beau, it was as toxic as swamp gas in the Restricted Acres or as malignant as Drumpf's creed.

"That fat slug has mommy issues. He's blaming all females for *his* inadequacies." I seized the paper. It had bullet points underscoring my argument.

- *Males were created in God's image; ergo, we are perfect. Females have the great honor of being formed by our creator to accommodate us.*

- *They require constant supervision and protection from others and themselves. They must be controlled. A Guardianship System should be implemented, so they learn to behave correctly.*

- *They have smaller brains and are less intelligent than males; consequently, their presence inside classrooms beyond 10th grade provides no merit to* *them and decreases the academic benefits for males by increasing the ratio of students to teacher.*

- Females are physically and mentally weaker; they're overly emotional and hypersensitive and thus unfit to enter the employment market. They need to be managed; therefore, they are incapable of ever being effective managers and would hinder an employer's success by vying for undeserved promotions and impeding the company's progress.

- Their ultimate goal, by nature, is to ensnare a male, so their provocative presence (e.g., wearing calf-length skirts, breastfeeding in public, etc.) is distracting, causes males to make bad choices, and detracts from a productive work environment.

- They're taking jobs from males who need to support their families.

- Their duties are to be obedient homemakers who serve their husbands and procreate. This is what makes them the happiest. When husbands decide it's time to have children, wives must acquiesce.

- Birth control for females, including pills, tubal ligation, diaphragms, or other intrauterine devices, is against our Lord and deprives them of the sole thing that makes them feel complete.

- Feminine products like tampons should be banned. Inserting an object dissuades females from guarding their chastity and encourages fornication. Also, gals don't comprehend how to use the products correctly and succumb to infections because it prevents them from urinating.

"What an idiot." I tore the leaflet in half. "He thinks the urethra and the vagina are the same thing."

"That's a big clue why he doesn't have kids."

"I can think of a smaller one." Agares wiggled his pinky. "His slogan should be *Ebel Drumpf is a tiny little chump.*"

The pamphlet's backside provided a brief biography on Drumpf. It described him as a former resident of the conservative Omunkar, a preacher-turned-politician, a segregationist, a gender supremacist, and a traditional family patriarch. Although, judging from newspaper articles Grandpa read to me over many weekend brunches, Drumpf was a con artist. He had no children, and his wheelchair-bound wife was persistently absent. Occasionally, he'd roll her out and use his purported faith healing ability, a.k.a. snake-charming parlor trick, to pray her to her feet. She used her temporarily regained bipedalism to douse soda on a reporter who inquired whether the Drumpfs used missing money from the treasury to fund their lavish lifestyle during Mr. Drumpf's momentary stint as a commissioner on the city council.

"Fake news!" Mrs. Drumpf shrilled when she was arrested for unbecoming conduct. "I tripped, and the reporter spilled her drink on her own head! *I'm* the victim." She returned to her wheelchair, and charges were reduced to paying a fine. All the details were beneath her colorless mugshot in the paper's Crime section.

Her husband was soon ousted by citizens for malfeasance and for dangerous rhetoric attacking civil liberties. His posts on the city council's media page read like erratic manifestos. He authored legislation attempting to criminalize miscarriages as either murder or desecration of a corporeal entity and force the offender to plan and pay for funeral services. His baseless and asinine asseveration was "the cunning female uses abortion as birth control and no other reason."

He falsely argued ectopic pregnancies could easily be removed from the fallopian tubes and reimplanted into the carrier's uterus. He wanted doctors who refused to do the nonexistent and physiologically impossible procedure to be incarcerated for what he termed *abortion murder*. He made the preposterous and scientifically untrue claim every female carried not microscopic genetic material but a diminutive and nearly fully developed fetus inside her at all times, minus the brain, which he said was created by the entry of sperm. He proposed females should be flogged for every menses they had because, he said, it wasn't a uterus shedding unneeded tissue; it was denying life to a future child. Outraged voters signed a recall petition and voted him off the council.

Undeterred, evidently by depthless egomania and a general inability to read a room, he announced his run for city manager. His longshot bid, which rapidly fizzled, seemed more a stunt to gain publicity for his entry into Bune Town's mayoral race. He was rivaling Danjal Jinn, the city council president and acting mayor, who Drumpf said was an elitist insider solely responsible for orchestrating his ousting. The narcissistic voice inside his head had to say it pretty loud to mute the caterwauling of those pissed-off housewives and single moms canvassing neighborhoods for recall signatures. One bevy spent thirty minutes explaining to us why Grandpa needed to sign their petition.

Drumpf labeled the allegations against him hoaxes,

the same thing he'd called the latest flu epidemic. He unsuccessfully sued a newspaper for defamation after it printed a paraphrased quote from Jinn dubbing Drumpf an insignificant sore loser whose rightful expulsion accrued him nothing. Suing the paper espoused Jinn's characterization of him. Jinn was already standing in for the incumbent, Raum Orcus, during his recovery from arterial bypass surgery and was a shoo-in to succeed him.

Lessons in civics class taught me about both Orcus and his heir apparent, and how their legislation could impact schools. They were career politicians, educated, well dressed, and had perfectly coifed salt-and-pepper hair, stating, *we're mature and wise but not too old.* They were daemons in the Kyriote party who ruled more by civil regulations than by religious law. They endorsed the secularization of public schools, citing polls and studies proving religion's detriment on young brains.

I read one study in a stack of medical books in Mr. Moroni's vet clinic while Josa got surgery to extricate wads of socks she'd been swallowing. Therapy hounds were used to combat depression and mood disorders in religious abuse survivors. A twenty-year study done by East Realm scientists on children and adults who grew up in sternly devout homes showed them to be more gullible, fearful, angry, and more addiction prone than their peers. They subscribed to spiritual possessions and refused medical treatment for auditory hallucinations because they believed they heard voices from a god, even when the voices told them to commit crimes. For health and safety reasons, Mayor Orcus had pious symbols replaced with plaques avowing *Indoctrinating children, particularly with shaming methods and psychological manipulation, is tantamount to child abuse and prohibited on school grounds.*

The Wechboros, an anti-choice party with which Drumpf had interned, appealed the mayor's ruling. While they slogged through the courts and had supporters phoning their representatives and picketing outside city hall, a disillusioned Drumpf relocated to the radical party's frayed fringes. He lobbied for swifter and harsher action—defunding education, organizing protests, marches, and riots. He incited violence under the guise he was "just kidding with whimsical banter," like when he said somebody should poison the mayor's IV bag…and then somebody tried.

He seemed to have gutted the city's infected underbelly and released its toxins onto the streets, contaminating the community. He proselytized a controversial ideology persecuting those he referred to as *the others*—atheists, agnostics, non-Gabrielites, daemons, and hybrids. "Our Founding Fathers shouldn't have allowed the treacherous foreigners into our realm," he'd said on his old tv ads. "They're criminals who live off tax-payer funded government assistance."

What was mystifying is his voter base, those who placed his campaign posters on their tenement housing, didn't have a problem taking handouts from the government, and a slew of them had criminal records. Drumpf allotted them permission to celebrate their hypocrisy, and they worshipped him like an oracle. "Our sympathetic forefathers caved to the begging mothers who brought this pestilence upon us. Females have no place in critical decision-making."

He espoused gender-specific bills to subjugate all non-males with curfews, stricter ordinances, and a dress code that incorporated a variation to a beekeeper's suit. He aspired to deny females education and employment, leaving them beholden to males for financial support. It was a smart strategy convincing witnesses and your slave that your boot must be kept firmly on her neck for her benefit, and you keep her underfoot because you care.

"Celestia is a false goddess sent to test our faith," Drumpf proclaimed into the microphone stand by his kiosk. "Beware infidels who follow the Morning Star. Gabriel is God's one divine prophet."

Some passersby spurned his leaflets. "Screw off, bigot." Others ripped them apart and the pieces scattered like snowflakes.

"Behold the heretics," he preached to his scant, mostly male, and largely overweight flock. "We must draft legislation to protect them from themselves and their ignorance."

"You're ignorant, flat-earther!" A heckler hunched, crossed one eye, and let his tongue dangle, personifying Drumpf's ignorance. Flat-earthers discredited scientific facts and astronomy regarding our spherical planet. They premised Earth was a disc encapsulated in a thin ice dome.

The heckler's companion laughed and added, "Yeah, educate yourself, needle dick!" She and her buddy then pranced by each holding their thumb and index finger centimeters apart to indicate the minuscule size.

"Ah, a bigmouthed gal." A disingenuous smile slithered across Drumpf's pudgy countenance while he waited for the couple to move beyond earshot. "I bet she breastfeeds in public for attention. Breasts are for sex, not for babies. Somebody should buy her formula or rough her up, eh?" His chortling congregation emboldened him. "As Gabriel's disciple said, 'No female shall be a queen. Bow and honor your king.'"

"As Danjal Jinn said," a voice declared, "'Democracy bows to tyranny when religion and state align, all judgment, criticism, and facts are abjured, and only those displaying absolute loyalty are praised as faithful patriots.'"

Wow. An agitator who fought with tact. I pondered what other truth bombs he'd drop.

"And your mother called from Avern," he hollered, "she regrets *not* aborting you!"

Never mind.

Drumpf retreated from the dispute and huddled behind another subject. "Abortion, spontaneous or not, and miscarriages, which females bring upon themselves by sinning, should be criminalized without exception, as implied by our lord and stated in my pamphlet."

A paragraph titled *Females were Created to Serve Us* read, *By default, a female cannot be autonomous because she's able to carry another inside her. Her rights are superseded by the rights belonging to the fetus since it may be male, and ergo, more paramount. Henceforth, females should be referred to as Zygote Chambers and their medical records opened to inspection. Their menses will be charted. Feminine hygiene products shall be attainable by a physician's prescription and doled out at communal menstrual huts. Mandatory pregnancy tests will be administered monthly to every Zygote Chamber of reproductive age.*

If a pregnancy is suspected, they'll be surveilled by government workers to ensure they do nothing to endanger their precious cargo. Expelled material from alleged miscarriages must be retained for inspection and testing to see whether criminal charges are warranted. Offenders will be detained within internment lodges.

Basically, females deserved no rights to privacy or decisions regarding their own bodies. They forfeited any right to say no. Resistance would be met with imprisonment and apparently a truckload of IOUs since Drumpf provided no feasible budget plan. He said non-male healthcare was covered by prayers and those seeking medical care were subject to shunning for committing religious bigotry.

"Praise the Lord," his flock squawked. "Praise Drumpf." He was a quacksalver, a grifter always attempting and failing at new business ventures. They reacted as though he was an oracle.

"They should fall to their knees and pray for forgiveness."

"You get on your knees to suckle pillicock!" two older teens raced by yawping.

Their female companions scudded along beside them, giggling, "Fowl-fucker!"

"See my brethren," Drumpf said, "another hysterical female. That's why you have to get those mouthy fillies while they're young, twelve to fourteen, so you can mold them and teach them how to ride."

The repulsive males swung around their caps and yee-hawed Drumpf's statement about grooming and child molestation. I assumed a half dozen or more of them was the motive behind the state creating the Child

Protection Service Unit of the police department. Those who refrained from cheering merely smiled, conveying a casual indifference toward predatory sexual behavior.

"When a male chooses to breed with a female and bless her with his seed, she's obligated to consent."

"That's rape!" yapped a detractor.

"Whores can't be raped." He looked to his drones for confirmation. They nodded and raised their beers to toast his assertion. "It's their penance. They relished the freedom of surrendering to desires then woke the next morn regretting having cheated on their beaus. Regret doesn't equal rape. Females don't have the same urges we do; they don't know they enjoyed it, but if they spread their legs for one, they'll spread them for all."

Drumpf was a clown whose claims would've been laughable if they weren't dangerous. Prostitutes can't be raped? Their livelihood is transactional sex, so why would they give out freebies? Plus, considering how many of their corpses were found in creek beds when floodwaters receded, it was safe to conclude they'd tried to say no.

Females wanting to and engaging in sex are tramps, yet they're too ignorant to know whether they enjoy it, so it's impossible to define it as sexual assault? Saying yes once negates the ability to ever say no in the future? Drumpf's antithetical postulations were too myriad to unscramble. Perhaps that was his goal.

The blonde in front of us asked her much shorter spouse, "Hubby, is he saying once a female has sex with a guy, she never turns another one down?"

"His math definitely doesn't add up." He scratched the circular bald patch on his scalp. "Not in my experience."

"He's saying he's a disgusting rapist who should be shot!" Agares blurted.

"Oh my." The blonde's palm went to cover her gaping mouth like she hadn't already heard the appalling phrases Drumpf had belched.

Eleleth apologized for the language. The blonde relaxed her hackles, and it somehow raised mine.

"Sentiment still stands." We shouldn't have to beg pardon for speaking against a bloated toad who got a free pass to vomit lies and vitriol. "And we didn't say he should die; we said he should be shot."

"Yeah," Agares concurred, "right in his shriveled ball sack."

The blonde's mouth gaped once more as if she envisioned Agares grabbing his naked crotch.

"Honey, the kid's right. Drumpf's a flatulent tool. Let's go." The duo held hands and walked away.

"Can you believe her?" I said. "Acting like she's never heard the words *ball sack*."

"I can't believe this." Eleleth brought our attention to the fat sack of crap holding the microphone.

"Those saying they didn't give their doctor consent before he drugged them and performed unnecessary pelvic exams, so they try to sue him for cash and their name in the paper." Drumpf blew out his jowly cheeks, rippling his neck wattle. "They went there asking for it. It's bonkers."

What was bonkers was requiring and expecting females to guard their virtue, yet not report when it was trampled on by knuckle-dragging Denisovans, then slut-shame them into silence or recantation, blame them for being victimized, and accuse them of seeking fame and money.

"Oh, come on!" yelled the ring toss operator as his line of prospective players dwindled. He grasped his cap and threw it. "You've gotta shut it, Drumpf!"

"Who needs to shut it is wives dreaming up the notion of marital rape. Gals and their date rape fantasies. We need harsher penalties for those filing false testimonies, and they should be billed for all those worthless exams they take because those trollops want doctors rooting around their private parts."

He perverted the facts and twisted them to reinforce his narrative. Of the hundreds of reported sex assault cases, one female was covertly recorded, agreeing to recant her accusation against her ex if he acceded to dump his new love and go back to his accuser. Drumpf chose to omit facts the self-proclaimed victim had mental health issues. The facts were discovered in the mandatory psychiatric evaluation every accuser was subjected to. This practice allowed the accused to brand his victim unstable, which translated to untruthful and ignorant to what rape was. Thus his assaulting her should be judged as less of a crime because it wouldn't impact her already damaged mind.

"Female circumcision will shut 'em all up!" asserted one apparent psychopath. His filthy clothes were tattered. His tangled hair and scraggly beard had missing chunks that appeared to have been yanked out by the roots, leaving inflamed spots on his skin. He kept muttering, "Cut 'em, cut 'em, cut 'em." Mutilating genitalia was an illegal practice exercised by barbaric tribes to control and penalize females by denying them sexual pleasure or comfort, but more often resulted in an excruciating demise.

I felt unsafe. I hooked my arm around Eleleth's and guided us nearer to Agares.

"Yaaaas, them thar guppies nearly ruin it for afwetes."

Drumpf's expression contorted as he deciphered the boozer's statement. "Ah, true. We've had sports stars almost lose their careers because they got a tad overzealous with their fans."

There were too many athletes who'd violently sodomized females in dormitories, cars, and hotel rooms to know of whom he referred. Their talent level denoted the leniency of their punishments, usually a flaccid apology saying they were sorry their victim didn't realize or accept the encounter was consensual. Though it's impossible to consent with a forearm garroting one's esophagus.

"Last spring," Drumpf resumed his egregious monologue, "the judge in Omunkar was spot on when he dubbed those thirteen-year-olds the sexual aggressors and rendered a light sentence to their so-called attacker. He was their uncle, for Gabriel's sake!"

"Das true," slurred a drunk congregant, "and gropin' zah compliment. I've a right to 'spect merchandize afore buyin'." Laughs gurgled around him. "If da wraitrish wantz 'er tip."

"Yes, sir," Drumpf continued. "A female only works outside the home to find a husband. Why is it a crime to show her you find her attractive? They toil to get our attention, and when we reward them, they cry rape. Bruises heal, okay. A young male's future shouldn't be ruined because *she* said *he* misread signals, and she's suffering mental anguish." He rolled a doughy fist at the corner of his eye. "Boohoo-hoo.

Her error in judgment isn't *his* fault. We should talk about what she was wearing and why she put herself in such a position."

"Wha…I don't…I…" Eleleth was dumbstruck. "This is nuttier than squirrel turds. I can't comprehend how females can be complicit in this insane logic."

I couldn't tell her it was for the same reasons she tripped over her own feet chasing males who didn't reciprocate her feelings or why Agares' mom wouldn't divorce her abusive and alcoholic husband. A combination of brainwashing, indoctrination, and fear of ostracization for questioning a universally accepted institution of beliefs kept us in line. "It's the fake fundamentals of femininity, right? If you can't be attractive, be amenable. Judging from the untied shoelaces and misaligned shirt buttons, I doubt there's a revolutionary amongst them or a basic ability to string two thoughts together. They only know how to do what they're told, like trained pets who'll do anything to please their owner, so they don't get whipped."

"It's self-preservation. Anything to nab a husband. Look at 'em." Agares winced. Numerous wrinkled mugs squinting through their cigarette smoke constituted Drumpf's fold. Broken capillaries furcated under their skin in red cobweb patterns. "Nobody's lining up to inspect *their* merchandise."

"That and reproductive laws won't affect them since, thankfully, they're too old or unhealthy to reproduce."

"Or too ugly," Eleleth said. "Tons of busted-up faces in the crowd."

"Exactly. Those ugly females think pretty ones are sluts, and pregnancy's their punishment as if the social concept of homeliness is a safeguard from sexual assaults." The anti-choicers didn't value life; they yearned to control it. They didn't donate to charities for orphanages, foster care, early education, or children's pre/postnatal healthcare, nor advocate for the betterment of those institutions. They threw their resources behind candidates campaigning to ban birth control and force females of every age and status to suffer through pregnancy, labor, public judgment, and mounting medical bills when maternity nearly killed them. Their message was clear: Only males had the right and privilege to enjoy sex without repercussions or privacy invasions.

"And ugly men with little shafts who can't get laid except by force really support Drumpf," Agares added. "He's advocating for the legalization of rape and starving infants to death so he can bust a nut on their mother's boobs. The sicko's entire candidacy is about controlling tits and slits."

"I wish they'd find a cure for the tiny penis epidemic and solve everyone's problems. They'd massively reduce the number of gigantic trucks currently taking up two parking spots in the lot because their owners are overcompensating." You'd see a lifted truck with a dual axle spinning four rear tires, loudly blowing black smoke from its exhaust pipe, and you'd hear a mature female say, *Oh, look. There's a male who can't sexually satisfy his partner.*

"Hey." Eleleth nudged me. "Now you know what to wish for when you blow out your birthday candles."

"You're hilarious." My retort, an inflated guffaw, was contrived and coated in sarcasm.

"Check out that booze hound," Agares said.

A slow-blinking male wobbled in place, "The trebble sharted aft they 'pealed the dome... domicile... chased law."

"Repealed the Domestic Chastisement law," Drumpf corrected him. "Yes, husbands can't teach their wives anything if they can't discipline them. That gabby wife whose corpse they found dumped in a silo wouldn't listen to her husband, or she would've known how to gratify him, and he wouldn't have been seduced by a harlot from Leyak. He needed comfort after his missus caused her own miscarriage."

"Damn degenerate!" A hunk of mud rocketed into Drumpf's chin. His menacing bodyguards unholstered their tasers and brandished them recklessly.

"Life begins at menstruation," his Little Prick League repeatedly chanted the foul phrase, squishing it past their dental cavities. They pretended all life was precious but were fine with a husband murdering his wife and dumping her out like a bag of garbage because he wanted to marry his mistress, whom they blamed for *his* acts.

One goofy fanatic clapped along with a cigarette filter lodged in the vacant slot in his shit-eating grin. "Death to the heathens!"

Not cowering to intimidation, an ensemble of protesters hoisted their fists and sang back, "Vote for Danjal Jinn! He knows how to win! Vote for Jinn! Vote for Jjjjjjj..."

The guards discharged their tasers. The metal probes were viper fangs pumping electrical venom into their victims. Their muscles first went as rigid as statues before they collapsed onto the grass in convulsions.

Onlookers screamed, "Females aren't disposable!"

A melee of punches, kicks, and hair-pulling ensued between the opposing groups.

Beyond the diversion, I saw a specter flitting for cover behind the kiosk. I blinked and strived to focus. The ghostly characteristics appeared familiar. I nudged Eleleth and Agares. "Is that creepy Russelifeld between the booths?"

"Where?" Agares followed my stare.

I gestured at the shifty figure partially obscured by the canopy's tassels. "Over there." I hoped he'd assure me it wasn't.

"Could be."

Darn it. He was our prime suspect for the theater light sabotage, and he was sure acting guilty, or stranger than usual anyway.

"Nah," Eleleth said. "He's in jail. Remember what Mrs. Beliel said?"

"He could've paid bail or something." He'd robbed from his sick brother, so surely he could afford it, and he was skilled at eluding punishment. Our complaints that he was a peeping perv were always flouted. The superintendent said the school would be sued for wrongful termination due to unfounded allegations. I tugged on her arm. "Just look!"

"Okay!" She snagged a glimpse before he got spooked and retreated from sight. "Maybe, if he escaped the bail warrantor and got a tan." She chuckled.

"Well, wouldn't he need a disguise if he'd escaped? Self-tanning lotion is easy to get."

"Holy crap, yes!"

"Why would he risk coming to a public place, though?" Agares stayed fixed on the last spot we saw Russelifeld.

Why indeed? I considered tailing him to find out what he was up to.

"Reconnaissance mission?" he asked as if he'd heard my thought.

"Quit reading my mind."

"Let's go." Eleleth jabbed our backs.

Vasiariah's abrupt presence held my feet. She nibbled on her breaded sausage without disturbing her vermillion lipstick. "What are y'all talking about?"

Peth, correctly assuming we were up to something, shook his head, reminding us of the agreement we established earlier.

"Nothing important," I lied. "Just curious why security isn't breaking up this fight."

"I'll find out." Eleleth dashed around the kiosk and between the booths—not toward security—to pursue Russelifeld.

"What's happening?" Mahlen loped up. I'd forgotten he was meeting us after work. "Is Fay okay?"

"Fay?" Agares asked as he took backward steps to follow Eleleth. "Who's he talking about?"

I waved him off and pulled Mahlen aside. "Not 'Fay.' Play. A big light fell on the stage during the show and nearly hit the actors."

"Oh, that makes more sense." He crossed one eye. "Autocorrect had me confused."

"This is serious." I checked to ensure Peth was distracting Vasiariah. They were sampling each other's food and beverage while watching the brawl. I lowered my tone, "We don't want to upset Vasi, but we think Russelifeld could be responsible."

"The spooky custodian?"

"Shh." I led us farther away. "Mrs. Beliel got him

arrested, and he was supposedly in jail, but we just saw him behind that kiosk, and it seemed like he was disguising his appearance."

"Show me."

We darted after our friends already in pursuit. They posed dorsum to dorsum, scanning the grounds.

"You lost him?" I turned to Mahlen, "They lost him."

"Lost who?"

"Crap!" we both exclaimed.

Vasiariah had sneaked behind us. "Y'all looking for Russelifeld?"

Peth, still chewing his breaded sausage, shook his head. The rest of us stumbled and stammered. Had she been playing dumb the whole time? She *was* an actress.

"It's okay. I'm peachy. Although my beau," she thumbed at Peth, "thinks I'm a fragile flower in a hailstorm."

"Babe, I was looking out for you."

"I appreciate that, but I'm not helpless. I prefer to be proactive against the bleach-huffing perv who spent more time by my locker than I did."

"What now?"

"I'm pretty sure he was the one drawing penis pics on it." She outlined a phallic symbol in the air.

Peth's face ignited like a lit match. "I'll beat his ass 'til it turns blue and falls off. Then I'll make him apologize."

"Good luck finding his ass," Mahlen said.

"I know how we can find him." A helpful and chilling revelation. "I can get his address from my mom's appointment book. She keeps all her patients' emergency contacts in there." She gave a melodramatic curtsy. "You're welcome."

"Uh oh, Peth," Mahlen teased, "you might have to make good on that threat." We'd ascertain whether his boast was anything more than a grandstanding beau defending his gal's honor. "We can take my car." He clasped my left hand to walk me through the carnival's exit gate. I sandwiched his digits between mine and felt his hubris swell as his thumb grazed the promise ring he'd gifted me. "You must not have gotten my text? They rescheduled the college tours in East Realm."

"No, the service sucks here, but Eleleth told me earlier."

"Can you go? I know it's short notice, but can you?"

"I'm teaching at dance camp. They can't find a qualified substitute this late."

Pride deflated in his forlorn countenance. "I guess what I meant is, did you even *want* to go?"

"Yeah, of course. Thelema U." I wielded my right fist as if gripping a sword. "Go fightin' Thracians."

He squeezed my hand tighter and smiled. "That's my gorgeous gal."

Chapter 5

The Beliels lived on a cul-de-sac in a lovely two-story brick house built by Vasiariah's father. He owned a construction company. The homes on their block had virtually the same layout.

"My mom is at the salon, so she won't have her address book. It'll be in our home office or in Mom's bedside nightstand." The bedrooms were upstairs, and the office was to the foyer's left. "Be discreet. I'm not supposed to have friends over when my parents are gone."

"We know, come on." Eleleth and I snooped around the office while Vasiariah searched upstairs. Her footfalls creaked on the uncarpeted tier above us. Mrs. Beliel disdained carpet. She said it was a petri dish for bacteria and allergens, and looked cheap. She placed mats underneath bulky furniture to prevent scuffing the flooring.

"Is every floor polished hardwood now?" Eleleth asked upward at the ornate plafond.

"Yep. Mr. Beliel makes kiss-my-butt money. He can build or remodel everything, look." Drafting sheets cluttered a tabletop. Eleleth leafed through the piles. I combed through drawers, finding a leather-bound book with *Addresses* engraved on the cover. I flipped to the Rs, and Russelifeld's information was listed. "I found it."

"Great. Let's get Vasi."

"Hey, you think that was Mrs. Beliel's car, and the janitor busted its taillights?"

"For sure." She examined a paperweight sculpture. "Isn't that why we're doing this? To scour his place for some kind of evidence proving he's a criminal."

"I don't know about breaking and entering, though." I hadn't wholly formulated our plan or motive. I wanted a reason to keep our group together. Solving a mystery seemed like an enticing method.

"I'll do it. I ain't a scaredy-cat."

"Curiosity kills cats, even non-scaredy ones." Two automobile doors shut outside. "Didn't we tell the trio to stay in the car?" Peth, Agares, and Mahlen were supposed to be waiting outside parked inconspicuously in the absent next-door neighbor's driveway. We'd taken Mahlen's hatchback versus Peth's UCV because it was an unremarkable model. Three creatures loitering on the Beliels' property would be remarked upon.

"Yep." Eleleth peeked through the window blinds. "Hide! Hide!"

"What?" She liked to prank us. I figured she had a joke brewing. She'd undoubtedly concocted a jump scare.

"Get under the desk! It's Vasi's dad and somebody else."

We abruptly straightened what we'd disturbed and scurried beneath the big, L-shaped desk. We were hidden unless a bum sat in the swivel chair and scooted their knees into the space presently occupied by our faces.

"What if he comes in here?" My syllables glided on a whisper.

Her finger went to her pursed lips.

A key unlocked the bolt, and Mr. Beliel entered. "It's on my bureau. I left the veranda sketch on the wrong pile."

"You're so forgetful," said an unknown male.

"That's why I keep you employed. To remind me."

They walked into the office, bringing scents of cologne and licorice root with them. I was thinking of a lie should they discover us. We could say we were playing hide-n-seek. Vasiariah wouldn't be in too much trouble with her father for breaking a rule. She was his doll, and he doted on her.

"Is that why, or something else, boss?"

We heard kissing sounds. Eleleth and I stared at one another, stupefied.

"Knock it off, Leo. My daughter could be home."

His acquaintance huffed. Papers rustled above us. We could see the tips of their steel-toed boots through the low gap dividing the backside of the desk from the shag rug its stubby legs squatted on.

"Got it. Let's go." Their footsteps receded to the egress.

The latch clicked, and so did the reality of what transpired. Vasiariah's father was cheating on her mother with an employee...a male employee. The Beliels seemed happily married. Vasiariah hadn't mentioned her parents disagreeing about anything. They were a picture-perfect family, literally. Their photo hung in Bune Town's portrait studio.

"You think Vasi has a clue?" I asked.

"That her dad's a cheater or that he's doing something that could get him exiled?"

Our dialogue reverberated off the surrounding

wood. "Both. Either."

"We underestimated her before. She suspects more than we give her credit. I love her." She tapped her palm to her chest. "But you know, I think she plays dumb sometimes. I guess to make males feel smarter. She *is* the most popular gal in school."

"True." Vasiariah raised her hand only to ask questions and feigned cluelessness when called upon to answer a teacher's query. Gals who were wiser than average and had ambition were deemed suspicious. You had to be extra cautious when dealing with male teachers, mainly middle-aged or older. They held badly hidden resentment toward intelligent young females and went to humiliating lengths to convince themselves they were shrewder.

One flustered P.E. coach randomly exclaimed in front of his class, "Everybody knows I'm smarter than you," to a gal who'd devised a winning basketball play for her team. He fixated on her for the entire semester, asking others about her or calling out her name whenever he saw her saying, "Jerah, correct your ＿＿＿ (fill in the blank with attitude, clothing, etc.)." His obsessive behavior became so disturbing he was ordered to resign. Jerah and the rest of us learned to enshroud our aptitude and cleverness to preclude derision, thus making it difficult to know who was genuinely naïve.

"I think," Eleleth added, "you'd be the most popular, except you sometimes answer questions too quickly, and you harp about feminism, or maybe it's because you lost your last baby tooth in eighth grade, and it took a spell for the permanent one—"

"Yeah, yeah, yeah." I wasn't taunted about the

temporary missing cuspid, but I was self-conscious about it. "Should we tell her?" She might call us liars, or if she found out we knew and hadn't told her, she'd say we're disloyal friends.

"Would *you* want to know?"

If I revered my father how Vasiariah did, this news wouldn't change my affection for him, but I would hurt for my mother, and I wouldn't want to be burdened with keeping it from her. Plus, homosexuality, or adults engaging in homosexual deeds, was an offense punishable by excommunication and exile from the realm.

I was six when they banished one of my first dance instructors to the Barren. Valac was the son of the studio owner and substituted for her while she nursed a sprained ankle. Someone suggested, "Young lads seeing a male dancer will encourage 'em to join dance class, lead 'em into gender confusion, and turn 'em queer." That quote snowballed into an avalanche of accusations. I was still haunted by the townsfolk's signs and wretched chants—*Gabriel hates fags!*

Valac was hauled from my class to a group shackled in the bed of a truck. They were forced to wear prison jumpsuits with various letters on their backs; B, G, I, L, Q, T. I knew my ABCs, but letters were missing, and they weren't in the correct order. "What's happening to the alphabet creatures, Mommy?"

"A mistake. A terrible mistake." She hurried me toward the car to drive us to safety from the gathering mobs. The metal plates on my soles tapped swiftly across the pavement. We hadn't tarried to change my shoes. "Stay clear of the windows!"

Curiosity prodded me to peek, but I didn't. I sat buckled in the middle rear seat with my shaky little hands covering my eyes. I clanked my nervous feet together so I couldn't hear the perplexing pandemonium outside that accompanied the banishment of adults.

Minors received a lighter sentence. Extreme conversion therapy. We could be subjected to reparative counseling merely for being earwitnesses. The therapeutic counseling was done by electrodes hooked to your genitals. "We can't *ever* let her or anyone find out we know."

"Agreed. We overheard nothing." She proffered her pinky for me to shake on it and seal our pact.

That settled, we arose from the desk hollow. My cramped legs had fallen asleep. I shimmied them awake on our path to the foyer.

"I guess Dad didn't see you." Vasiariah descended the staircase. I wondered had *she* seen *him*.

"Nope. We hid in the office, which is where Amitiel found the address book."

"Who's ready for some espionage?" It was the proper term to use since we'd already inadvertently spied on Mr. Beliel and his furtive tryst. I felt guilty about it and for feeling a whit happy Vasiariah's family was as dysfunctional as the rest of ours.

***

The book listed Frag Russelifeld as an employee for a maintenance company. It contracted out workers like him to schools and other commercial buildings or facilities. He lived far from town in a trailer court in the rural district where mostly ranch hands and farm laborers resided.

The farther we drove on Fern Street, the starker the contrast. The weedy roadside was strewn with litter. Potholes eventually outnumbered the intact asphalt. Chunks had broken off and tumbled into the ditch.

A half dozen ramshackle houses, stitched together by poison ivy, seemed one windy day from complete collapse. Consecutive vacant lots were cemeteries of their former neighbors abutting a dense forest. Sprawling limbs shook hands over the double blacktop lanes.

Mahlen slowed his speed to gawk. "Was this tract the original realm settlement?"

"What's left of it and the refuge encampments." I loosened the uncomfortable lap belt. I wasn't used to sitting in the middle. "Creatures who didn't already live here migrated here to escape the war and constructed shantytowns."

"I must've missed that paragraph in history class," Peth said from the rear seat.

"My grandfather used to tell me about the olden days. He was a kid when he and his parents fled the wars." He'd retold the story so much it had almost become *my* experience. He'd sat in the rear middle seat feeling heat radiating through the windows as flames lapped at their speeding car. "Aur'ell, make yourself small!" His father had urged him from the driver's seat, his fingers digging into the steering wheel, relinquishing for a brief second to drag a palm across his sweaty brow before returning to the helm. "Keep your head down," his mother warned. He lay petrified on the floorboards, hearing explosions and screams and seeing wings flap past the glass.

"My grands don't tell me anything except to get a

109

haircut."

"This area looks familiar. Grandpa retired as a manager from the metal factory that used to be off a side road somewhere at the end of this street." The owners worried methane vapor seeping from the swamps was poisoning the employees and relocated the plant.

"If it goes that far." Agares hung his head from the opened passenger window. "Lumber trucks have torn this place apart."

A log-hauler grumbled by kicking out rocks and sticks. They caromed off the car's fender.

From the backseat, Eleleth grasped his shoulder. "Get your face inside and roll up the window before you get hit."

"Okay, Mom."

She quickly withdrew into her spot. In the rearview mirror, I detected a scarlet blotch on her cheeks. Equating Eleleth to her mother was the worst affront for her.

Agares sat back beside me. I opened the glovebox to get the city map and smacked his knees.

"Ouch!"

"Sorry." I wasn't. I handed him the map. "We don't need to go to the street's end. Maple Avenue is off this road. There."

"I see it." Mahlen steered onto the graveled path. A worn sign read, *L be ty Trailer Court*.

"Liberty," Vasiariah filled in the missing letters. "That was the name in the address book."

We jounced onward. Untended shrubs delineated the property lines around each mobile home lot. "Peth, your UCV would've been too hulky to drive between these lanes." He eased off the accelerator as we approached the next aisle.

"Number 15, that's it." I pushed his chin toward the dilapidated structure with the cracked skirting.

"Oh, yeah. That looks like the sort of shack he'd live in." He parked the car on number sixteen's unoccupied pad.

Agares leaned across us to peer through a hole in the five-foot shrub wall, "How does a maintenance worker not maintain his own house?"

"Right!" Eleleth craned her neck from the rear seat. "I see a light on."

"Get down," Vasiariah said. "I saw movement."

We all ducked. The trailer's front door swung open. Russelifeld emerged bearing two stuffed garbage bags. He pivoted to lock the door, tripped, caught himself by straddling the warped and rickety handrail, then somersaulted down the stairs.

We suppressed our laughter.

"Goddang-it-to-Avern-son-of-swamp-witch-bastard," he cussed his way to his beat-up van. After multiple attempts, the engine cranked, and smoke plumed from the rusty muffler.

"Quick, let's hop out," Eleleth said to Agares. "We can search his place. Ya'll follow him. Pick us up later by the dying pine tree at the gravel path's end." They exited in crouched positions and gingerly closed their doors.

"Don't get caught," Mahlen warned.

"You either."

Mahlen reversed and trailed the van several minutes away from town. "Where's this fool headed? There's nothing out this far except some logging trails."

" 'Til the marshland gets too spongy," Peth said. "The academy stopped training here years ago. The city blocked the place off with fencing."

"There's an old junkyard. They used to get discarded scrap iron from the factory for cheap and resell it." Grandpa brought me along when he recycled our broken shed and bought me some training wheels for my bike.

"Maybe he's selling something for scrap." Vasiariah was optimistic. "Probably whatever he stole from the light fixtures."

The van rounded a curve and navigated into the junkyard's rutted driveway. "Mystery solved," I said. The tall perimeter fence precluded us from seeing anything else. "Let's get back to the trailer court and see if Agares and Eleleth found anything."

"Yes, madam," Mahlen sounded irked. He rapidly wheeled off the dirt lane, onto the grass, and then into the road to retrace our original path.

We picked up the snoop duo by the dying pine tree. "Russelifeld's house is disgusting," Eleleth said. "Filthy and stinks. I wouldn't touch a thing. Did you all see what he was up to?"

Peth moved over so she could enter the backseat. "It looked like he was recycling something at the scrapyard."

"Probably some stolen equipment," Vasi said. "He wasn't trying to hurt anyone, just make a few bucks."

Agares sat in the passenger seat. Something sharp in his pocket poked me.

"Did you find anything?"

"Not really," he lied.

"Well, this was fun. I'm glad it's over." Mahlen

accelerated down the road toward the school where we'd all gathered after the play. "I've got cleaning duty at the club in about fifteen minutes."

"Can one of you take Am home?" Eleleth typed on her phone's keypad. "I'm meeting Vehuel for dinner."

"I can't be late for work. I'm cutting it close dropping you three at school and those two at the carnival."

Already getting ditched. My bad dream seemed to be a premonition.

"I can take her. Let these lovebirds finish their date." Agares smacked Peth's knee.

"Thanks, bro."

"You're all still going to the parade tomorrow, right?" Vasiariah helped paint and decorate a float advertising her father's company, and she wanted, nay, demanded we see it.

"Of course," we unanimously answered.

"I'll be there on Cherub's booster club float." Mahlen and his teammates would ride on their platform with signs asking for more school spirit donations and game attendance to support the athletics department. He dropped us off at the school, gave me a fast peck goodbye, and sped toward the carnival grounds with Eleleth close behind on her scooter.

"She's back with Vehuel?" Agares led me to his truck.

"I guess so. You jealous?"

"Nah, I knew I was merely a piece of meat to her." He grinned. "I'm happy for her and overjoyed I don't have to keep pretending I'm unaware she's into me to keep things from getting awkward."

"You knew?"

"She wasn't remotely subtle about it."

The corner of something peeked from the top of his pants pocket. "Whatcha got there, in your pocket?"

"Maybe I'm just very happy to see you." He unlocked his doors, and we climbed in. A plethora of mint wrappers overflowed from a cup holder. Either he was addicted to sugary candies, or he snogged lots of gals with dragon breath. Gross.

"Seriously. What did you find, and why didn't you say in the car?"

"Everybody seemed to want to put this to bed." He inserted his key into the ignition but didn't turn it. "You heard what Vasi and Mahlen said, and Eleleth was too busy texting her beau to search Russelifeld's place."

I pondered if she was really into her ex, or was she trying to pique Agares' interest by showing him he had competition? It wasn't working.

"I found a heap of jerkoff mags and pictures. The models looked young. He had photographs of our classmates too." He buckled his seatbelt, and I followed suit.

"Who?"

"I don't know all their names." He fished through his console for a mint. "I saw Vasi, Caim, and Eleleth. The others were, um…" He unwrapped his candy and popped it into his mouth. "Succu and one from her brood, maybe her stepsister or half-sister or sister-aunt. The inbreeding is confusing on so many levels."

"Does she look like her jaw lost its battle with gravity?" You could virtually smell her bad breath across a room, and it could knock you off your feet.

He snickered. "Yup."

"Slack-jawed Jiki, her half-sister. She's another C

114

U next term."

"Oh, my. The almost C-word." He reached into his pocket. "I found you too." He handed me my photo with SAMPLE stamped on the top.

I felt queasy thinking about what that revolting creep was doing with my picture and how he obtained it. "Did he steal photos from the yearbook office?"

"I assume, except Succu signed the backside of her pic, 'To my white knight.' She dotted the *I*s with hearts."

"What in Avern is she doing giving him her photo?" I counted the number of instances she'd spied on us. I could foresee myself falling down a conspiracy rabbit hole.

"No idea, but this is weird." He relocated his mint from inside one cheek to the other. "He used some photos as bookmarks in a poetry anthology. He'd marked the page with the poem, 'A Reply to the Spider,' by B. Tany Fieldz. You remember it from literature class in middle school?"

"Not really." In middle school, I had an unrequited twenty-minute crush on Agares. I figured it was the notion of him being the bad lad daemon, the rebel, that attracted me. And because everyone else liked him, I'd hopped on the bandwagon too. I saw him much differently now. "I didn't know you liked flowery prose." I wasn't a fan of poetry or insects or poems about insects. I preferred history over entomology and ballads.

"It's not something I advertise."

"'Cause it might impact your alpha male status in school."

"No." He cut his eyes at me, "I think we *both* know

it's pretty rock solid."

"Well, don't strain your rotator cuff."

"What?"

"Patting yourself on the back." I acted out the movement.

"It's not like that. My dad says," he mimed guzzling a beer, "'males who like poetry are thumb-sucking sissies.'" Then he fake burped. "Well, thumb-sucking is the insult he uses when he's sober. I won't repeat the drunk one. Anyway, this poem isn't flowery. It's about deception."

"It maybe sounds familiar. Can you give me a verse or two?"

He shut his eyes and declaimed it from memory.
Walk into my parlor,
The spider says to me.
He calls it a pretty parlor,
Although I've no desire to see.
There are things to show me
Just up a winding stair;
Yet for all his claims,
I simply do not care.
Thinking me soft in the head,
He welcomes me into his bed,
To tuck me under a fine sheet.
From his pantry, he offers a slice
Of what he says is very nice.
With compliments, he is replete.
He speaks of his warm affection.
His words are a misdirection.
His wickedness he cannot hide,
Still he urges me to step inside.
For his cajoling, I'm not fond.

"Oh, no, thank you," I respond.
"Regardless of what you say,
I must bid you a good day."
The eight-legged bug returns to his den,
Weaving his little webs of sin.
He hopes to dine upon my carcass,
Sprinkled with sweetness and finesse.
Alas, such a witless old thing,
Singing false flattery to kiss my hind wing.
He thought my robes of blue had more of a purple
hue.
That spider foolishly mistook a wasp for a fly.
I'll plant maggots in his belly and watch him die.

"Oh. Wow. If he's directing that towards us, it's bone-chilling."

"I think he stole the pictures and some checks. They were made out to cash from Vice Principal Melek and the Cherub High bank account dated after Russelifeld was fired."

Photos of young females bookmarking pages about murder prose were more imperative to me than whether or not he stole checks. "Maybe it was part of a severance package."

"Could be. I'm going to call Isham. He made detective a few weeks ago." Isham was Agares' maternal first cousin once removed, but they were near in age. Isham's granny was the much older sister to Agares' mom.

I'd interacted with him at school and watched him lead our football team to a sector championship. He was the taller, darker, less debonair version of his younger cousin. He'd joined the police force after graduating high school. I speculated he was a medium by which

Agares obtained his information on the declaration rituals.

He dialed a number and switched on his phone's loudspeaker so I could hear. A voicemail recording played. "You've reached Detective Isham Buer. Leave a message."

A beep sounded. Agares asked if they could get together to discuss an important issue.

"Sure." Isham's reply startled us. "I've been meaning to call you."

"Why're you pretending to be your voicemail?"

"I'm waiting to hear back from my date last night, and I don't want to seem too available. But ne'er mind that. Do you know what happened to some photographs of mine that disappeared?"

I suspected the mutilation pictures originated from him. He was evidently an unwitting source for Agares.

He responded with a fib phrased as a question, "Are you missing a family photo album or something?"

"Ne'er mind. They'll turn up. What's your important issue?"

"Can you check out a criminal named Frag Russelifeld? He was a janitor at our school, and we think he's harassing some students."

"I know who he is. When I was a beat cop, I arrested him for drunk and disorderly conduct, but his attorney got the case thrown out, claiming the arrest was due to a discrimination bias. Total horsecrap. We call him grease pig around here because nobody's ever gotten his charges to stick, and he must be greasing the right poles, or ya know…"

"Yup, I get it," he interjected. "So, you'll check on him?"

"I've got a large caseload with the larcenies and stabbings, but if I get time, I'll look him up."

"Thanks, buddy." Agares ended the call and stashed his phone in a dashboard cubbyhole.

"Did he say *stabbings*?" I emphasized the second S. "As in plural?"

"It could've been a slip of the tongue." He cranked his engine. "Or the stabbing at Club Pinion may not have been the isolated incident cops said it was."

"That's unsettling."

Raindrops sprinkled on the dingy windshield. He flicked on the wipers. "Let's go before we get caught in a flash flood." The worn rubber blades made streaked double arcs across the glass as we drove through the empty lot.

"Well, on the upside, we'll never see it coming through this." I tapped the windshield. My fingertip left a clear dot behind.

"Oh." He decelerated. "Would Her Royal Highness prefer to wade home?"

A lightning bolt streaked the sky, and its subsequent boom rattled the windows.

"No, sir, she would not."

Chapter 6

Flooding in West River, and all its branching tributaries, was common. Timeworn dams would crack, overrunning sandbag barriers. Insurance companies wouldn't insure businesses or homeowners if they built too near the banks and didn't put their structures on stilts.

Sixteen months ago, at the finale of a summer's long drought that aided winds in eroding topsoil and levees, Bune Town and Leyak were deluged with copious rainfall. Water engulfed the shambly bridge connecting the two cities. Lots of drivers were hospitalized. Emergency room staff were overwhelmed with patients, including my mother. She'd gone to the ER with a severe headache fearing it might be a bulging vessel about to rupture.

Inundated with hypothermic car crash survivors, the medical staff either overlooked or dismissed Mom's history of aneurysms. They diagnosed her with a bad migraine and told her to wait. Her texts updating me became muddled as she jumbled words together. When a nurse finally got around to calling my mother's name, Grandpa and I had arrived, and Mom was unresponsive in her chair. She'd languished in a vegetative state ever since.

The All Life is Precious Bill, which convicted murderers were using to postpone their executions, wouldn't let us turn off her ventilator so she could die with dignity. She was relocated to a long-term care facility and forced to waste away. We were only allotted short, monitored visitations to prevent our freeing her from a living death. In my worst nightmares, she'd wail and sob and beg me to pull the plug while convicts outside banged on her window. I dreaded falling asleep.

Losing Mom was the hardest thing I'd experienced. There were no goodbyes, no hopes of reconnecting; it was just gone. I didn't see the point in our being born, loving only to suffer pain and tragedy, all the while creeping closer to our own demise. I strived to find joy in my life, yet there was always a void there, an empty seat in the room, a silence where there should've been laughter, and there my heartache has resided—a black beast of despondency reminding me how much happier I could be. Grandpa recommended I see a grief counselor. I preferred not being stigmatized as mentally unstable.

"Am, did you hear me?"

"Huh?" I'd zoned out again.

"What's the plan for the parade tomorrow?" Agares clicked on his blinker to signal his turning onto Sycamore. "Who's riding with whom? I'm fine with driving us."

"Well, Mahlen's on a float for his basketball team, and Vasi's on that stupid one for her dad, so they have to be there early. Peth'll probably be up her butt somewhere. I doubt Caim's going."

"Grieving over her sister or because Tannin can't go?"

"Why can't Tannin go?"

"The fireworks trigger his autism seizures."

"You're confusing that condition with epilepsy, neither of which Tannin has. He'll tell you himself he was a mean kid whose parents wouldn't discipline him, and they used it to get government assistance and other freebies."

"Crap on a cracker!" He smacked his thigh. "I was in a store with him and his folks when we were ten or eleven, I think, and he wanted a toy, but they said no, so he threw a tantrum, crying, kicking, screaming." He thrashed an arm around. "His dad told the freaked-out clerk he had autism, so she gave him the toy for free to shut him up."

"Yep. They're terrible. Tannin said ninety percent of the kids he met were little a-holes because they were allowed to be and had been misdiagnosed by naïve clinicians, greedy parents or guardians, and lazy teachers who didn't want energetic kids in their classes. After he outgrew the baby stuff and wanted to date Caim, he behaved himself to get moved into her class. His folks said it was the divine miracle they'd prayed for."

"Of course, and nothing to do with the fact that once he turned eighteen, he'd have access to his money and would stop them from getting it."

"By that time, they had his younger sister, who they said was autistic too. She was in my Tiny Tappers group. If she wanted a classmate's spot in line or their row on stage, she'd shove them. I heard her mocking Daevah Yanek's younger sister because of her stutter, and that was the last straw. I made the little brat apologize publicly to every single dancer in class, and I told her if she ever bullied anyone else, I'd have her permanently removed. Her condition cured itself within milliseconds." I snapped my fingers.

"Horrible parents doing a disservice to their own children." Agares was an authority on horrible parents.

"Mmm hmm. Taking resources from the kids who really need it. Speaking of a kid with bad parents, I don't know what the status is on Eleleth. She's probably going to the parade with Vehuel. You bringing anyone?"

He flashed a sly grin. "I may have mentioned to somebody I'd be there."

"We're taking separate cars then?"

"We'll figure it out." Agares drove to my house and dropped me out at my driveway's end. "I'll let you know once I hear from Isham."

I wouldn't hold my breath, figuring his cousin was preoccupied with whoever was his date. "Call me on the landline. My cell battery needs to charge."

"Okay. Stay dry."

"Yeah, see ya." I gave the door a shove, but the truck's momentum forward shut it. I surveyed the sky. The light precipitation was already tapering. I unlocked my front door and walked into the house. It was dim and silent. I secured the deadbolt and flicked on a light.

"Papa?" No response. He must've gone to his rummy game. I hung my keys on their hook and kicked off my dank shoes. "Josa?" She scampered from her parlor bed to greet me. "Did I wake you from a nap?" I scratched behind her ears. "Let's get you fed." She trailed me into the kitchen, anxiously observing me fill her food and water bowls.

A crash emanated from my grandfather's bedroom. Josa yipped at the noise.

"It's okay. It's the trophies falling." Grandpa's over-weighted trophy shelf periodically ripped itself off the wall.

She growled and woofed toward his room.

"What's wrong? You think he left his window open again?" His screen was torn, and he'd come home to find a squirrel running amuck.

Josa concurred with a bark. Her hackles were up, and so were mine. She wasn't an aimlessly barking hound. The last time she was in her attack stance, she killed two coyotes who'd ventured into our backyard.

In case something bigger than a rodent was in there, I should call animal control. I retrieved my cell. It had zero percent power. I picked up our telephone. The landline was dead. Storms were notorious for severing our lines. We were on our own. I could run outside, shrilling like a dork, or I could let my dog exercise her badassery.

"Shhh." I clutched the pan used to cook scrambled eggs. "Come!" I ran down the hallway with her at my heels and flung open Grandpa's door. "Get 'em!"

Josa raced past me into the darkness. I switched on the light. Before my pupils could adjust, she was biting and chomping a masked intruder, swarming him like a legion of hornets, and I was clobbering him on the head.

He yowled and frantically went for the open window, gliding on some fallen trophies and ramming into a dresser. He got his knees onto the dresser's top and his torso half out the window when Josa clamped her jaws on his waistband, tugging his jeans downward, exposing clusters of her bloody teeth marks and his hairy butt. I proceeded to spank him on his butt. "Get…

out... of... my...house!"

"I'm trying!"

"Release, Josa, release!" She let go, and he tumbled to the ground. "Get out of here!" I shouted.

Josa barked and leaped after him, nipping his calves while he rapidly hobbled over the fence into the murky night. I stood there panting as my epinephrine levels waned and the seriousness of the situation dawned on me. I giggled, then cried, then giggled when I cried.

"Amitiel," Ms. Vanth called from her screened patio. "Are you all right?" She was a neighborhood watch member and a sweet spinster with a bad knee who baked us cookies because I'd bring in her Saturday paper. I'd forgotten to do it today. "I didn't know you were home, or I would've warned you I saw a prowler." Her residence was catty-cornered to mine, providing her a broad view. "I phoned the police."

"Thanks, Ms. V." I dabbed at some snot with my sleeve. "I'm okay." I could hear sirens nearby. They were doing extra patrols due to the burglaries. "I'll go get your paper."

"You come stay here 'til they get there. I'll brew some herbal tea."

"Yes, ma'am." Still clasping my weaponized skillet, I exited the sliding glass door, slipping into my flip-flops on the way outside. "Josa, come." The squashy ground rose up around my rubber soles as we plodded to Ms. Vanth's house. She served me a hug, a cinnamon bar, and lemongrass tea. I had no appetite. I took a bite and a sip so not to offend her hospitality. My taste buds must've been on a trauma-induced hiatus because two of the most potent flavors in nature tasted like the paper cup from which I drank. I sneaked the dessert to Josa at my feet. Her appetite was fine.

"Do you know a number where we can call your grandfather?" She readjusted her silky headscarf, which concealed some hair rollers.

"They're all in my contacts list on my phone. He should be finishing his card game soon and coming home. He's not a night owl."

A blaring Bune Town Police car whipped into my driveway. Two cops emerged, drew their flashlights and guns, and walked the perimeter of my residence.

Two more officers arrived. They interviewed Ms. Vanth and me inside her patio. She was back and forth, bringing beverages and snacks. I worried she'd offer to cook a seven-course meal, and they'd never leave.

"We've got dispatch trying to reach your grandfather," the higher-ranking cop said. "So, you can't describe the burglar other than a male of average height and weight covered in dark clothing, gloves, and a ski mask?"

I must've seen his skin when Josa semi-pantsed him, yet I couldn't recall his color. I shook my head.

"You were very brave and lucky you have a good guard dog, but we don't recommend assailing intruders. For peace of mind, keep your doors and windows locked...not that we think this burglar, in particular, will return."

His pimply-chinned partner guffawed. "Unless he wants another spanking."

"Be respectful, rookie." Isham opened the creaky screen door. He entered, and his towering presence filled the room.

"Detective Buer, are you working this case?"

"Yep, you can go now. Leave a copy of your notes on my desk."

The uniformed officers, apparently miffed by Isham's brusque manners, let the screen door slam behind them in a coarse rat-a-tat-tat.

He placed a paper sack on the wicker table near my pan and sat diagonal from me. "Hello, Amitiel."

"Hi, Isham. Do I have to repeat everything to you?"

"Nah, I heard." He loosened his tie. "Sound really carries out here."

Ms. Vanth entered from the adjoining kitchen. "Hey, Detective Buer." She touched his shoulder. "How's your mom? I haven't seen her since I tore my tendon during our doubles tennis match."

"She's well. Practicing for the next tournament."

"I'll be rooting for her. Can I offer you tea, coffee, or some hot cocoa to match that handsome complexion?" She gave his shoulder a squeeze.

If he blushed, I couldn't tell. "Yes, please. Anything with caffeine."

"Dealer's choice then." A whistling kettle beckoned her to the stove.

"Do you recognize this?" From inside the sack, Isham extracted a transparent plastic bag containing a mud-caked, unfolded pocketknife. The shiny metallic blade glinted on his bronze skin, and I speculated whether the intruder would've used it to slash mine, like what befell the daemons outside Club Pinion.

"I've never seen it. You'll have to ask my grandfather. I know he carries one, but the knife I've seen is smaller and has a different handle."

"I found it in the muck below his window. Your

pup there," he motioned toward Josa lying in the corner, "may have caused the perpetrator to drop it. It looks like it was used to saw out the exterior screen. It's the same method used in the previous break-ins. This, however, is new." He extracted a second plastic bag containing a bundled pair of muddy cotton underwear.

They bore a resemblance to the hipster style, which I owned, along with bikini-cut briefs and thongs to eliminate panty lines. "Maybe if they were clean, I could tell whether they're mine."

"Or the guy's a perverted weirdo who walks around with a pair of loose underpants in his pocket." His stoic countenance failed to express whether he was being sarcastic or making a statement.

"I don't know. You ever pull laundry out of the dryer, and static cling makes the clothes stick to each other? You put your foot down a pants leg and out pops a sock. It could've landed somewhere random, and Josa used it as a chew toy. Or maybe they blew off somebody's clothesline. I'm in no condition to hypothesize." The sanctity of my home, and possibly my underwear drawer, had been breached. I wasn't comfortable knowing my knickers would be examined as evidence by umpteen strangers.

"Fair point. I'll write *unclaimed stray article* on the tag." He returned the objects to the sack.

I held up the pan. "You need this? I hit him with it."

"We already secured a swab of his blood from inside the bedroom."

A clinking spoon on a mug preceded Ms. Vanth into the patio. "Here you go." She produced Isham's steaming cocoa and a napkin. "I'm out of marshmallows."

"Thank you, ma'am. This is grand."

She tarried, waiting for him to taste it.

He sipped his drink. "Mmm, delicious."

She blotted together her recently glossed lips. "I'll be in the living room, doing my stretches, should either of you need me." She patted my head. "The couch is a pull-out. You can stay the night if you need to."

"Thanks, Ms. V."

"I can escort her back here when we're finished." Isham gulped his beverage and rose from his chair.

"What's left to finish?" I wanted the ordeal to end.

"You have to list stolen items and photograph any damages. Your granddad will need to sign some forms which he can use to file a claim with his homeowner's insurance company. They may reimburse him for things like electronics, depending on his coverage and deductible amount."

"I don't know whether we have insurance." It would've lapsed if Grandpa forgot to pay it.

He drained his cup. "Ahh. In any case, standard procedure dictates we do the paperwork."

"Does it also dictate wiping off a chocolate mustache?"

"Oh, crap." He swapped his cup for a napkin and cleaned his face. "Better?"

"Yep. Let's get this over with. Josa, come." We ambled out of the patio. She ran to play in the yard.

Isham shadowed me and extracted a vaping pen from his shirt pocket, "Mind if I smoke?" He put the device to his lips.

"It's your funeral." An increase in lung illnesses coincided with the popularity of e-cigarettes. They were also known for spontaneously exploding. Carrying them in a pocket near your genitals was really tempting fate.

"You're right." He inserted it back into his pocket. "I switched to the vape pen because I thought it would help me quit smoking, but all it does is get me coughing more. Agares says it makes me look like a douchebag anyway." He retrieved a paper cigarette and stuck it between his teeth. "He should be here soon."

"What?"

"Yeah, he says I'm like a giant baby with a strange pacifier or a toy flute." He patted around his pockets, presumably for a match or a lighter.

"No. I mean, yes, you do look douchey with the vape pen, but you said Agares should be here?"

He paused his search, "Uh, first of all, ouch. Second, I called him earlier, which I definitely regret now, to tell him I had some info to give him, but I had to investigate a burglary here, and he said he'd be right over because you're his friend."

"You got something on Russelifeld?"

"You know about the janitor?"

"I was with Agares when he called you today." Standing in my driveway, I began detailing to Isham what transpired from the play to the carnival to the subsequent pursuit and home invasions—Russelifeld's and mine. Agares' truck rumbled up. "There he is. He can tell you more."

He got out, leaving the driver's side door ajar in his haste to hug me. "You okay?"

My ribcage popped a little under the pressure. "I just chased away a burglar. Josa did most of the work. I'm fine." I broke our embrace before my spine cracked like a peppermint stick. I also didn't feel I warranted being consoled. "I was telling your cousin about the janitor."

"Uh, huh." Isham lit his cigarette. "You broke into a guy's house?"

"We didn't break in," Agares corrected him. "It was unlocked."

"Mmm-kay, so you let yourself into a guy's house without his permission or knowledge and found some sort of proof of something you don't know what it is yet?"

"He had jerkoff magazines next to pics of high school students all over his house and checks made out to cash rather than…"

"None of which is unlawful unless it can be proved the checks were stolen or the photos were nude minors."

"I didn't see any."

"His argument could be he has worked at schools and could've developed harmless friendships with the students in the pictures?" He looked at me. "Were you one of those students, then he passed you over for another, and you're aching for revenge?"

Was he joshing? "Ew, no!"

"But he had your picture. Did you give it to him? A smoke show like you probably gets lots of attention from older fellows."

"This was a mistake." Agares trudged to his truck door to close it.

"I'm only busting balls," he yelled at him. "Sweety, tell your beau to calm down." He took a drag from his cigarette.

"I'm not your sweety. I don't tell Agares what to

do, and he isn't my beau."

"Then why would he care so much that some random turd-stain was jerking it to your photo?"

"Because he's one of my best friends, and he cares about others. Isn't that part of your job?"

"I can check into this possible pedophile, Russelifeld…"

"He's going to investigate the perv," I called to Agares.

He crossed his brawny arms. "What's the catch?"

Isham tapped the ash from his burning cigarette. "If…"

"Here we go."

"You get me a dinner at Vasiariah Beliel's house."

"Forget it," I said. "She's underage, and she's seeing someone."

"I ain't interested in her. I like her mom." His bushy eyebrows danced.

Ms. Vanth's flirty behavior made sense now. Isham liked older females. "You want us to get you a date with Mrs. Beliel, who's married?"

"Am I to assume you two amateur sleuths aren't aware she's in an open marriage?"

We both shook our heads, Agares truthfully, and I in a pretense I hadn't overheard the kiss between Mr. Beliel and his male employee. Perhaps they did have an open marriage.

"You get some valuable info on the creepy custodian first," I said, "and we'll get you a group dinner with the Beliels."

"Deal. I'll get the insurance forms for your grandfather." He walked toward his car with a baseball-sized dent in the bumper.

"I can't believe it." Agares shook his head. "You just pimped out Mrs. Beliel."

"I merely agreed to facilitate a meeting. She's an adult. I'm sure she'll turn him down." Mr. Beliel, on the other hand, might not—but I wouldn't tell Isham that. "You think he'll investigate the janitor?"

"Hard to say. He's torn his drawers with me too many times to count."

A pair of headlights shone in our direction. They irradiated the slightly bent stance of a bipedal creature striding toward us. I recognized Grandpa's oncoming silhouette by his gait. Somebody dropped him off. "I heard what happened. I'm so proud of you." He kissed my forehead. "You are your mother's daughter."

"Thanks, Papa, but Josa's the heroine. She chewed the burglar a new butthole."

He chuckled. "I bet she did." He stuck out his palm. "Agares, right?"

"Aye, sir." They shook hands.

Isham, carrying a folder labeled BTPD, introduced himself to my grandfather and accompanied us into the house to fill out paperwork. We did a walk-through before sitting at the dining room table with a stack of blank forms. Our electronics—nothing was new, and jewelry— nothing was real, were untouched. It was almost embarrassing we didn't have a thing worth stealing.

Perhaps Josa and I thwarted the robber before he had a chance to steal anything. It was partially true. I wouldn't mention my unmentionables sealed in a baggie when I updated my pals on the situation.

Our landline service hadn't been restored, but my cell charged enough to dial the phone company to report our outage. A recording said service would return soon. I dialed Mahlen next. His phone rang and rang until his voicemail answered. I didn't leave a message. He was working, and it would be too late to stop by when he got off. I also calculated his astuteness in somehow using the incident to his advantage in our marriage argument, saying unmarried females are more vulnerable than married ones. I clicked *END CALL* prior to the beep. I'd phone him later.

Vasiariah sent a text saying she'd heard from Peth, who'd heard from a guard services member who must've heard from someone on the police force my house had been burglarized. She wanted to come spend the night, but her parents said she had to prepare for tomorrow and couldn't miss her beauty sleep for a pallet party. She apologized, then had me promise via text I'd be at the parade to see her float.

I called Eleleth, who vowed to come over if she had to sneak out. "Ms. Beliel is worried you're going to be more popular than Vasi," she said through the phone. "You've got the sympathy factor plus the badass factor now."

"You know I don't care about that."

"Vasi's mom does, and her seeing you as a threat won't bode well for our friendship with her."

I didn't care to discuss conjecture. "Hurry up and get over here. Did your parents say it's okay?"

"They're nodding. I'll be there in a few. 'Kay, bye."

I gnawed the periwinkle polish off my nails, waiting for her to arrive. I couldn't sleep alone in my bed, which was presently a mental snare disguised as a full-sized mattress awaiting my slumber. I'd close my eyelids and see that sticky-fingered pervert rifling through my drawers, sniffing my underwear.

"Detective Buer, can you recommend a reliable surveillance camera system?" Grandpa was going to install equipment worth more than anything in our house. We'd record the burglar stealing our cameras.

"Yessir." He went on listing various brands and where to buy them.

"Cameras record home invasions," I said to Agares. "They don't stop them."

"No, but you stopped it. You and Josa. That was a gutsy thing to do. That burglar will never come back here."

"Tell it to my nerves." I lifted my jittery hand.

He wrapped both of his around mine. "Would you feel better if I asked your grandfather to let me sleep on the living room couch? I'll tell my folks I'm at Peth's." He glanced at his wristwatch. "They'll be tipsy enough to be agreeable and not drunk enough to be confrontational."

"I don't know." Gums would flap saying it looked improper having a male stay over right in the front room. "My neighbor tends to gossip, and Eleleth will be here." I wouldn't risk our friendship on her misjudging me as a romantic rival. "She might get the wrong idea."

"Yeah." He grinned. "She'll think I'm here for her because I'm like a big brother to you. And as long as she thinks that, your reputation remains unsoiled. She won't tell anyone because it'll look like she was the one sneaking around with her secret crush and behind Vehuel's back. Can you imagine the talk?" He clutched an imaginary string of pearls and fanned himself.

Each knot in the hearsay nexus would twist another

lie. "Grapes would explode off the vine."

"You know it." He lowered his tone, "And I can't sneak over here tonight because the last thing you need is taps outside your window or a friend seeing me sneak in."

Isham and my grandfather began to say their valedictions.

"All right. Don't ask 'til your cousin leaves."

"I won't."

"And another thing." I knew Ms. Vanth's vision was sharp as a hawk's. "Don't park near my house should Grandpa say okay, which is highly unlikely."

"Okay," Grandpa said when we asked him. "Extra creatures here tonight will give us some peace of mind. But don't park…"

"Near the house," Agares finished his sentence, and too quickly.

"Yeah." My grandfather's one-eyed squint surfaced. "I'll be leaving my bedroom door open, and I'm a very light sleeper."

"Yes, sir." He hurried out to his truck.

I recommended chewing my nails and watched him reverse from the driveway. Eleleth beeped her scooter's horn to stop him from backing into her. Her three-wheeled mobile sat in most drivers' blind spots.

He waited and let her roll up beside him. "Sorry, hot wheels. Didn't see you." She started to say something, but he interrupted. "Hold that thought. I'll be back in a minute." He eased onto the road and drove off.

She put her helmet into her side compartment and met me in the front entryway. "Did he say he's coming back?"

"He's staying over because everybody's shook up about the burglar."

She walked in and kicked off her sneakers. "Did you ask him to?"

"He offered." I closed the door and locked the bolt.

"Before or after he knew I was spending the night?" Her gears were moving again, clicking toward the answer she craved.

"After." It was the truth, although she'd perceive the timing differently.

"I suspected as much." She removed her backpack and held it by its top strap. "Too bad for him my ex and I are already talking."

"Hello, young miss," Grandpa greeted Eleleth as we passed the dining room.

"Hi, Mr. Aur'ell."

"We'll be in my room, Papa."

"Uh-huh." He resumed reading the numerous forms Isham had left.

Cautiously, I flicked on my bedroom light switch. My hypervigilant state expected to see an intruder. My pupils saw nothing and told me to calm myself, to think of something else. "How *was* your dinner date with Vehuel? Is he taking you to the dance now?" Was she replacing Agares, trying to make it a throuple, or simply adding one more buddy to our group?

"And have him be the seventh egg to our happy half dozen? No." She tossed her bag onto the floor.

Odd metaphor. "Are you using one to make the other jealous?"

"Does Mahlen know Agares is staying over?"

"Are you insinuating that's what I'm doing? Because that's ridiculous." I felt testy. "I'm not advertising this."

"No, course not." She grasped my hand, "I just didn't want to slip up and mention it to someone who isn't supposed to know. I won't say anything to anyone. What's important is how you're doing." She gave me the once-over and gasped. "Look at your nails! I'm giving you a manicure tonight."

Chapter 7

"Can we slow down?" Eleleth, in her peep-toe pumps, click-clacked on the fractured sidewalk behind us. Her balance in stilettos was notably impressive. She managed not to get stuck in the fissures or stumble over the loose pebbles scattering from the craters. A clever chalk artist incorporated the dark pits as black pips on a white domino. It was the 3-4 tile. The next concrete square had a big red strawberry with its seeds represented by multiple smaller craters. "Please?" her click-clacks coupled with the swooshing of the tufts on my corduroy pants provided an interesting percussion.

"We're almost there." Agares panted for the fifth time. His engine trouble postponed our leaving when we'd planned. We had to park two hilly streets away from the parade's route and stop at a couple stores on the way so Eleleth could drain her bladder of the five glasses of apple juice she'd had for breakfast. "Peth is saving us a spot, but his willingness to hold out dwindles fairly quick under a large crowd."

"I'm getting a blister."

"You insisted on wearing high heels knowing we'd be walking and standing all day." I'd tried talking her out of it, or to at least wear flats. She said Vehuel liked her in heels. She'd spent her whole life seeking her mom's validation. Striving to impress a mate was par for the course, even if it meant changing herself, and nobody could persuade her otherwise.

"I'm not a soothsayer. I couldn't predict Agares' truck wouldn't start, and we'd be forced to hike uphill from a million miles away."

"Or stopping at every store to pee," he mumbled.

"What?"

"We're here." We topped the hill where Pecan Avenue intersected Main Street. We were next to a bus stop bench and four stinking portable toilets. Agares motioned at a spindly arm waving above the crowd several yards away in front of the flower shop. "There's Peth."

"Thank the gods." Eleleth sat on the bench to rub her foot. "You see Vehuel anywhere?"

Peth was elbowing him and pointing at us. "Yeah, he's there." She could see him herself, if she'd wear the glasses that corrected her nearsightedness.

"I'm using the latrine really fast." She held her sniffer and went into the stall.

"Ugh, that's heinous." We moved away from the stench. I scanned the growing mass and saw a few moony-eyed gals with Agares in their sights. "Weren't you meeting someone?"

"I was. She sent a mad text saying I stood her up. She didn't believe my truck wouldn't start."

"Has she not seen that rust bucket?"

"Seeing it parked in your driveway probably didn't help."

I yanked his sleeve. "Did she?" The last thing I needed were rumors I was an unfaithful floozy...or a faithful one. Either was bad. Or that my grandfather was an unfit guardian. "Did you tell her?"

"Whaaaat?" His mouth was agape. "And sully my

reputation?" He fanned himself. "What would the neighbors think?"

"I'm serious."

"You're too serious. All the tea-spilling gossipers are going to talk about is you surviving a masked intruder, or did you forget that?"

I had. The night prior, Eleleth talked my ears off about her date while she filed and painted my nails. She asked if I preferred tansy over periwinkle, and tansy flowers made me think of Tany Fieldz, the poet whose work was bookmarked by the creepy custodian. I couldn't scrub away the image of a wasp planting maggots in an arachnid's belly to watch it die and why it resonated with Russelifeld. Was it a clue into his demented psyche?

After everybody went to sleep, I rifled through my mother's literature collection. I found two other poems by the author. "Do you remember telling me about the spider poem yesterday?"

"I like poetry; I'm not apologizing for it."

Males could be so sensitive. "No, dummy. I'm not teasing you about it. My mom had a book with poems by the same writer. One's called 'Rage.' It's good. It goes,

My rage is a dragon, lulled to sleep with time.

Yet even after decades, this wrathful serpent doesn't die.

Agares joined my recitation.

It's sustained on bitterness, nourished from malice & lies.

One day my dragon shall awaken & burn those who fed it.

"Oof, I'm detecting a common theme with this

poet. Anger, deceit, revenge, and death."

"There's something else too." I retrieved a note from my pocket and offered it to him. "I copied this one. It was too long to memorize."

He read the title aloud, "'The Smiling Viper.'"

Beware the smiling viper, the fanged bedside savior.

While we pity the old and sick, he views an opportunity.

When the feeble need care, he hisses, "Allow me."

When they cough, he eagerly awaits their death rattle.

Beware the smiling viper and his venomous babble.

Though he vows not to bite, the vein of gold shines too bright.

A poisoned mind. A quick flick of his pen,

To take everything fast before they mend.

Slyly, he coils to bask in his spoils.

Smirking, he slithers to his pit of forged wealth and sin,

Wearing the mask of kith or kin,

Because it's never the snake in a bare field one sees,

Only the rustle of the leaves.

"Doesn't it seem like a play-by-play of what Russelifeld did to his sick brother?"

"Because he stole from him?" He returned the paper to me. "You think he's using these poems as a guidebook to life, like he believes the poet is speaking to him, telling him what to do?"

"He sure ain't using pictures of high schoolers to mark prose about cupcakes and kittens or ill-fated romances. These poems are fraught with vengeance and homicidal desires. You said he had my picture."

"I knew I shouldn't have told you." He made his pensive expression where he gandered upward while his tongue maneuvered around the inside of his cheeks. "You think he broke into your house?"

"I don't know, but until whoever did gets caught, I won't be sleeping well."

"I guess I'll be on babysitting duty then."

I was infuriated he'd referred to himself as my babysitter. "After all the times you've crawled to my house, you have the audacity to call me a baby?"

"Uh, nope." His eyes enlarged. "Nah-uh, not what I meant."

"I don't need to be chaperoned."

"Okay." The door on the portable toilet stall opened. "We can go."

"We should hurry." Agares took enormous strides to cross the asphalt and extricate himself from our conversation. "I can hear the trucks."

Our friends beckoned to us. They and hundreds of parade-goers packed both sides of Main Street behind interlocking steel-barred barricades. Eleleth carefully climbed over first, and Vehuel helped her.

"You made it," he said. "I was about to go get a big pretzel from the vendor down that way. You want anything?"

"I'd love a cheese and pepper one. Amitiel, you hankering for a soft pretzel?"

"Cinnamon and sugar if you're going." I scaled the top bar about four feet from the ground. Agares moved to assist me. "I got it!"

"Are you in a mood?" He easily stepped over the barrier.

He knew very well I was in a mood. He'd put me in one. "Don't you need to go get some snacks to keep your fawners at bay?"

"Fawners? What the…"

"Hi, Agares." The devotee from Friday's Young Independents meeting manifested as if kismet heard me. She fluffed her mousy mop of ringlets and poked out her jugs.

"Kara, hey." They shared a clumsy side hug. She postured beside him in an unmoving muteness akin to a big-boobed mannequin. He didn't bother introducing us, nor did they bother conversing with one another.

We observed the decorated floats roll by, their flatbed trailers transformed with fringe and garland, fabric bunting and foam, glitter, and metallic floral sheeting. Nearly every small business had a garish float advertising their services. Riders waved to the crowds and tossed baggies with hard candies, trinket toys, gift cards, and fridge magnets embossed with their business information.

The cavalcade had no discernible order. The lead float was a confectionary store. They tossed bite-sized chocolate discs wrapped in plastic. I caught too many to eat. The remainders would melt in my pocket, so I passed them to the children nearest me.

The fourth wheeled platform was Beliel Construction Company. It was designed to look similar to a two-tier log cabin with glittery streamers and dangling ribbons. Vasiariah, wearing a flowery crown, poised on the balcony garnished with matching flower wreaths.

"She looks like a princess," Eleleth said.

"*My* beautiful princess." Peth blew Vasiariah a

kiss. She pretended to catch it and put it to her bright pink pucker.

Four of her father's employees, rose boutonnieres pinned to their lapels, tossed real flower petals with their business magnets. If a bee swarm flew by, all five passengers were dead meat. If the one who smelled like licorice was up there, he'd be the biggest target.

"All right, we've seen her, and she's seen us see her," Agares said. "Can we go before the storm clouds roll in?"

"Relax." I tied my cardigan sleeves around my waist. "The weather will hold. The wind isn't even blowing yet."

"Unlike this parade."

"What's got your panties in a twist?"

"I'm bored with flagrant capitalists, and I need to be home practicing for the debate."

"Aren't you running unopposed?" Was I alone in the assumption he'd automatically be named class president?

"The deadline to enter is still several days off."

"I need to pee again." Eleleth shifted her weight from foot to foot. Her mom had mentioned she'd gained a few pounds and suggested she go on a diet.

"You've got to stop the juice cleanses, the detoxes, and the solid food fasting trends. I mean it."

Agares agreed. "It's not healthy, especially when you're already slim enough."

She took his remark as a compliment and a sign he'd noticed her physique. She smiled from ear to ear as if she were a mischievous lynx who'd outsmarted a fisher and snagged a bass from his trotline. "I did ask Vehuel for a pretzel." She hadn't admitted she was trying to make Agares jealous, but her subliminal message reminded him her ex was bringing her a treat. "It'd be rude not to eat it."

"It would, and we haven't seen Mahlen yet. He's on a float coming up." I gestured to the most sparsely decorated platform. It was behind Ebel Drumpf Ministries' gaudy monstrosity extolling Gabrielism. A pulped paper statue of the alleged prophet was the centerpiece surrounded by males bowing their heads and females on their knees. All of them wore tacky Vote for Drumpf sashes. "Can you hold it for two more minutes?" I wasn't leaving, no matter her answer. She could take her toddler-sized bladder to the lavatory inside the ice cream parlor.

"I can wait, yeah."

The fifth parade truck towed a shimmery double-decker platform for Acting Mayor Danjal Jinn. His armed security team, akin to a pack of stone-faced watchdogs, rode on the lower level. Above them on the upper deck, his aides lobbed candy wrapped in stickers saying Vote for Jinn. Confetti guns and firecrackers spewed from their float in colorful bangs. Onlookers oohed and aahed.

The engine accelerated to climb the hill between the delicatessen on the north side of the street and Petal Pushers on the south, where my chums and I gathered. As the truck topped the crest and should've decelerated, its front tire blew. The driver swerved, lost control, bounced off the curb, and careened into the preceding float's rear bumper. Vasiariah and three of the four others on her platform managed to hang on and withstand the jolt.

"Vasi!" Peth hurtled over the barrier and sprinted

to her platform.

The unlucky employee thrown to the pavement lay static on his side mere yards from us. His limbs were unnaturally bent like a discarded ragdoll. An expanding scarlet puddle pooled around his head and a clear fluid leaked from his ears.

Previous oohs and ahhs were supplanted by screams. Countless adults prayed aloud. Children were sobbing. A police officer darted into the street to stop the progressing floats.

"We need help!" somebody shouted.

"Is there a doctor in the crowd?" yelled another.

They ran to render aid. One started dialing on a cell phone, presumably calling an ambulance. I expected to see Vasiariah's mom run to the victim or at least toward her daughter. She didn't. She must've been in a shocked stupor. I, too, felt numb and couldn't believe what I was witnessing. Was this an appalling hoax?

"Let me pass." A hulking figure bulldozed through the obstacles of bodies and steel bars. "I'm a paramedic."

To aid his entry, Agares and I detached the connected barricade in front of us. Lying beside the post's leg, I saw a bifold wallet and picked it up. I flipped it open, and the cloth material emitted a bittersweet scent similar to aniseed or fennel. The identification card's photo resembled the victim, Leonar Mammon. *Did he go by Leo?* I sniffed the wallet again. Licorice.

"I'll ensure that gets to the hospital with the casualty." Mrs. Beliel extracted it from my clutches and hurried after the paramedic. "I'm a nurse."

"Get him on his back, easy now," the medic

ordered. He and the first two responders slowly turned Leonar to initiate cardiopulmonary resuscitation. They swapped around who would provide breaths and perform chest compressions. It was a nail-biter speculating how many pumps the medic's beefy forearms could give before cracking the recipient's sternum.

Vasiariah's mother circled the victim, periodically kneeling and rising but never participating, and eventually left to check on her daughter. Did Mrs. Beliel know who Leonar was...who he really was? Was this a happy accident for her?

"Sniper!" A security guard shouted. He stood beside a hole in the window of Danjal Jinn's truck.

A female shouted, "Someone shot at the mayor!"

"Acting mayor," trumpeted a male's voice.

"Are you actually male-splaining to me right now, smartass?"

It seemed an assassin had ambushed the acting mayor's float, assuming he would be aboard, or perchance to merely frighten the politician into quitting the race. It was anybody's guess which deranged Drumpf zealot was culpable. My bet was on someone from one of those berserk conspiracy theory groups who professed Drumpf to be the Chosen One to defeat the fire monster-worshipping pedophile cannibals. Of course, his campaign would apply their political spin and claim to be the real targets that the sniper had missed while aiming for Drumpf's float.

"Over there on the roof!" A guard unsnapped his holster, drew his pistol, and fired at the deli's rooftop. "He's on the move!" A second and third guard commenced blasting at the sniper fleeing across the rooflines. Police officers joined in.

Shrieking bystanders dropped to the pavement as the contagion to fire caught on. Parade riders and walkers dove underneath their floats. Vehuel and his pretzels were nowhere to be seen. Kara knocked a kid down in her haste to scram.

Eleleth and I pasted ourselves to the flower shop's wall. My hair snagged on the textured brick. I was sure I'd be leaving some strands behind and taking with me the indentions of the mortar grooves on my backbone. When it was a daily tug-of-war against anxieties cautioning you to not leave the house and you wrangling down your irrational fears, something like this happened and reinforced all the negative worries.

"Those cops are going to shoot innocent bystanders!" Agares dragged two weeping children toward safety beside us. They left trails of melting ice cream on the concrete walkway.

Eleleth held my hand too tight.

"Your nails are digging into my palm."

"Sorry." She eased her grip. "Hey, I don't have to pee anymore, but side note, can I borrow your sweater?"

I spied a darkening patch on her jeans. She'd peed herself and required a coverup. I untied my cardigan and gave it to her. "Keep it."

A cop hunkering in his patrol car squealed orders on a bullhorn. "Citizens, remain calm."

No one did. Everybody freaked out, fleeing inside nearby businesses, or crying and pleading to their deities to rescue them.

"Officers are pursuing the shooter." What if there were multiple shooters? We heard staggered shots in the distance and a siren wailing closer. "Clear a path for the ambulance."

Some creatures had remained flat where they fell, and their legs or arms poked beyond the barricades into the road. The emergency vehicle honked until the stray extremities were retracted. It was then steered toward the burly medic in the midst of giving CPR to the injured party.

Mahlen and others, using the brief interlude in action, dismounted their platforms and headed toward safer areas. The short lull was ended by hail barraging the tin roof on the hardware store. To panic-stricken minds, it was machine gun rounds. They fled behind vehicles or rubbish bins. Mahlen ducked underneath the deli's delivery van.

A ferocious gale blustered in, spewing ice pellets in every direction. The weather wasn't holding out at all.

"'Winds aren't even blowing yet,' isn't that what you said?" Agares made sure to remind me we would've already left had I not delayed us.

He always had to be right. It was an additional agitating trait he had. "Blow it outta your ass!"

"Stop it, for Celestia's sake," Eleleth pleaded. "We're being shot at!"

"We're not being shot at," Agares corrected her. "Not anymore."

"See," I said, "he always has to argue and always has to be right!"

"I do not!"

"Let's get out of here!" Eleleth, in her urine-soiled jeans, eased along the bricks. "There's Mahlen."

He'd somehow gotten to the corner of the antique store on our side of the street. He called to me and motioned for us to run toward him. "He's probably parked nearby." He was also in the opposite direction from where the police were chasing the shooter.

"Come on then!" Eleleth slipped off her heels, and we three sprinted past the donut shack, a consignment shop, and a wholesale casket place which was terribly ironic at the moment.

"What about Vehuel?" I asked.

"Let's just go! I'll buy you a pretzel another day, like when I return your sweater."

"Ohhh." Pee pants could put a damper on a fledgling courtship. "Gotcha."

"I'll text him later."

Mahlen held open his arms, and I ran into them. "It's all right. We're okay. My car's in the lot over here."

We piled inside, scrambling over one another and a bag of extra booster signs Mahlen's team failed to post onto their float. "Ow!" Agares shoved the duffel onto the floorboard. "This stupid poster gave me a paper cut!"

"Oh, poor thing." Eleleth feigned sympathy. "Maybe the paramedics can tend to you, after they save the guy with the fractured skull!"

"Direct your sarcasm elsewhere. *I* didn't ditch you."

"Vehuel didn't either. If anything, I left him, and I feel pretty crappy about it!"

"Mahlen, please get us outta here," I said. "Take me home."

He maneuvered into the road dodging pedestrians and other drivers. "Heck of an epilogue to your burglary story, huh?"

He'd heard the news and not from me. "I'm sorry the gossips told you before I could. Your phone kept going straight to voicemail."

"It's fine. I'm glad you're safe." He detoured through side roads for what seemed like an eternity, finally steering us into my driveway.

From the parlor window, Josa stared out at Grandpa. He was holding a cordless phone to his ear and pacing across the concrete. He hustled to our vehicle and moved pretty swiftly for an old dude with zero cartilage in his knees. He impatiently tugged on the handle as I opened the door.

"I was worried sick, calling hospitals." He hugged me. The clunky phone he held dug into my spine.

"I'm okay, Papa."

"The news said there was a sniper at the parade, multiple injuries, and a fatality."

I guessed Leo, who smelled like licorice, didn't survive. "It was horrible." I stepped out and closed the passenger door. "A carpenter for Beliel Construction was thrown from his float right in front of us, blood everywhere."

"Well, he's still alive. The cops killed some fella named…" He fished in his pocket and snagged a piece of crumpled paper. "I wrote it down." He was smart about taking notes and avoiding the embarrassment of forgetting. He unfolded the note and read aloud, "Kamael Erlik. He's a teenager from Bune. Do you know him?"

"Holy sh…sure do. He's in our history class."

"Not in the last few days," Mahlen said. "His house was burglarized."

"Or so he claimed," Eleleth chimed in. "He was

always stealing stuff at school. He could've staged the burglary to cover up the fact he's been the one breaking into houses."

"They found a stolen rifle on him and gobs of undergarments. They're doing the, the ah, watcha-muh-call-it, ballistics testing on the gun. I don't think they're doing anything to the underwear, though."

"Stealing and murdering are two vastly different things," Agares said. "Why's a teenager shooting at the mayor?"

"Why does anything happen, Agares?" Eleleth's tone was terse.

"I'm just saying, but screw me, I guess! Mahlen, your car smells like piss. I'm out." He exited the rear seat and slammed the door.

Eleleth got out after him as if she meant to escalate the dispute, but Vehuel drove up and called her over. "I'll talk to you later, Amitiel." She entered his car, and they departed.

"I've gotta go too, babe. My parents are probably losing their minds." He reversed his transmission and sped onto the road. He hadn't bothered to kiss me goodbye, and I suppose I hadn't troubled myself to kiss him either.

"The reporter called him a young father."

"What, Papa?"

"Kamael, the sniper. They said he has a newborn with special needs on the way, and the family is begging for donations."

"Oh, I forgot about the paternity suit. An attorney served him legal papers right before summer break." His sixteen-year-old ex's parents sued him for prenatal embryonic support and for a judge to compel him to take a paternity test. He maintained he wasn't the father and said he told the gal to take a pill, which she wanted to, but being a minor, couldn't get the medication. "I hadn't heard anything else about it. I thought they dropped the lawsuit, or she miscarried."

"They were praying for it. Neither one of them wanted to be parents, and they shouldn't have been," Agares said. "I'm pretty sure they were first cousins."

"I guess you need a ride to your truck, young fella."

"I can call a buddy of mine."

"Nonsense. I'll get the station wagon going. Let me put this phone up, and I'll open the garage." He headed into the house.

"Papa, really, he said he can call—"

"Amitiel." His voice was stern. "Everyone else is busy with their families. I'm not leaving him stranded here without his truck."

Agares looked at me while he spoke to my grandfather's receding form, "I appreciate it, sir."

We obediently followed Grandpa through the front door. He petted Josa then took a few tottering steps into the parlor, where he experienced a partial fainting spell. His puffy recliner intercepted his falling body.

"Papa!" I ran to his side. Agares helped me straighten him into a comfortable sitting position in his chair.

"You all right, sir?"

"Just light-headed and dizzy." He rubbed his temples. "I didn't eat much today."

"We're taking you to the health clinic."

"And have my insurance premiums raised? No, thank you." He shut his eyelids and leaned on the headrest. "It's low blood sugar, and the stress of worrying about you at the parade got to me."

I wouldn't hear his excuses. "You're due for a checkup anyway, and I'd sleep easier knowing you're fine because if it's something serious..." I couldn't finish my sentence. He was my closest last living family member, my father figure, my mentor. He loved me even though I was mixed blood and his relatives disowned me for it. I loved him all the more for it.

"If the doctor thinks so and declares me unable to be your guardian, you'll be sent to foster care until you're eighteen. I'll hold 'til then. You can take me on your birthday." He traced an X over his chest, "I swear upon my beating heart. Now fix me a peanut butter sandwich before you take Agares to his truck, please."

"Before *we* take him. I'm not leaving you alone."

"Amitiel."

"Ah, bup-bup-bup," I cut him off. "This is the best compromise." I padded into the kitchen, glad to get my focus on a constructive activity and off the alternate conclusion of what could've transpired had I not been around when Grandpa fainted. What if he'd seriously injured himself or worse? What would happen to him if I'd been shot and killed today? I'd have a nice cry about everything later.

Grasping a knife in my trembling fingers, I slathered creamy peanut paste on two wheat bread slices and poured a cup of milk. The expiration date on the carton was nearing, but it smelled fine. I added it to our grocery list and affixed it to the fridge with a homemade magnet. It was a teeny kitty I'd painted orange in art class years ago and given to Grandpa because it resembled his Ginger Tom.

"Should we swing by the market and pick up some things?" Agares fixed himself a glass of ice water. "Maybe some vertigo medicine?"

I placed my grandfather's meal and drink on a tray. "Are you inquiring as my babysitter or my grandpa's?" I hadn't forgotten his comment prior to the parade.

"Ugh, here we go." He set his glass on the counter with a loud clink. "I didn't mean anything negative when I said that. We take care of each other. I just meant it's my turn to watch out for you. You can't really be mad."

I didn't have time to waste being angry. Grandpa's health was the priority. I lifted his tray and proceeded to walk around the island counter.

Agares pivoted from the sink to block my path. "Are you mad?"

I was busy, and he was impeding my progress. I carefully sidestepped so not to spill any milk.

He mirrored me. "You know I'm sorry."

I stepped to the opposite side.

So did he. "Nah-ah. Not until you say you forgive me."

I already did, but I was enjoying our improvised foxtrot. I took a bigger step, and he matched it.

"It was a figure of speech, Am, a dumb turn of phrase."

I decided to deliver him from his misery. "Like how I'm a ball-buster who's just messing with you because I love to dance?"

"Maybe you are now, but..." A realization light bulb seemed to click on above his head. "Oh, you know what, I'll take it as a truce."

"How 'bout you take this to my grandfather." I

gave him the tray. "I'll back out the station wagon."

"Don't chip the paint."

"Um." I opened the interior side door leading into the garage. "You're still skating on thin ice."

"Son-of-a-," the door closed on his last word, prematurely punctuating his sentence with a hinge squeak.

Once in Driver's Ed., I'd grazed an ill-placed fire hydrant causing a two-inch scratch on the rear fender. It was a harmless accident that kept me from behind the wheel, not because I didn't get my license, but because driving made me edgy. Today, however, I would tromp down my consternation and drive the crap out of the wagon so Agares wouldn't have the satisfaction of thinking he needed to babysit me.

I liberated the automobile's key from its hook and tapped the garage door button. The panel sections loudly gobbled up their vertical track until they were parallel to the unfinished ceiling. The naked insulation often vibrated loose and had to be shoved back into place between the wooden beams.

I eased around the mammoth wagon and its obnoxiously large chrome bumper. It was a tight squeeze to open the car's door without hitting the wall. Had I any junk in my glute trunk, I wouldn't have been capable of gliding into the driver's seat. The aged vinyl creaked, and the old tears pinched at bare skin.

The trapped air inside smelled musty, and the interior needed a thorough vacuuming. I drew the seatbelt across my body and joggled the latch plate until it clicked into place. I hoped I wasn't strapping myself into a mobile coffin.

I cranked the fifteen-year-old engine. It sputtered,

and I revved it like a racecar to keep it running. I dusted the mirrors before cautiously reversing into the driveway. Gas. Break. Gas.

I feared Josa would one day leap behind the wagon's rear end, and I'd run over her. Break. Mirror check. Gas.

Once outside the stall, I clicked the remote opener affixed to the visor and initiated the garage door's closing. The noisy motor grouched and ground itself shut. I rolled down the window to breathe fresh air and disregarded the already mustering tension headache that would soon prance its cleated soles upon the turf of my meninges.

I parked and honked the horn to notify my passengers I was ready. Agares emerged from the front door, preceding Grandpa, who locked it. He stepped away, then turned back to check he'd secured the upper bolt and doorknob lock.

Agares opened the passenger door. "You driving this tanker?"

"Backseat." I thumbed at the lumpy rear cushion with unraveling seams.

He climbed aboard. "Okay. I'll be your navigator." It was a reluctant acceptance for one always preferring to be the pilot. He'd resort to fisticuffs when he didn't get to steer the ship's wheel on the playground in elementary school. "With the parade route blocking streets and cops cordoning off areas, traffic is going to be tricky. You might have to take some unfamiliar roads."

"I'll do fine." Grandpa was at the driver's side. Healthy color had returned to his visage, although I wasn't sure he was fit to drive.

"Papa, you had a fainting spell. You shouldn't drive."

"This is my car." He opened the door. "I'm not sitting in the passenger seat with a spring poking my butt, and I get carsick in the back, especially with a full stomach. Scoot over."

"Swear you'll tell me if you feel light-headed?"

"Yes, ma'am. I appreciate your concern, but I don't need a babysitter."

Is that how I made it seem? Was I a hypocrite, stubbornly refusing help but lording it over another? I pressed my seatbelt's release button. It didn't yield.

"Come on. Over." He tapped my arm.

"I'm trying." I tussled with the buckle, repeatedly pressing the button and tugging, but it wouldn't unfasten itself.

Grandpa yanked at the strap. "Quit screwing around."

"I'm not." The faulty clasp finally unlocked, and I was free. As I scooted across the sofa seat, I glanced at Agares in the rearview mirror. His smug expression exuded vindication from our earlier misunderstanding. I loved my grandfather so deeply. I'd do anything to keep him safe, even if it made him feel like a child and me his caretaker, and I did sometimes begrudge the situation. I was an orphaned teen saddled with the responsibility of caring for my aging guardian. It wasn't his fault. I'd appointed myself. Agares was in the same boat, frustrated with caring for both his parents and feeling as though the friend he looked to for support now needed to be babysat.

Grandpa repositioned the seat and, with some maneuvering, buckled himself in. He focused intently on the dashboard instruments through his spectacles. He shifted the steering column lever until the needle landed on R. "We'll have to take the long way." He stared over his shoulder while reversing from our driveway. "News said there are barricades and detours a mile in every direction from the parade route."

"That far?" I thought they reported police shot the sniper, or he was found dead.

"They're ensuring their suspect acted alone, gathering, watcha-call-it, evidence." He shifted into drive. "Whatever covers their asses, since they dropped the ball and let a shooter target practice at the mayor."

"Acting Mayor," Agares mimicked the stranger who'd yelled it at the parade.

"Not the time," I said.

"It was funny. Bullets were flying, and a dumb a-hole couldn't resist correcting somebody."

"It's funny now. Things *are* in hindsight when fear subsides, and you aren't cleaning the crud outta your corduroys."

Grandpa lurched us into drive. "I know some old logging trails we can take. Bootleggers used to use them too, making rotgut bathtub gin."

"How do you know about that?"

"Your ole Papa has a storied life." He meandered along Sycamore and steered onto a side street. He took several more turns, left and right. Paved avenues transmuted into gravel lanes. Weedy ditches were supplanted by thistle plants and brambles. Grandpa dazzled us with the saga of renegade moonshiners covertly manufacturing grain alcohol in hidden stills to sell illegally and tax-free. He gestured to carpets of underbrush. "They'd hide their equipment there, boil their hooch, and nobody was the wiser." His tall tales were matched in height by lofty trees wearing capes of woven vines, their outstretched limbs cloaking the forest's secrets. "Back when these were dirt paths, bootleggers would've traveled them at night under the shine of the moon. Hence the name, moonshine."

I doubted moonlight could penetrate the overgrown vegetation. A timber company had sprung up and laid claim to these acres subsequent to the original settlers planting roots in the realm. The company was good about promptly replanting after it felled trees.

We'd roved far beyond the semi-kempt pebbled lanes and onto narrow muddy backroads hewn into the ginormous flora. I was confident we were lost in the woods. "This is nowhere near Main Street."

"Where are we?" Agares rolled down his window. Other than our motor and its periodic fanbelt squeak, it was quiet, with no city racket. "Do you smell rotten eggs?"

"Um, it's a broader detour than I planned." Grandpa looked around, squinching behind his lenses. "Maybe that fella can give us directions."

"Who?" Was somebody else directionally challenged, or were Grandpa's eyes playing tricks on him? In the boxing match that retired him, a jab to his temple nearly detached his retina. The illusionary forest shadows were also deceptive. I'd seen what appeared to be marmots riding horseback and pointy-hatted witches stirring a cauldron.

Our trail diverged into two other paths. Grandpa steered toward the farthest one. There, I strained to see a towering figure puffing on a cigarette. He leaned casually on his car, visually inspecting its flat front tire and raising his phone into the air. He waved his arms to flag us over.

Agares poked out his head. "Isham?"

It seemed like my grandfather had intentionally driven us to what we thought was the middle of nowhere. "Papa, were you meeting him here?"

"I called him while you were at the parade to see if he knew anything. You were driving up, and he told me we should meet him out here but keep it quiet because he's on a case." Grandpa parked perpendicular to the disabled car and shut off his engine. "You need some help, Detective Buer?"

"Yes, sir." He nodded. "I'm not great with tools, and my scissor jack broke." He motioned to the broken mechanical device on the ground.

"I got one in the trunk." He jiggled his seatbelt until it unbuckled. "Along with wheel chocks and a safety jack stand." He got out to rummage through the boot.

"What case are you working this close to the Restricted Acres?" Agares asked his cousin. "Can you tell us?"

"Tailing the janitor." He walked over and squatted by the door. He had a grease blotch on his chin. It was juxtaposed against the crispness of his clean white shirt. "I was doing pretty well, followed him from his cruddy house to the marsh where he dumped his garbage, but it was like he was expecting me, or someone, the squirrelly way he acted. I dunno." He inhaled through his chewed filter, causing the lit end to burn brighter. He held his breath briefly then exhaled smoke. "That walking chalk stick came right up to me, asked why I was following him. I said, 'I'm an investigator, and you're a custodian, right? You have access to lots of different places around town like hospitals, morgues, and schools? There was an incident, and your name was mentioned.' He got a panicked look and said he didn't hurt the gal; he only got rid of the lab test results."

"What's that mean, lab results?" I couldn't ask whether it had anything to do with the photographs he was unaware Agares had stolen from him.

"Best I could piece together from his rambling is he was led to believe quack technicians created a virus they can't cure yet." He snuffed out his cigarette in the dirt. "So rather than alert authorities who'd warn the public, they're getting rid of the evidence and preventing mass hysteria. He thinks he's doing a good thing. Or, at least, he's convinced himself of it. He was also guaranteed a remedy for whatever ails him."

"A remedy for albinism?" Were they dangling a promise of skin-darkening melanocortin injections to him? The trunk lid closed. Grandpa, arms loaded with gadgets, walked to Isham's car and readied it for a tire change.

"Full disclosure." Isham opened the back door. "I'm in over my head." He climbed inside, cramping the interior next to Agares, and shut the door. "I made detective way too fast, and I've an inkling it was done for a reason." He glimpsed himself in the visor mirror and wiped the grease blotch. "The janitor knew he was followed, and he confessed to me like he has nothing to fear. It makes me think I do, or I should."

"You throwing in the towel already? Is that why you still live with Auntie Sylla?"

"I don't live *with* her. I pay rent."

"It's the same thing."

"No." He shook his head like a wet dog shaking water from its fur. "It's not."

"You gotta cut the cord, dude."

"I ain't a mama's boy." He backhanded his cousin's arm.

Agares returned the gesture. "Yes, you are."

To avoid the rogue spring in the seat, I shifted my bum, in which the two squabblers were becoming an added pain. "What did he throw in the swamp?"

"It sank before I could get to it. I don't carry a pair of rubber waders in my car, and I'm not getting my nuts bitten off by whatever's in that nasty bog." He placed a palm over his crotch.

"You didn't ask him what he dumped?" I began to understand why he thought he made detective too fast.

"If he's telling the truth, it's evidence. Or it's his weekly garbage. Without special equipment and a court order to trawl the wetlands, we can't find out."

"You think telling us this is enough to get you a dinner date with Mrs. Beliel?"

He canted his head. "It's at least worth a lunch."

Chapter 8

With Sunday's alleged parade sniper dead and detectives saying he acted alone, Monday was business as usual. Our hopes for a school cancellation were dashed. We did, however, get promised an early release. The exact time was to be announced following the debate assembly. It was scheduled after second lunch period for candidates to argue and explain why they'd be the best class president.

Agares was writing his speech across from Mahlen and me in the mostly unoccupied study hall. Vasiariah and Peth were making out at a table near us. "Do you really need me to proofread your acceptance speech?" I asked Agares over the smooching. "Aren't you merely thanking your classmates for their votes and pledging to do a good job?"

"Yeah, dude." Mahlen took a break from playing footsie at me below the table. "Just speak off the cuff. You got this."

Agares wouldn't gander up from scribbling. "It's an opening statement, not an acceptance speech. I don't have an automatic expectation to be granted something."

"Hey!" A crimson-cheeked Eleleth burst through the double doors. She slapped a flyer onto our table. The blistering fury in her visage was spreading, and her mane might've ignited into a curly brushfire. "The bald prick strikes again!"

"What's wrong?" I examined the paper. *VOTE FOR ME* was written in bold type above a picture captioned, *Daggon Yarhibol, angyal.* He posed with a double thumbs-up, his hair shorn nigh to the scalp and a sneer pulled over his protruding incisors. "He's such an anal wart."

"Yeah, one who's running against Agares for class president," Mahlen said. "Is there a cure for anal warts?"

Agares read the flyer and snickered. "I welcome the competition. That four-foot sucktard will definitely win at humiliating himself. He's as crooked as the nose on his face."

"Didn't you see the asterisk at the bottom?" Eleleth pointed at the star preceding a minuscule sentence, "It says, 'Angyals are superior to daemons.' It's a racist smear campaign."

I concurred. "We need to take this to the principal."

"Already did." She flopped into her chair. "He said it's free speech."

"Hate speech is free, huh?" Would the principal be so forgiving had it stated daemons were superior?

"The debate should be a mud-slinging fiasco." Peth curled his arms around Vasiariah, "We'll be there."

"He's banking on me losing control and threatening to kick his ass so he can say daemons are too quick-tempered and hostile to be capable leaders."

"Aren't they, though," Mahlen joshed.

"I'm very levelheaded, bro. Ask me again, and I'll hold yours under water 'til the bubbles stop."

I cocked my head. "Will you be able to keep your cool? Doesn't Daggon have a relative who ran for city manager on a pro angyal/anti-female platform?"

"Yeah, his Uncle Ebel," Vasiariah said.

"Ugh, Drumpf!" Eleleth crumpled the paper and flicked it into the trashcan. "That demented rape-isn't-a-crime-because-procreation-is-ordained-by-god guy?"

"He also said gals are too flaky to know what they want." Mahlen's comment seemed directed at me specifically.

"And female orgasms are a myth?" I blurted. My rhetorical query was a broad subliminal message to him, although I realized too late everybody else would hear it and draw their own conclusions to my meaning.

Before the embarrassment entrenched in the faux Values of Femininity could catch me, Vasiariah intervened. "Just because dumpy Drumpf's unable to give them doesn't mean they don't exist."

Without making eye contact, she and Peth subtly high-fived.

Eleleth giggled. "Probably why he got himself recalled."

"And he lost in a landslide defeat," Agares said. "Something he and his nephew will have in common."

The bell dinged, signifying the end of lunch. Students who weren't already excused from the assembly, like Mahlen for basketball practice, mustered in the auditorium. I had to work backstage for credit in my audio-visual class, ensuring microphones and speakers worked. I milled around the stereo system, obscured by a massive velvet curtain and rows of old wooden sets.

Listeners could almost hear the blast from a starter pistol as the two debate competitors took off. Agares' opening statement was dynamic and concise. He listed problems and their solutions. It was a nice balance of positivity versus negativity.

Countering that was his opponent standing behind his lectern on a concealed apple box. Although he was actually taller than four feet, his stature was greatly stunted next to Agares. To compensate, Daggon spoke loudly and fast, utilizing exaggerated arm and hand movements to appear larger. He zigzagged across incoherent lanes of thought, recycling and regurgitating propaganda from his uncle's failed campaign. He equated what he termed the seductive female gender with mental retardation, then contradicted himself by saying females were conniving, guileful, and devious. In his distorted mind, we were calculating geniuses bent on destroying male kind, yet so mentally handicapped it was unsafe to permit us to make decisions for ourselves or let us perform anything more than limited menial tasks.

I nearly shut off his microphone. I peeped through a window in the sets that lined up with a curtain hole. Appalled facial expressions convinced me to let him keep talking.

He was derailing his own candidacy. He made blatantly untrue statements. He called Agares a "conspiracist" and accused him of fearmongering by spreading rumors hybrids were being abducted, tortured, and executed, which his rival flatly denied.

"You're exaggerating stories to fit your narrative," Agares said.

He raised his index and middle digit. "I suppose there's two sides to every tale."

"No, there's not. There may be multiple perceptions, but there's one set of facts." He raised his first finger, then aimed it at Daggon. "You seem allergic to them. You're a liar, a bigot, an idiot, and an embarrassment to creature kind."

We clapped and cheered. The moderator, Mr. Ubach, banged his gavel.

"I'm not a liar. You're a liar, liar." Daggon groused. One could practically see his feathers ruffling.

"Poor decorum can lead to disqualification for both of you," Mr. Ubach cautioned. His woolly lampshade mustache accentuated his lengthening frown. "Next question. Daggon, what're your policies for combatting discrimination?"

"With one race, you have no racial discrimination," he replied. "I support the bill one of our legislators proposed fourteen months ago. Wellness Triage for Females."

"W-T-F?" Mr. Ubach inquired.

Universal laughter erupted at the acronym usually reserved for the phrase, *what the fuck*.

"It was formally called I-F-A, but there's been a lot of improvements."

"The Incubator Farm Act?" Agares asked.

Spectators gasped, jeered, and spat expletives. The controversial bill was racist and cruelly misogynistic. It suggested herding females into internment camps, subjecting them to rigorous pelvic exams and medical tests, and treating them as nothing more than zygote chambers used to birth the supreme race, which certain proponents believed would be *their* particular species. It was a less scientific version of gene editing and an equally barbaric version of ethnic purging.

"That bill was oppressive and intrusive. It was a state-sanctioned dystopia, and the reason your uncle, who we," Agares waved his hand across the audience, "all know is the legislator you're referring to, lost his bid for reelection to the city council."

It evoked memories of the time my mother and my eleven-year-old self went to the grocery mart. Mom stood perusing the newspaper rack, and I was near the register when the male cashier held a box of extra small feminine napkins and said, "Hmm. Somebody's all grown up, eh?"

I felt exposed and violated that a stranger knew my intimate business and believed he had the right to comment on it. I was mortified and too abashed to tell my mother. Luckily, she overheard. "Mind your own business, pervert!" she shouted.

He was unaware my mom was in earshot. His surprised face flushed bright red, and his eyeballs couldn't have bugged any farther if he were a frog and she was smushing him.

She marched up to the counter. "Apologize before I have the manager fire you." Mom didn't shy from confrontation. She was a barrister who knew the law well and was used to arguing her case, even if clients initially mistook her for a secretary. She set them straight. I yearned to be brave and self-assured like her.

"Sorry, ma'am." He bagged our items with lightning speed. "Sorry, miss."

When we got into our car, she hugged me and said, "That pedophile's deviancy is his shame, not yours, darling. You deserve to be respected. Always defend yourself."

I understood what feminism was on that evening and how certain males would exploit their power if females didn't assert themselves. Furthermore, I discovered creatures were really terrified by my mom.

Daggon was another male who seemed terrified by females. He swabbed his sweaty bald noggin, which removed concealer covering his acne. "Well, I have it on good authority the city is reconsidering the mandate with new provisions. Contraception will be illegal since life begins at menstruation."

"Moron!" a distant speaker yelled. The crowd guffawed.

"Is this a debate or a joke?" Agares gandered all around as though to verify he was indeed on stage. "You can't be serious! Not only have you proved yourself shamefully ignorant about biology, but you're publicly admitting to endorsing a bill, which was struck down, because essentially, it advocated for baby mills!"

"I advocate for the survival of the fittest. It's a test for the best race. The strongest embryos survive, and the strongest females will survive carrying them to term."

"What happens when they can't? You're going to have a lot of angyals, daemons, and hybrids bleeding to death in your police state."

"Only the weakest species will die. We angyals have nothing to fear."

"How dare you!" Agares slammed his palms atop his lectern. "I know females from all three races who died after they were denied life-saving medical interventions because savages like you valued your deranged beliefs over their lives!"

Agares' sister, Marid, two years his junior, was kidnapped en route to her bus stop when she was ten years old. She was beaten, raped, and left in a ditch. A utility worker found her twenty-four hours later and called an ambulance. A nurse's aide, who barged in without knocking, told the Gamigins it wasn't necessary for Marid to take an emergency contraceptive pill because, he said, "The body has a way of shutting that whole thing down." His patronizing insinuation was a *real* victim is incapable of being impregnated.

Obviously, he was wrong. Magical sperm ninjas didn't scale down Marid's cervical walls to attack the rapist's semen. Her belly soon distended. Her distraught mother took her to a clinic where she was told it was fluid buildup, and it would eventually drain. When it didn't, she took her back three weeks later and was informed her daughter was merely gaining weight and to alter her diet. Mrs. Gamigin waited another week before taking Marid to a different clinic, where a doctor informed them of her pregnancy. At four months gestation, it was too late for abortive medication and illegal for her to surgically abort, even though brain-damaged ten-year-old children aren't equipped to carry a fetus. By her twentieth week, she suffered a concealed placental abruption and bled to death. The Gamigins were forever changed.

Daggon slicked his tongue over his gapped teeth. "If my creator decided those females deserved to be ravaged and atone for their sins, so be it."

An angry vein jutted from Agares' temple. He flew into a rage and attacked Daggon, throttling him from head to toe. The spectators applauded. Four teachers sprinted to haul him off and drag him backstage.

The moderator banged his gavel and shouted, "Agares, you are disqualified from this campaign!"

Boos gushed.

"Unless a new candidate submits his or her name,

Daggon will be running unopposed. I'll allow a two-minute respite for any potential challengers to decide."

I hit the play button on the stereo to broadcast intermission music before approaching Agares. "You can't keep getting into fights with everybody!"

"Why? Why can't I?" He rubbed his fist. "They're begging me to punch them, and I may as well oblige!"

"Because they win." I inspected his reddening knuckles. I doubted he'd have a bruise since Daggon's soft nasal cartilage absorbed the majority of the impact. "Even though they lose the physical fight, they win by proving you're some violent daemon who can't control himself. They get everyone's attention by getting your attention. Don't you see the game they're playing?"

"I know the odds are against us, but I can't keep ignoring how we're treated."

"Use your brain to fix it." I poked his skull. "Don't sink to the level of stupid creatures who goad you into fighting."

"A leader leads, and I want my kindred to fight. Either you're with me or against me."

"Is that an ultimatum?"

"You can't remain neutral your whole life."

I averted my gaze.

He slapped his palm on the wall next to my head. "You will have to make a choice at some point."

"I choose to leave." I turned away from him and his meaty forearm to make my exit.

He slapped his other palm on the wall in front of my face, boxing me in. "Wait. Wait," he dehusked his gruff voice.

I could feel his exasperated exhales thrashing my ear. "What for?"

"This music sucks, and I'm sorry I yelled."

I jumped as gavel bangs boomed from the acoustic transducer near me. "The time to enter has expired. Any challengers should make themselves known."

"I'll do it," a faint speaker proclaimed.

"Who's that?" I shoved his arms down and spied through the curtain hole.

"Eleleth Gremory is running." She sprang to her feet. "I hope my opponent has a better understanding of anatomy thanks to the butt-kicking Agares generously awarded him."

Laughs exploded throughout the auditorium.

"Your protégé is taking your throne," I said.

"She can have it."

She ascended the platform steps. "It's terrible when someone puts your body through something you didn't ask for, right, Daggon?"

He wiped the blood off his swelling face with a handkerchief and lugged himself up to the podium. "I think…"

The audience chanted, "Eleleth, Eleleth, Eleleth."

"I think," he began again.

"My body, my choice," Eleleth said. "My body," she paused and pointed to the crowd.

"My choice," they responded.

They continued the call-and-response pattern until Daggon thrust his lectern, toppling it over, and stomped off stage.

"The debate is postponed indefinitely," the moderator said. "This assembly is adjourned."

Students and faculty departed the auditorium. The public announcement system crackled, and the school secretary ordered me to report to the principal's office.

"What now?" Agares asked.

"It's the secondary confab about my declaration. Melek told me we'd meet again."

"They're trying to wear you down, whittle you into their perfect angyal."

"They picked the wrong day. I'm not in the mood for their petty crap."

"I'd go with you, but I need to get an icepack on my fist." He displayed his swollen hand. "Maybe if it doesn't look so bad, I can tell them Daggon fell and only score myself a one-day suspension."

"Your punishment was disqualification, and only because you wouldn't finish the debate, which delayed Mr. Ubach from leaving early for his smoke break. You were a casualty from a missed nicotine fix. All you'll get from the principal is a high-five for exercising your masculinity."

"Sheesh, I hope it's with my other hand."

"Ugh!" I turned my back on him and the double standard. Males were coddled and encouraged to embrace their nature, violence and all. Females were castigated for being their natural selves or for actions society solely allotted to males. We were told we were wrong, improper, dirty, or sinful and had penis envy if we challenged gender-specified traits or rules.

Things like skirts, high heels, and cosmetics were deemed feminine. Because if makeup or certain garments were sentient, they'd have vaginas? No. Stuff to make one attractive was directed at females since our purpose was being desirable at all times. We were to be one-dimensional, mild-mannered nurturers, soft and meek who strictly adhered to impossibly high standards of beauty and likeability and didn't fuss, fart, burp, or mention our periods…ever.

You were chastised and shamed for venturing from your designated gender role. Caim's penalty for defending herself with a book slap to a stalker was a three-day school suspension, which affected her grades and her transcript submitted to colleges. Agares lost control, tackled and repeatedly punched Daggon on stage before witnesses, and he'd get a celebratory pat on the back.

I stomped through the hall, bypassed the secretary's vacant desk, and knocked on the principal's office door. "Come in," filtered clearly through the hollow core.

I entered and met with a three-creature panel scrutinizing me. Vice Principal Melek, Principal Nakir, and the pink-eyed school receptionist, Secretary Gadreel, appeared to be visually dissecting me. Each crispy blink of hers extracted another layer.

Cherub High's vice principal spoke first. "Amitiel Zephon, seventeen-year-old senior with high marks in all subjects. Our board welcomes you."

Welcomes me. Ha! The school board decreed seniors participate in the declaration ritual, or we wouldn't be permitted to attend our own graduation, intimating our transcripts and diploma may be indeterminately delayed. I camouflaged my inner eye roll with a polite smile. "Thank you."

"You are mixed, correct?" He flipped through stapled pages, straining to read words over his moly nasal hump.

He knew my race. Was he aiming to insult me? "I'm a hybrid."

"Aye, a mixed blood." He said it with a negative

connotation, as if the assemblage of vowels and consonants left a sour aftertaste. "Be ye angyal, or be ye daemon?"

"How're you allowed to ask me that question? School is meant to be a secular institution focused on education and separate from religion."

"Schools may be desegregated; society is not. If you try to straddle both worlds, you'll find yourself very alone."

"It's a simple, innocuous query." Gadreel dabbed her crusty socket. "It brings order to our world."

"No, it's not. It's a loaded question whose reply may come with consequences. How can I answer honestly to a panel of angyals looking down on me, daring me to say anything other than I want to be an angyal too? I disdain your judgment and your labels."

"Excuse me?" They leaned backward as though jostled by my statement.

"You heard me."

Gadreel's eyes would've ballooned if not for her partially glued lids. "Are you a heathen? Do you not worship or pray?"

"Has praying done anything for your conjunctivitis?"

"How dare you!"

"Calm yourself, Mrs. Gadreel," Melek advised. "She's immature. She doesn't fully comprehend what it means to be ostracized from a community."

Ostracize. Oust. Excommunicate. Exile: Scare tactics. Perhaps banishment wasn't the penalty they made it out to be. Nobody returned from the Barren to tell us. Although, citizens were departing West Realm in droves.

"Are you not a creature of faith?"

Believers viewed an atheist with suspicion because one detractor, one dissenting voice of reason, could bring down the cult's whole system. "I'm not playing your arbitrary game." I stood and walked out, pursued by threats.

"You will answer!"

"You must choose!"

"You'll answer at the Fateful Inquiry!"

Ordering me to do something tended to have the opposite effect. The day my Fateful Inquiry arrived, I plotted to take the stage under the guise I'd be announcing my official declaration: Angyal or daemon. I'd say, "I was born of both angyal and daemon blood. I've been called a hybrid all my life. I've felt a kinship to each side. I've thought about what it means to be a Gabrielite or a Celestian. Will I choose one or the other and vow my loyalty to that faction, or will I remain a hybrid? I'm here today to decide." Either choice I made would be a lie. I was neither pure angyal, nor pure daemon. I was both. "But someone, some shadowy group," I'd boldly announce, "has been performing ghastly experiments on teenagers to prevent our coexistence."

I didn't care if they tried to withhold my diploma. I'd received an advanced copy of my transcripts because Daevah, my friendly purse twin, worked as an assistant to the school receptionist and had gotten into the files. She'd even pressed it with the official seal. She said it was thanks for defending her younger sister against the bully in her tap class.

"What happened now?" Eleleth was outside the receptionist's office. "Did they ask about the fight already?"

"No, it was the second meeting. And no," I said as her mouth opened, "I didn't give an answer yet."

She walked beside me toward my locker. I could hear her thinking about what to say as she fiddled with her bookbag straps. "Wanna skip school, get some frozen yogurt, and talk about Daggon's butt-kicking?"

"I do!" I swirled the dial, inputting the numerical sequence into my combination lock. "I'm also curious how I should address you."

"Address me?" Puzzlement furrowed her brow into grooves.

I filled in the jigsaw pieces. "Commander in Chief or Madame President?"

"Oh, neither." She laughed. "They postponed the debate."

"Is Grand Empress Gremory too posh?"

"Quit it." She playfully bumped me with her bag. "They'll cancel the whole election or rig the vote before they let a female be class president."

"So you don't want to be?"

"I'm not ready for the flack that comes with it. Today was fun because the audience took it as a joke. When the novelty wears off, and I don't withdraw, they'll call me a rug-munching virago. I'd be a social pariah."

"You'd be great, though." I retrieved a notebook and closed my locker. "Eminence Eleleth."

"Hmmm, I actually like that one."

She drove us to the ice cream parlor near where we'd witnessed the parade shooting. Revisiting the spot was cathartic. We weren't in danger. Guns weren't firing. Crowds weren't screaming and crying. All my friends were unharmed. It was placid. My choice for a vanilla cone reflected that. It was plain and boring and purely sweet comfort.

We kept our chitchat mundane, focusing on her upcoming choir performance, the Serelia dance, and our next game night. I didn't bother Eleleth with what may be Isham's nothing burger about the weirdo custodian, even though I was dying to reveal her nemesis, Succu, was having a clandestine relationship with him. I also couldn't say Isham had acquiesced to investigate because I'd promised him a date with Mrs. Beliel, whom he said was in an open marriage. I couldn't broach that subject without our talking about Mr. Beliel's forbidden kiss with his male employee and that employee getting his head cracked open at the parade where we could've been shot.

I also couldn't tell her anything without revealing all the time I was spending with Agares and his cousin. She'd crap a brick and fart clay for a day. Reclaiming Vehuel as her beau wouldn't make her any less territorial over Agares. She wouldn't truly believe our innocence unless I told Mahlen there was nothing to tell, and he'd absolutely believe something was going on because I didn't accept his damned promise ring as fast as he wanted.

A fire truck whizzed by. "Wonder where he's going?" Eleleth sipped her sugar-free, fat-free, artificially flavored milkshake.

"Probably to help Omunkar." I finished my single scoop and nibbled at the wafer cone.

"Why?"

"Ever since they deregulated safety restrictions, that city has caught fire every other week and never has enough trucks or firefighters."

"If only there was another realm without that problem," she not so understatedly hinted.

"I already told you I'm thinking about enrolling at Thelema University there. You're preaching to the converted."

"Well, amen, sister." Her straw sucking an emptied cup signified she was ready to go. She tossed it into the trash receptacle. "Come on. I'll take you home. We killed enough time; my mom won't know I skipped class."

"Ohmkay." I finished eating my cone as I followed her outside. I buckled my borrowed helmet and settled into the sidecar. I pressed my notebook tight in my lap so the wind wouldn't blow out my pages. I was glad I managed to get through the chat without spilling my guts about everything, but I was guilt-ridden I couldn't share it all with my best friend. Among the other reasons, there was a chance we were barking up the right tree, and our quarry might be more dangerous than we anticipated. It was better not to involve anyone else.

She dropped me at my house, and we waved goodbye. From my front entryway, I could hear Grandpa cussing and joggling the television cable. "You need help, Papa?" I shut the door and kicked off my shoes.

"I'm trying to get the news channel to clear up. A silo imploded and killed a ranch hand. Frag Ruh-so-and-so."

"What?" It couldn't be the creepy custodian. "Was the last name, Russelifeld?"

"Could've been." He glanced from unscrewing the cord. "You heard about it?"

"I saw a firetruck go by earlier, and someone mentioned it." I had to phone Isham. I rifled through the paperwork he'd left to find his number. I called, and he answered.

"Detective Buer speaking."

"Isham, this is Amitiel. Is it true about the silo explosion?"

"Implosion, but yup." Just like his cousin, he couldn't resist correcting me. "The janitor, or former janitor, was working in a chemical fertilizer silo. They say it's highly combustible and are likely ruling it an accident. They found most of his corpse on the farm and peeled some of it off the nearby barn. So ne'er mind interrogating him about the fishy goings-on we discussed."

"Doesn't his death seem really convenient for whomever he worked for?"

"Oh yeah. He was a Grade A creep, but he wasn't a criminal mastermind. He was either a patsy or mentally ill. Now, how about that lunch I was promised?"

Getting laid seemed more important to him than solving this mystery. "I'll call you back."

"Brunch then?"

I hit the END CALL button. I expected to hear some semblance of a triumphant tone since the crook he labeled "grease pig" finally got stuck with the repercussions of his deeds, even if they were currently sticking to the side of a barn. I dialed Agares. He answered mid-ring.

"Am, you heard the news?" His excitement was audible. "That weirdo blew himself into a million pieces! How crazy is that?"

"I know! I talked to Isham, but he's more

concerned about lunching with Mrs. Beliel."

"He can't figure which head to think with. I don't know how he made detective."

"Neither does he. Remember what he said in the woods after blowing his surveillance job?" A good investigator, at minimum, would've tried to locate what Russelifeld dumped in the wetlands. I couldn't connect the tiles yet, but he was an interlocking piece in a much larger puzzle. "You want to go back out there, retrace his steps?"

"I dunno." His verve ebbed. "If Isham saw anything, it was likely a common case of illegal dumping by a petty criminal. I'm not wading balls deep into a swamp for an unknown item—probably household garbage—that you know isn't even there anymore."

"I bet Isham will do it." I baited him. "After I guarantee I'll let him read in real time my text to Vasiariah to schedule a group lunch date at the country club, his lust will override his fear."

"Fear? I'm not afraid." He took the bait. "I'll conference him in." He dialed his cousin's number. I needed to get Isham on the hook too. I counted on their familial rivalry goading them into the clandestine excursion.

After three rings, Isham answered. "Hello, cuz. I assume you're phoning me with details about the lunch with Mrs. B."

"First, settle a bet for me."

"Okay." He seemingly chewed on a pencil into the receiver.

"Amitiel thinks you're not brave enough to go out into the woods where we fixed your flat, but I said you're *definitely* not brave enough."

"Very funny. I'm not playing this game."

"See, Am. I told you he wouldn't do it."

"He didn't say he wouldn't yet."

"Crap, you got me on a conference call?"

"I said I'd call you back. You have my word you can watch me text Vasi about scheduling a lunch date with her mom if you lead us to wherever the janitor dumped something."

"Uhhh." He tapped the pencil against his teeth. "And should she refuse?"

"I'll drive you to her house myself for an impromptu get-together."

I could hear him breathing into the phone, the notion swimming around in his mind. A quick remark would snag him. "I know it's super scary, so I totally understand."

"Fine. I'm in." Reeled in. "I'll be at your house in an hour." His line clicked.

"Agares, you still there?"

"Yup. Are you actually going to get him a date with Vasi's mom?"

"It won't be a real date. It'll be a group gathering at best, and it depends on whether Isham is full of it."

"We'll soon find out. See ya in a bit."

Chapter 9

I hadn't registered how simple it would be to get Agares and Isham to provoke each other into venturing back into the forbidden woods. As slaves to their emotions of anger, pride, and self-esteem, they couldn't yield to a challenge to their masculinity. They hadn't been trained to tamp down their temperament.

Males tended to act or react before thinking and would fistfight over the most minor disagreements. It was astonishing they hadn't driven our species to extinction. I had to tread prudently, reassure the cousins they were both brave, or else we'd end up in a two-car race barreling over logging trails until one of us splintered a tree, and the other proclaimed himself the courageous victor.

I decided riding with Isham would fare better. I could keep him calm and on track by fluffing his ego. Agares would be less foolhardy without a competitor directly egging him on.

"You're serious?" he asked me through his driver's side window as I stood on the curb. "You're gonna sweet talk him with tales of a Mrs. Beliel lunch all the way to the bogs?"

"Yes. Please don't rev your engine or tailgate him. We don't wanna get into a wreck."

"He's the one with a big dent in his bumper and a trunk-load of flat tires from running off the road." He thumbed at his muscly chest, pumping his pectorals up and down. "*I*, however, know how to drive."

"Drive on my nerves, maybe." His peacocking was silly and in no way underpinned his allegations regarding his driving ability.

"Exactly—drive you crazy with my pec pumps."

"Not what I said."

"And I can handle my truck with expertise."

"Prove it." His acting recklessly would make me right, and he hated when I proved him wrong.

"I will."

"Uh-huh."

"I'll prove the crap out of it."

An automobile resembling Isham's rounded the curve on my street. The driver clicked his high beams on and off to confirm his identity.

"Bet you won't." I got in the last word before clunking over to Isham's car in my galoshes. A pine-scented air freshener hung from the rearview mirror. It swung furiously after I had to slam the door to ensure it latched. "Lead the way, Detective, and please don't break-check him."

"He needs to learn to drive better. We *are* trying to outrun the twilight here."

I gave him a reality check. "How'd you get the dent in *your* car?"

"Touché. Very nice deflection." He steered onto a dirt trail leading into the dimming woods and reduced his headlights to the fog lamps. It decreased our visibility to mere yards. "Incognito mode." Agares followed suit behind us. We passed numerous signposts: *NO PUBLIC ENTRY. KEEP OUT. NO DUMPING. VIOLATORS WILL BE PROSECUTED.*

NO PUBLIC ACCESS. "We're officially trespassing, so I'd appreciate you sending that text now."

"Fine." I transcribed a brief text to Vasiariah and sent it.

Isham read it aloud, "'Hey, Vasi. Can we schedule a group lunch date at your mom's country club?' That's it?"

"What else you want me to say?" Did he think I was going to write *Booty Call for Mrs. Beliel*?

"Say I'm scouting venues for a possible department fundraiser."

"I will, once she replies and you take me to the dump spot."

"Deal." Isham pointed to a shining plate affixed to a tree: *PROPERTY OF SNG TIMBER Co.* "You know who owns this lumber company?"

"No. Who?"

"Sachiel and Nanael Gold. S-N-G."

"The governor and his wife?"

"Ding, ding." He rang a pretend bell. "They've got their dirty fingers in a ton of pies. We'll need to concoct a lie if anybody on their payroll stops us."

"Aren't cops permitted to patrol here? You're a detective investigating a case."

"That's the last thing I'd want the Golds knowing. They'd call my boss demanding an explanation and get me suspended without pay or complain to the mayor and get me fired."

"Isn't interfering with an investigation illegal?"

"Anything goes in an election year. Local politicians cave to pressure, particularly when it's an entity with power, influence, and money to back your opponent." He jerked the wheel to miss a stump. "Jinn has some principles, so he'd want to resist their interference, but with the amount of uneducated bigots and closeted pedophiles crawling from underneath rocks to support Drumpf the clown, Jinn can't afford to also have the governor openly campaigning for him."

"You think Gold is secretly campaigning for him?" Drumpf aspired to recreate Bune Town into angyal-catering Omunkar's restrictive image. If the governor over all four realms wanted that too, unknowing citizens were fighting a battle that had already ended.

"For a shady con artist so dumb he can be manipulated like a puppet? Yes. Which is why we need a good lie. We'll say you and your jealous ex with irritable bowels just broke up and we got lost in the woods while unsuccessfully trying to get away from him." He gestured toward the rear. "Start wailing and randomly babbling, saying your heart is broken because he cheated with your nine-toed sister-in-law or something really dramatic."

An irritable bowel and nine toes? "What was your prepared lie when you were alone?"

"I'd say a crime witness was meeting me and feared being seen by the perpetrator, or I was romancing a married dame, and we needed privacy."

"You do that very much?"

"What?" The steering wheel spun through his loosely curled fingers as the car turned. "Trespass and lie about it?"

"No. Romance married, older dames?"

"Because of my interest in Mrs. Beliel?"

"Her, and Ms. Vanth. She drooled all over herself when you were there, like when I dangle bacon in front of my dog."

He snickered. "The mature ones have always been crazy about me. Ms. Vanth is too old for my liking, but thirties to mid-forties." He whistled. "They know what they want. I don't mind taking orders, and they know how to give them. How about you?"

"What about me?"

"Do you take orders or give them?"

"I'm not having this conversation."

"Agares is a boss, but if he's like me—"

"*He* has a slew of females wooing him, none of whom are me." Isham was muddling portions of his faked story with the present. "My beau's name is Mahlen."

"Does that mean we're having this conversation?"

"No! Shut up and drive the dang car."

"Mmm, I think I got my answer." A roguish smirk keeked from his profile.

"Are you going to behave 'til we reach the swamps?"

"Yes, ma'am." He stopped and killed the motor. "We're here."

We sat amid endless columns of gnarly trees and a row of mile markers resembling gigantic carrots in an ogre's eerie garden. "Still looks like the forest to me."

"It's the Restricted Acres. That's what the markers are for, alerting truckers to stop. We can't drive right up to bogs or we'll get stuck. Hence the phrase bogged down."

"Is that right, professor?" I sarcastically put my fists beneath my chin and braced my elbows on his center console as if enthralled by his intellect. "Enlighten me with your knowledge. Does your dictionary also have the word *condescension*?"

He smiled. "Keep acting like that, and I might expand my age bracket."

"I see charm and a wanton libido runs in the genes."

"Does it?" He opened his door to the scents of pine, fir, and spruce. He grabbed a flashlight and handed me another. "Don't slide off the seat thinking about what runs in my denim kind."

"Ew. Your denim jeans? No wonder you prefer older females. They probably like your dad jokes."

"Among other things." He clicked his tongue. He didn't beg forgiveness for his coarse language or treat me like a prudish nitwit. I liked his candid bawdiness. He stepped out in his tall rubber boots and signaled his cousin to park in the trail running perpendicular to ours. "Between those two oaks. You can fit."

Agares settled into the shrouded woody alcove and shut off his truck. The luminescent circle from his flashlight disclosed his movements. It darted around like the alien spaceships in the comic books he used to loan me to read. He walked toward us wearing thigh-high waders. "How far are we hoofing it?"

"Not too far." Isham shined his light around before crunching down a nearby trail. "Come on."

"You think he knows where he's going?" I switched on the flashlight and secured its strap around my wrist.

"He couldn't find his ass with both hands and a map, but we have no alternative to locate the janitor's trash bog."

We followed Isham and the timber company's prohibitory signposts. We deviated to avoid brambles and briars until the forest abruptly ended. Soil disintegrated beneath my shoes. A floor of vegetation plunged like an earthen elevator whose rooted cables had been severed. Gravity yanked me south. Air rushed past my body, sending my arms flailing above me as my butt crashed onto the crumbling ground and continued to slide along a steep incline.

"Am!" Agares zipped by me, his hands floundering for a lifeline among the foliage avalanche. He gripped my ankle. I felt myself falling faster down the slope until fingers clenched my forearm. They jerked me to a stop, nearly wrenching my humerus from its socket.

"My bad, guys!" Isham held me in one hand and a bowing tree branch in the other. We hung precariously askew from nature's jungle gym.

Our heavy panting filled the interlude. Moist dirt packed against my lower dorsum. Instinctively, I grasped Isham with both hands, forgetting the flashlight attached to my wrist. It slid to my elbow and conked my head. "Ow!"

"You gotta watch your step." Isham's bright bulb seared into my eyes like one from a cranky playground usher spotlighting me with condemnation. "I forgot to mention the ground is fickle here."

"Damn it, Isham!"

"Isham?!" I kicked my free foot at Agares. "You were taking me down with you!"

"I didn't mean to. Stop kicking me. I didn't know what I was grabbing!"

"There's a big root to your left," Isham said. "Use it to climb back up."

Agares traded my ankle for the exposed meshwork of chunky rootlets, and he began his laborious clamber. I latched onto Isham's forearm and climbed as he helped lug me upward.

The woods had spat us out like a meal it didn't agree with. The herbaceous canopy had opened up, and we could see the disused metal factory. The gloaming cast an ominous red tint over it. *KEEP OUT NO TRESPASSING* signs hung from a twelve-foot-tall cyclone fence. Barbed wire strands were braided through the chain links. Razor wire coils spiraled along the top and bottom. The fencing surrounded a second cyclone fence bordering the perimeter around multiple buildings.

"An absurd level of security for an unused sheet metal plant," Agares said.

"No kidding. And are we downwind of a slaughterhouse?" It was a godawful amalgamation of rotting animal carcasses, decaying food, feces, and burnt hair. I pinched my nose. "What in Avern is that stench? Was this converted into a new sewage treatment plant?"

"I heard they're building a theme park. Maybe it's the portable toilets construction workers use?"

"A theme park?" I asked in a nasally voice. "What's the theme? Concentration camp meets menstrual hut?"

"Incubator farm," Isham said.

The I.F.A. It gave me sickening chills. The legislative petition proposed by Drumpf for state-sanctioned inseminations to be scheduled at internment camps had been dismissed along with its bestial petitioner. "What the…"

"Fuck," Agares said.

"Yeah, W-T-F. Wellness Triage for Females." Isham folded his arms like he was cradling an infant.

"A baby mill."

"That bill wasn't passed."

"Because it was never voted on. There's no law to prevent building the camps or permitting," he made quotes in the air, "'volunteers,' from participating in their experiments."

"What experiments?" Those black and white photographs of mutilated creatures snapped through my mind.

"Population control. Pureblood angyals are ensuring their line stays untainted. They combine male and female DNA, sperm and ovum, impregnate unconscious females and force them to carry the embryo to term, even if the pregnancy or delivery kills the mother. Then they do it again and again for those who survive."

"That can't be true."

"My department has been investigating fascist groups for months, and this deranged stuff pops up on their message boards. It's coded language, but we've deciphered their interpretation of the W-T-F, a.k.a. the I-F-A."

"Why haven't you arrested them P-D-Q?" Agares was Pretty Darn Quick with snarky quips.

"For chatting about a bill a politician submitted?" He shook his head. "They have to conspire to commit a crime or attempt to commit one, and not merely talk about hoping one comes to fruition."

"So there's nothing we can do?" I was sick of feeling powerless.

"Don't go flapping your gums about this. We're keeping the investigation under the radar."

"But creatures need to kno—"

"If you tell anyone, you'll not only blow my case, you'll find the Establishment comes down hard on gossiping trespassers."

"Isham, what's your angle?" his cousin asked him.

He extracted a square pack of cigarettes and unwrapped the foil top. "You asked me to bring you."

"We asked you to bring us to the bogs. Why did you bring us here?"

Isham carefully unsheathed a cigarette and dragged it under his nose, taking in its tobacco scent. "You both go to school with a kid who's a junior fascist and posts anonymously on the message boards." He bit the filter and held it between his teeth as he lit the opposite end. "I'd appreciate you surreptitiously finding out who it might be and giving me a name. There's a pay perk it in for me, and maybe fifty bucks for each of you if your tip pans out."

"Are you taking us to the bog or not?" I asked.

"Send that second text, and I will."

I checked my phone. "I don't have any service."

"Well." He glanced at the dusky sky. The burnt sienna hues were minutes counting toward sunset. "We're losing daylight." He inhaled his cigarette, held it, then exhaled. "We can make it if we hurry."

We marched onward, creating a chorus of snapping twigs and sticks. Thorns pricked at my clothes. The sun was convening at the horizon, and I pondered whether Isham was aimlessly misleading us in circles. Walking behind him, I smelled his cigarette smoke and then his flatulence. "Gross, Isham. You could've warned me."

"About what?"

"You just farted."

"No, I didn't. The spoiled egg stench means we're

nearing the swampland." From his collar, he pulled on a lanyard and drew a compass from underneath his shirt. "This way. We're close."

The earth became spongier, the atmosphere more humid. Blood-sucking mosquitoes buzzed around my ears. My galoshes made sucking sounds as we entered the edge of the swamp.

"That's it, there." Isham's bulb spotlighted the corner of a white garbage bag. It clung to a log against the bank. Using a loose branch, we fished it out.

Agares carefully uncinched the top and listed the inventory. "Cell culture dishes like we use in biology class. Vials. Specimen cups." He jostled the sack. "Latex gloves. Goggles. Surgical tools."

"It's a pile of medical waste?" I shined my light inside and removed a second smaller bag.

"Watch the syringes. They may not all be capped."

"This is only papers." I read the headings in their calligraphy printed font. "It's a bunch of birth and death certificates from Saint Gabe's Hospital." I extracted the stack and fanned them out like poker cards. "No names. Cause of death: Premature. Preterm. Brain bleed. Stillborn. Undeveloped. These are for fetuses, hours to days old."

"Are they copies with typos or something?" Agares scrutinized the pages.

"You see an M.D.'s name on anything?" Isham rifled through the bags. "There was an office raid on a physician who had admitting privileges at Saint Gabe's. He was implicated in an opioid scheme, forging official documents and baby trafficking. If you wanted to sell one, buy one, or alter records because the mother was too young and obviously the victim of sexual abuse, you'd go to this doctor."

"So the janitor disposed of evidence?" I thoroughly inspected the bag's interior, unsure of what I was searching for, but I had an inkling this could be the doctor administering those hormone injections.

"Unless he didn't know what he was disposing of?"

"Agares, he threw it in a swamp."

"I'm submitting these bags as evidence to the district attorney tonight." Isham took them from us. "You two keep all this info to yourselves, or you could blow the case."

"Our lips are sealed." Agares pretended to zip his mouth closed.

"I'm serious. You kids don't know who you might be screwing with. Take her home and don't contact me for a while." Isham shambled over our previous trail.

"We're keeping your flashlight," I called after him as though it was some victory even though he was leaving with a sack of evidence he wouldn't have found had I not badgered him into looking.

"Can we stop this amateur detective crap now?" Agares put his hands on his hips. "Isham is a real cop who's giving the evidence to the D.A. and we're just teenagers with a hunch. We could've been seriously hurt in that fall, and my tuxedo won't fit over a cast."

"You're right." I took deliberate steps along the path to avoid another mishap. "I've been listening to my grandfather's conspiracy theories too much, trying to find something interesting in this stupid town."

"A cabal of junior fascists is rather interesting." Agares' boots crunched behind me. "What do you care about this place? You'll be leaving for college in East

Realm next autumn."

"I don't know. What if I didn't?"

"But you will."

"Maybe I won't."

"You should tell Mahlen then because he's got y'all's whole future mapped out. Love, marriage, you *and a baby carriage*," he sang the latter four words. "Isn't that how it goes? He's probably going to propose at the dance."

I needed to change the subject. "What about you with Kara and her big jugs?"

He did a short whistle. "You jealous?"

"Of a chick who knocked down a kid so she could run to safety? No." We moved up an incline, and I began to pant. "But I am curious why you didn't ask her to the gala and instead are going with Eleleth."

"You know very well she asked me."

"Seems like you're leading her on."

"I'm perfectly content telling her to go with Vehuel."

"So you can take Miss Fun Bags?"

He grabbed my shoulder and turned me toward him. The flashlight illuminated his countenance in an eerie glow. "Are you trying to start a fight with me? It's like you're always testing my friendship, and I'm getting tired of it."

"Well, I'm pretty tired of everyone assuming they know what life choices I'm making." I pushed his hand away. "Which college I'm going to, what race I'm picking, who I'm marrying. This wild goose chase was so we could all spend more time together, and now we probably *have* stumbled upon something serious!"

"I didn't mean to pressure you," his timbre

softened like a kindergarten teacher calming a kid having a tantrum. "Relax."

"Do not talk to me like a child." I shoved him. "You first introduced me to this grand conspiracy idea with those damn syringe photos! Scaring me thinking a secret Establishment was going to clip my wings or tail and inject me full of hormones. You want me to choose daemon. Mahlen and Vasi, and probably Eleleth too, want me to pick angyal."

"I don't think any of us should have to choose. The reasoning doesn't make sense." He slapped at a mosquito. I could see welts already rising on his arms from their bites. "Look, I believe the evidence. Zealots are plotting to eradicate hybrids by any means necessary."

"Listen to yourself. You're telling me ghost stories. Are Rawhide and Bloody Bones coming after me too?"

"It seems convoluted, and it's complicated to understand. I want to protect our kind and you."

"As if I'm helpless?" I shined my light into his eyes. "I don't need a babysitter, remember. Don't treat me like I'm your little sister."

His face tensed as if I'd stabbed him in the heart.

"I'm sorry. I didn't mean it." I'd jammed my foot right into my stupid mouth. "I wouldn't talk about Marid like that. I meant as a sister in general."

"It's okay. For the record, I don't see you as a sister." He walked past me on the trail.

What did he see me as…an asshole? I hustled to match his gait. "Agares, please don't be upset."

"Quit apologizing. It's fine." His large form moved farther ahead. Shrub branches snagged at him before boomeranging into their original positions and into my path.

I used my forearms as a shield. "You don't sound fine." He seemed almost to be swatting me with the twigs. "I didn't intend to hurt you that way. You know I wouldn't disrespect Marid's memory. I loved her."

"And she loved you. As we all have."

"What?" Have? Past tense?

"We're here." We exited the underbrush and stood in the alcove beside his truck. He said nothing.

The anticipation was harrowing. "I wish you'd just yell at me and get it over with."

"I haven't thought about Marid in a couple of days. *That's* what I feel bad about. Betraying her memory by forgetting her."

"I'm sor…"

"Stop." He raised his palm. "I realize what you're trying to get me to understand, and you're right. We've all been putting pressure on you, and it's stressing you to the limit. I won't do it anymore." He opened his door and gestured for me to slide across the sofa seat. "Do you recall the day in the library when you first met Mahlen?"

I guessed he was going to underscore how my immature outburst was similar to my beau's callow moods—he'd occasionally sulk if he reckoned someone took too many potato chips, or when he asked for salve for his chapped pucker, and I gave him my balm which, unbeknownst to him, was tinted, so he walked around with ruby lips. He was so flaming mad once he discovered it, steam was virtually shooting out of his ears. "Aye."

"Do you really?" His head tilted. "Because I remember you and I were there at the table on a study

Britt Field

date. You needed help with Algebra, and I was working up the courage to ask you to the Serelia gala dance. Then a bug scared you, and you literally fell for another guy."

"You thought it was a date?" I barely remembered our study session. Algebra was so mundane. I loathed it.

"You didn't ever have feelings for me?" He climbed in and sat behind the steering wheel.

I rolled my eyes. "Isn't the adoration of everyone else enough for you?"

"Answer the query."

"Fine." I deserved to be made a little vulnerable after my ill-spoken sister comment. "I had a crush on you once in middle school, but things changed. We grew up, became close friends, and I love you as a best friend."

"Sure. Best friends." He packed our flashlights into his center console. "I care about you. I can't let you make a life-altering decision without saying something. Once you choose to be recognized only as an angyal, you'll be consumed by it. The archangyals will make it their mission to blot out every part of you that was daemon. And that includes me."

"That's not true. I don't have to pick. I'll declare myself a proud hybrid."

"How many hybrids have you seen after they graduate?"

Of the few I knew, I couldn't recollect where exactly they'd gone. "They moved to East Realm."

"Mmm-hmm. Their numbers are disappearing. I don't want you to be among them." The dimming interior light added a dramatic effect to his already dark features.

"I don't want to talk about this anymore, these hypotheticals. It makes me anxious." My thumbnails had already begun picking at the nails on their adjoining index fingers.

"I'll take you home, and we won't speak of any of this again."

Chapter 10

The week slogged along like talons, gradually scraping down a chalkboard. The news about unsolved burglaries, a dead parade sniper, and an exploded custodian had been overtaken by the remaining Serelia festivities, plus the drama surrounding the presidential debate. Agares had gotten himself disqualified for beating up his opponent and paved the way for Eleleth to nominate herself. She'd be the first female elected if she beat Daggon. It was almost all she talked about, besides the upcoming gala.

"I'm excited." Eleleth spoke in a wide-open mouth while applying fuchsia powder on her eyelids in front of the mirror. The hue matched the stripes in her pantsuit. "I noticed Succu hasn't tailed us for days now, and she's been absent. I'm hoping we'll be free of her and her sisters during the dance."

"Me too." I surmised Succu's absence had to do with the blown-to-smithereens *white knight* janitor. The secrecy was killing me. "We should be harder to stalk wearing our masks."

"Pfft, she and her cronies can sniff us out like bloodhounds." She tucked her makeup compact into her clutch. "Speaking of craziness, I feel like I'm in a love triangle."

"Between you, Vehuel, *and* Agares?" I didn't tell her Agares had asked me about my feelings toward him, nor that I'd answered about having middle school puppy love for him.

"Duh. I'll see them both at the gala tonight."

"I'm sure Agares will find solace in the gaggle of females waiting in the wings when you go dance with Vehuel."

A horn honked outside.

"They're here!" Vasiariah put on her bejeweled mask.

Our suave dates, wearing tuxedos and identical black masks covering from their nose tips to their foreheads, arrived to meet us at Vasiariah's house. She greeted them in the foyer in a quadruple-layered white tulle gown with a pearl-encrusted bodice. She was an elegant wedding cake topper, a rich confection maintaining its shape against Mrs. Beliel's hot camera flashes.

"Y'all sure took advantage of Dandy's two for one sale," she said. "And Peth with a matching hanky? You thought of everything."

"It's for my cold." He sniffed.

"Lemme get a pic of you two." Mrs. Beliel directed them to pose by the staircase.

They stood on the hardwood steps. They sat atop them. They lounged on the balustrade. Peth interspersed each stance with a cough.

"Are you okay?" Vasiariah asked him. My inward feeling matched her outward expression, both pondering if Peth was using sickness as an excuse to bugger off and not have his sister seeing him with non-angyals.

"I wouldn't miss this for the world." He dabbed at his red nose, evincing a proven cold symptom.

We all exchanged corsages and boutonnieres amid camera snaps. Mahlen and I each wore mauve flowers to match my satin dress and his cummerbund. He adjusted the pleated sash. "You're as stunning as I predicted."

"You talking to yourself," I teased, "or me?"

"Can't it be both?" He leaned in to kiss me.

"Just a peck. Don't smudge my lipstick." My mask was already creating a makeup problem. It was surely rubbing off the foundation on my upper cheekbones, and my mascara-coated lashes kept hitting the eye holes.

He gently deposited a smooch upon my lips. "It's a free-for-all later, though. Lipstick or stain be damned."

We posed for a dozen pictures with and without our masks and finally boarded the limousine we'd all pitched in to rent. Our beaus sat across from us.

Mahlen tapped on the divider glass to alert the chauffeur to drive. He then asked Peth, "Has your sister been busting your balls over coming with us to the dance?"

Vasiariah's look shot daggers at him for broaching the subject.

"Nah." Peth chuckled. "I told her I was working on converting you all, and she seemed to buy it. I'm waiting her out. She'll get bored with theology, and we'll become a normal family again."

"That's right, honey. I'm looking forward to the barbeques."

"Did anyone else hear the funny thing about Boutique Ball Gowns?" Agares asked.

"Is it about the crypt keeper who works there?" Eleleth hadn't forgiven her rude behavior. "Is she scaring customers shitless?"

"I don't know, but shit *is* involved. A sewer pipe clogged and, rather than call plumbers whose repair work might've hindered their business during Serelia, the staff burned candles and incense to cover the odor. The smoke set off the ceiling sprinklers and caused a lot of water damage to their dry clean only apparel."

"Good," Eleleth said. "I hope it stays closed and loses a ton of money."

***

Our driver seemed to make countless extra turns until finally wheeling into the parking lot outside the gymnasium. He skidded to a stop in the line of cars trying to park. After having taken twice as long to get to our destination, he dropped us at the entrance.

Upbeat tunes streamed from inside the building. "Tickets, please." Two masked attendants sat at a desk posted in front of the double doors. "Here are your king and queen ballots if you want them."

We exchanged our tickets for the ballots, wrote in our choices, then slipped the forms into the locked box.

"These decorations are beautiful," Vasiariah said. "The committee did a great job." She chaired the committee and was instrumental in choosing the secret admirer theme. Knowing what I'd learned about her father, it made sense.

"Fishing for a compliment?" Mahlen mimed holding a rod and casting it into the air.

"Quit it." I nudged him. "Everything looks wonderful, Vasi."

We donned our masks and entered our school's decorated gym via an arbor swathed in a rainbow of hydrangea. The low lighting and artificial fog hovering ankle-high above the floor provided a mysterious aura for the masquerade ball.

"Would you gals care for some punch?" Peth asked. He'd spied his sister and Daggon by the refreshments table and may have hoped the joy of the evening tempered his sibling's ire at him.

"No thanks, babe. I'm not thirsty."

"Me neither." My clingy gown, complete with corset top, left no room to ingest anything. Plus, lavatory visits were an ordeal.

"I can't risk staining my white stripes before we do the professional photo." Eleleth swiped lint off her sleeve.

Vehuel whistled and swaggered up to her. "You are spectacular. You gotta gimme a dance."

"Hmm." She looked at her escort. This had to be a dream come true for her.

"Agares, let me steal her for a few songs."

He nodded his permission, and the duo boogied to the dance area. A gaggle of single females, like pigeons in a park, immediately congregated around Agares, hoping he'd toss them a crumb.

Mahlen whirled me across the floor. "Have I told you how phenomenally gorgeous you are?"

"You can never say it too much."

"Your mask, the dress, this ring." He brought the backside of my hand to his lips and kissed it. "You're perfect."

Eight songs, four stepped on toes, and two line dances later, the music stopped. A spotlight shone on the platform, illuminating Vice Principal Melek with an envelope in hand. He cleared his throat. "We have an announcement." The microphone squealed. He distanced himself from the mouthpiece. "The Serelia King and Queen are Mahlen Forneus and Vasiariah Beliel."

Applause erupted. Peth and I, with a smidge of reluctance, congratulated our beaming dates. Sustained clapping and camera flashes escorted them through the crowd and onto the platform.

Agares nudged me. "Do you ever feel like fate is pushing some together while pulling others apart?"

"What do you mean?" I watched Mahlen and Vasiariah kneeling to receive their plastic tiaras.

"Remember the three Fates in mythology? One wove our life's line, a second measured our line length, and the third snipped our string." His two digits scissored the air.

I knew the tale. The weaver, the allotter, and the cutter. The three deities controlled the destinies of mortals.

"Let our Highnesses lead us in a slow waltz." The announcer motioned to the disc jockey to play music.

"Yeah," I said. "It was an ancient polytheist's interpretation of birth, life, and death,"

A love song flowed from the crackling speakers, and couples resumed dancing. Peth, standing nearest to Eleleth, asked her to dance.

"Why a sudden fascination with the Fates?"

Agares clutched my right hand and slid his to my lower back. "It almost looks like some strings get braided together." We began to slowly waltz. The lessons I gave him at age ten were paying off. I'd agreed to teach him the three-count step pattern so he'd intervene if/when a guy I didn't like asked me for a dance at the junior high promenade. The principal made it obligatory for gals to say yes whenever asked. They taught females our right to say no or feel comfortable was superseded by the male's feelings and protecting his fragile ego. "Does the amount of time Vasi and Mahlen spend with one another ever bother you?"

As we completed a forward half box step, I recalled the numerous instances Mahlen had given her a ride somewhere and how we spent so much time together as a group. "They had a date briefly the summer before we met, but it meant nothing." They both told me it meant nothing, and I believed them.

"Doesn't matter." He shook his head. "Fate and society prefer beautiful, popular, blond-haired, blue-eyed angyals to be together."

My eyelids squinched in miffed skepticism. "Is that right?"

"Yup and a promise ring on your finger won't change it."

It was a silver band absent any promises. I hadn't pledged a thing. "He told you about the ring?"

"Obviously. He's positive you're declaring yourself angyal."

We did a left box turn. "I never said that."

"You never said you weren't either."

"I shouldn't have to say anything." I endeavored to loosen our clinch.

He compressed me tighter. "Nuh-uh. You can't run from this."

He was right. At some juncture, time would catch me.

"Does it worry you they're traveling together to East Realm, minus their significant others, and staying there for seven days?" He was really stirring the pot.

"Not at all." Why wasn't I concerned at all? Should I have been? Why did Agares care? "You're trying to rile me. It won't work." I squeezed him harder. "If my good friend and my beau choose to throw away our courtship so they can be together, there's nothing I can do to prevent it."

"You'd dump him, right?"

"There wouldn't be anything to dump because he would've already made his choice."

His eyes widened behind the peepholes in his mask. "You wouldn't be devastated by the betrayal?"

"I'd be hurt if they cheated, but if they were truthful and upfront about their feelings, I'd have to accept it." We completed a backward half box step.

"You'd still be friends?"

"Not a snowball's chance in a wildfire."

He tossed back his head in laughter.

"The same argument could be made that we spend too much time together."

"You and I?" His laughs abated. "You said, in my truck the other night, you only had a middle school crush on me."

"Uh-huh."

"Is the rumor mill grinding out salacious stories of unrequited love?" He thrust his frame against mine. "Tell me about this soap opera. Am I *pining* for you?" he whined. "Is it a forbidden attraction? Does the passion *burn* with heat from a thousand suns?"

I was offended. "Is it such a ridiculous idea?"

"Weellll, I mean…"

Splatters on the floor captured our concern. The twosome swaying next to us were vomiting magenta globs. "Gross!" I sidestepped away from them.

"Is the flu going around?" Agares asked, "Or did somebody spike the punch?"

Eleleth and Peth, each holding a plastic cup, strode over. "I reckon they can't hold their liquor," he said, raising the cup to take a sip.

Eleleth smacked it from his hand and threw hers down. "We don't know if that's what it is." She gestured to others, violently puking. "Could be bad punch or the snacks."

"Is it food poisoning?" I thought about the freak accident during Vasiariah's play, the amputation rumors, the stabbings outside the angyal club. "Or something worse?"

The electricity shut off. Screams and heaving noises filled the darkness. I clung to Agares.

"It's okay." He patted my back.

"What's happening?" *Something worse*, my neurotic psyche answered.

"I dunno. A power surge of some kind. Maybe a storm hit a transformer."

"Eleleth, Peth?"

"We're here," they said.

The electricity was restored. I released Agares from my embarrassingly tight bear hug and blinked until my pupils adjusted to the lights. The fog had settled. Muddled and bile-splattered attendees gazed around in squinted looks.

"Where's Poyel?" her brother asked. "Anyone see her?"

We surveyed the crowded area. I didn't spot her or Daggon among the dazed figures in fancy dress.

"She left with her escort," someone replied.

The answer put him at ease that his sister was fine

but put Daggon on my radar as the culprit behind this prank.

The screeching microphone again snatched our attention. "Remain calm," Melek's upbeat timbre had turned dour. His bowtie had gone askew, much like our night. "We had a minor circuit breaker issue, and someone thought it funny to spike the refreshments. Do not sample anything over there." He motioned to the back table. "A custodian is coming to clean the floor. Be mindful where you're dancing."

"Hey, babe." Mahlen was suddenly at my side. "Let's get some fresh air and some privacy." He grasped my arm and tugged me toward a rear exit.

"Uh, okay." Before my brain decided to go, my obedient heels were already clacking behind him.

He led me past reentering couples, each adjusting their bowties, neckerchiefs, or reapplying lipstick. We bypassed them and sneaked out to get away from the chaperones. What we got was a sight of Vasiariah and Peth, sans masks, tickling tonsils beneath the lean-to roof.

"Great minds think alike," Mahlen said.

"Oh, hi, hello." They both swabbed the saliva from their mouths. The lit bulb overhead highlighted their reddening cheeks.

"Didn't mean to intrude." I looked for a secluded corner we could claim. Two silhouettes stood at the parking lot's far edge. "Hey, isn't that Ms. Hashmal?" I saw the outline of her tummy. She seemed to be on break from chaperoning. "Who's with her?"

"Her husband or fiancé, maybe?" Vasiariah said. "Stealing off to live out an old high school fantasy probably."

The door opened. Eleleth stepped outside along with Agares. "Where did y'all go?"

"We needed to get away from the puke fest," Mahlen half lied.

This was clearly a make-out spot. Had Eleleth finally decided to throw caution into the tempest winds to put the moves on her crush, and why did that bother me now? I diverted the subject to the parking lot duo loudly arguing. "Looks like marriage trouble for them."

The shadowy figure slapped Ms. Hashmal.

"Oy, jackass!" Peth lurched forward, and his date seized him.

"He might have a gun. Somebody call security."

"On it." Mahlen swung his phone in the air. "No service!"

"The cops are coming! Leave her alone!" We hoped the faux warning would thwart the assault.

Ms. Hashmal scuffled with the male. He forced her into a car and drove off.

I ripped off my mask. "We have to do something!"

Agares flagged down the rent-a-cop working security at the function and recounted what we saw.

"What you're describing is a domestic dispute," the officer's condescending tone burned like boiling tar. "It's a disagreement betwixt a husband and his wife. We respond to crimes, okay, kids?" He tucked his thumbs between the top of his pants and the belt, straining to corral his fat belly.

"It was an assault," Agares corrected him.

"From this distance, you don't know what you saw." He craned his neck upward. "Oxygen's a little thin up there for you."

"Uh, sir." Peth interceded before the officer poked

the bear out of Agares. "Can you at least have a cop go check on her?"

He sniffed. "You kids been drinking?"

"What?" we asked.

"Y'all on drugs?"

"We're at our school dance." Eleleth removed her mask. "This is unbelievable."

"What's unbelievable is wasting my time to call in a false report. That's an arrestable offense."

"It's not a false report," Agares growled through clenched teeth.

The cop put a palm on his holstered pistol. "It's a case of not minding your own business."

"Sir." Mahlen threw up his hands to interpose. "We're sorry to have troubled you. Let's not waste any more of your time. I'm sure you have better things to do."

"That's right." His demeanor relaxed. He got inside his cruiser and left.

"Corrupt cops," Agares said. "We're on our own here."

Something occurred to me. "Maybe this seems off-topic, but Ms. Hashmal is Cherub High's last full daemon teacher."

"That can't be right." Mahlen ruminated for a moment. "What about Mr. Kroni?"

"Quit."

"Miss Ipos?"

"Transferred to Leyak Elementary," Eleleth said.

"Mr. what's his name?" He triple-snapped his fingers. "Uh, the P.E. teacher with the bad crew cut?"

"Fired or forced to resign because of his fixation on Jerah." Vasiariah donned her mask.

"Ms. Abyzou?"

"Maternity leave." I reflexively loosened the corset around my tummy. "Ms. Hashmal's pregnant too. We need to go to her house."

Mahlen shook his head. "We're not leaving our last Serelia dance to do *that*. We'd be the ones arrested for getting between a husband and his wife."

"I'll mention it to my dad," Peth referenced his guard commander father. "I'm sure Hashmal will be fine."

I was too flustered to argue. "Then let's go home. The gym stinks like vomit, and my feet are starting to hurt."

"No, you're not going already?" Eleleth's goggle-eyed plea implored me to stay.

I was about to relent. Then Vasiariah reminded us three of them had to get a booster vaccine in the morning prior to leaving the realm. Peth and Agares both agreed we should call it a night. Mahlen reluctantly acceded and called his father to pick us up.

Chapter 11

My wonky clock radio woke me from a restless night. The disc jockey's baritone resounded as though his booth was inside a keg. He was mid-story about a clash between protesters and counter-protesters. "Four adults were treated at hospital and released after a skirmish at the Drumpf rally."

I hit the off button and checked my phone. I had texts regarding Poyel. She hadn't returned home from the dance, and nobody knew where she might be. This wasn't the first time she'd broken her curfew, so her dad hadn't yet called the police.

I had an ill feeling in my stomach. It wasn't the full-scale *about to blow chunks* sensation. It was a general uneasiness. If I thought very long about it, the sensation had remained with me on some level since Mom was first hospitalized.

On top of always worrying something bad was going to happen and having it reinforced by events like Ms. Hashmal's domestic abuse and Poyel going A.W.O.L., the dreaded departure time for my friends had arrived. They were leaving, traveling across the Barren, to tour colleges in faraway East Realm. I'd endeavored ineffectively to coerce them into delaying their trip. Now I was armed with another reason to try and get them to postpone it.

I washed my face, daubed on a tinted moisturizer

to camouflage my sleepy mug, and hastily dressed. I laced up my shoes at the door. One heel had Josa's gnaw marks, but I didn't have time to change. I plucked the car key from its hook and said bye to Grandpa.

"It's nippy outside. Take a coat," he replied from behind his farmer's almanac. "Love you."

"Love you too." I grabbed my leather jacket. "Put a chew toy on the list for Josa." I went out, leaving tracks of my rubber sole bits, and fired up the wagon. I fiddled for three minutes with the unruly seatbelt. I was convinced it required an exorcism until it finally clicked.

I reversed onto the road and drove toward the depot. The car's fanbelt squeaked at passing joggers, bike riders, and speed walkers as I decelerated to study their profiles, seeing if they were Poyel. I assumed I'd see her on missing posters soon.

Merging onto the intra-realm highway, I saw billboards asking citizens to vote Danjal Jinn or Ebel Drumpf for mayor. Each had misspelled graffiti, labeling one a "commueniss/soshillist" and the other a "fashiss/raceist." I recalled Drumpf's deplorable rhetoric during the carnival and his nephew's regurgitated hate speech at the debate. It was enough to chase anyone from Bune Town.

I steered onto the West Realm Depot exit and followed signs to the visitor lot. I parked and carefully considered what words to say to my departing pals. The wind slapped my ponytail into my face hindering my hustle to the terminal.

Each running transport vehicle sat parked in its spot on the departure lane. Exhaust fumes filled the air. They swirled around waiting travelers and an employee checking their tickets.

The commuter vans were centered in the ten-car motorcade. I observed Agares helping our buddies load their luggage into their van as I approached. "Hey, are you three *actually* leaving with our friend missing?" The phrase was much more indelicate than I planned.

Eleleth snapped down the handle on her wheeled suitcase. "Hello to you too."

"Sorry, but a missing creature kind of overrides a need for salutations."

"Missing?" Her response was too sarcastic to simply say she rolled her eyes. She airbrushed a huge chartreuse arc with them. "Poyel has done this before. Besides, she isn't our friend anymore." Her words were as frigid and hard as the concrete pillar I leaned against. I couldn't help sensing she was mad at me—likely due to my cutting our gala night short and shredding whatever Agares smooch fantasy she'd dreamed up.

"Vasi?" I searched her powdered features for empathy. "It's Peth's sister."

"I know, and he understands I can't do anything." She blew him a kiss at his perch on the wall. He reciprocated. I wondered whether he even mentioned Ms. Hashmal's assault to his dad. "Eleleth's right, even if a little crabby from her booster shot. The needle was huge." She made an exaggerated circle with her thumb and index finger. Eleleth stuck out her tongue in response. "Anyway, Poyel made her choice to cut us out of her life. I'm not missing this opportunity to go search for someone who wouldn't do the same for us and is likely pranking her dad. She'll turn up."

They hugged me, said cheerio, and boarded the van. The chipper attitude was misplaced in the

217

melancholy mood.

"Honey," Mahlen said, "for all we know, Poyel has deliberately faked her disappearance to get attention for herself or Daggon's wacko causes."

He was probably right. I was sure Daggon was behind the spiked snacks and power surge at the dance. However, the nagging in my gut wouldn't cease. "What if Poyel *is* a victim though?"

"You shouldn't let your worry become paranoia." He gripped my shoulders as if to ground me, like I was so air-headed I might be blown away by a backfiring muffler.

I felt more insulted than comforted. His patronizing invalidated my concerns.

He slid his palms down my arms before clutching my fingers. His eyebrows squashed together, forming an eleven on his frons. "Where's your ring?"

"What?" With everything going on, who could think about jewelry?

"The ring I gave you. Did it slip off?" He scanned the ground.

"No, I just didn't wear it today."

He recoiled as though my retort was a tangible personal slight.

"All aboard!" a guard strolled by squawking. "All aboard now!"

"Yeah, Ifrit, I heard you!" Mahlen climbed into the vehicle. "Maybe this trip will be good for us. The time apart will show you how consequential our relationship is. We need a short break."

I was tired of his veiled threats and ultimatums. "Maybe what we need is a break, period. Goodbye."

The doors closed, shutting my view of his shock. A

sentry ordered the chauffeur to drive. The van rolled forward, revealing Agares standing on the other side. He hurried over the lane to beat the next oncoming vehicle. "Did you just break up with Mahlen?"

"I did." I tugged my jacket tighter around me. I'd gotten the anger off my chest, and it left me cold.

"It wasn't anything I said at the dance, was it? About the rumor mill, or you and me?"

"Not directly." I'd already been rethinking the courtship with my now ex-beau before Agares told me our ninth-grade study session was meant to be a date. I wondered why things couldn't be easy with Mahlen like they were with Agares. Did romantic love complicate everything? Was I being stubborn, or was I forcing something that wasn't there? "Things between us haven't been the same since he gave me the stupid promise ring and these little, I don't know, subtle conditions attached to it. You wouldn't understand." He'd never been in a long-term relationship. He was a hit it-n-quit it, love 'em-n-leave-'em guy.

He dug the toe on his big shoe into the gravel. "That it's less of a gift and more of a choke chain on a collared dog?"

"Uh, yes, kind of exactly that." He didn't have a positive opinion on courtships. Our parents had been bad examples. "Do you see yourself as the dog or the chain?"

"You wanna talk about it?" He raised one palm horizontal to the ground. "Or distract yourself from it?" He raised his other and lifted them both up and down like balancing scales.

"I have to teach a Tiny Tappers class, and I'm worried about our missing friend, but yeah, sure." I already felt overwhelmed.

"Come here." He stretched open his arms.

"Why?"

"You need a hug. Bring it in." He enveloped me. The slick fabric of his coat sounded loud as my ear brushed across it. "I know you want to look for her, and I'm with you, but if I'm honest, Eleleth and Vasi are right about Poyel. She doesn't want our friendship. She wouldn't look for us if we were the ones unaccounted for, and she probably *has* faked her disappearance."

I wanted to mention the vaccines; however, it would've made Mahlen right about me being paranoid. "Aren't you supposed to take my mind off of it?"

"You're right. Come on." We headed toward the parking lot. He kept an arm draped over my shoulders. "We could have game night with Caim and Tannin."

"Okay." I tried to sound enthusiastic. "You call them to set it up. Tomorrow. Not for this evening. I'm exhausted."

Our farewells were taken by a breeze as we parted ways in the lot. During my drive home, I assured myself my chums were right about Poyel. She would likely resurface tonight. I shouldn't have tried to guilt Eleleth and Vasiariah into canceling an important trip.

I texted an apology at the first yield sign. At the second, my phone tinged, saying the message was unable to be sent. I tried several instances unsuccessfully throughout the day to resend.

I tried prior to starting my tap class. I tried during dinner with my grandfather. I tried after we watched the nightly news, just before the anchor announced Poyel Harut was missing and considered a possible runaway.

Grandpa hawked and spat a wad of tobacco into his

can. "Is she related to the Haruts who have the summer barbeques?"

"She's their daughter." I'd been correct to fret about her. My friends should've been concerned too. I edited my apology text to add she was declared missing. *Unable to be sent.* "Her parents are divorcing, so they think she ran away."

"You don't think so?"

"A lot of peculiar things have happened lately." Stabbings, missing creatures, burglaries, a parade sniper who may have been the burglar, crazed politicians, scuttlebutt about hormone therapies, discarded evidence in the bog near a hidden facility in the Restricted Acres, an exploded custodian with secrets, and an awful time for communication lines to go down. "Anything's possible."

The landline telephone in the kitchen rang. I rose to answer it. "If it's Botis," Grandpa said, "tell him we aren't speaking 'til he admits he cheated at rummy."

"Okay." I brought the handset to my ear. I could hear a faint crackling on the line. "Hello?"

"You were right...about Poyel," Agares spoke in a stunned monotone. "Sorry, I was dismissive before."

"Authorities are still saying she's a runaway. Maybe she is." I held onto hope it was her decision to vanish.

"Maybe. I'm not so sure. Is your cell phone out too?"

"Yep. None of my texts are going through, and this connection doesn't sound great either."

"Crap." His palm went over the transmitter to muffle his parents' bickering in the background. "Um, I gotta go. I just wanted to tell you I was wrong, and you were right." The line went dead.

"Is it Botis?" Grandpa asked from his chair.

"No. Just a friend worried about Poyel." My concerns had been vindicated, yet I maintained a wish that I was wrong. The emotional rollercoaster was exhausting. "I'm off to bed, Papa. Goodnight."

***

Sleep eluded me. Under my covers, I was too hot, and out of them, I was too cold. I couldn't get comfortable. Thoughts cartwheeled in my mind, switching from one idea to the next, like pages flipping in an opened book.

I hadn't heard from my friends or Mahlen. Was it a storm? Had some deformed beasts rumored to roam the Barren chewed through cables? Was I choosing to be paranoid because I didn't want to admit to myself I wasn't hankering to hear from my ex? I tossed and turned from worry until my shorts wadded up my bum and the skinny straps on my top twisted into my collar bone.

I couldn't focus on relaxing, even with steady precipitation battering my roof. Creatures were going missing or ending up dead, and nobody seemed to care. Mahlen, Eleleth, and Vasiariah had left to tour college campuses as if things were normal. Meanwhile, the rest of us stayed behind to deal with a brewing unrest.

I saw my pals in a different light. It was similar to how my radiant nightlight cast distorted shadows of objects in my room. Dancing duos within the musical glitter globe atop my dresser looked like eight-limbed ogres projected on my wall. I regretted painting over the original charcoal color with lavender. It was supposed to be a calming hue; instead, it provided a perfect canvas for monstrous silhouettes to terrorize me.

I'd been sleeping with a nightlight since the break-in. Shutting it off would eliminate the shadows but replace them with the fear a burglar lurked somewhere in my darkened room. I clicked on my lamp to scan every corner. The monsters disappeared. My bedroom and bathroom were empty.

I clicked off the lamp and turned away from the projection wall. I ruminated on how fast my friends would change with the flick of a switch or the prick of a needle and discard me the way they discarded Poyel after she vanished.

The familiar rapping at my window was a welcomed diversion. I craved company. I slid open the drapes. Agares tarried below the eave. His drenched pajamas stuck to him while sleet poured from the sky. I lifted the sash. A chilly gust misted me with water.

Agares stepped in. His torn T-shirt, streaked with maroon splotches, flapped open from the collar. It bared a superficial slash amid his chest. He stripped off the wet cotton garment and laid it on the window's ledge. Soapy fragrance and steam rose from his muscular torso as though he'd just climbed out of a bath.

I inspected his three-inch-long scrape. "Agares…"

"Shhh." He lay his index finger upon my archer's bow to mute me. "His pocketknife barely made contact. He was only trying to scare me."

He was fearless to a fault, but his father's behavior scared me. He'd never used a weapon on his son before. The violence was escalating. I couldn't endure losing Agares. "Your dad's a sadist."

"We all have hobbies." He deflected with a joke. Humor was his defense against trauma.

I couldn't muster a courtesy laugh. "I'm sorry." I looped my arms around his taut waist, dampening my pajamas and not caring. I needed to comfort him, and I needed the comfort I found in his strong embrace. The rhythmic percussion of his heartbeat soothed me.

"You don't have to apologize. I needed this." He cradled me. His lower jaw whiskers brushed my crown.

"You're growing a beard."

"You like it?" He roguishly rubbed the bristles into my scalp.

I leaned backward to survey his newest attribute. He rotated his face showing off his stubble. I admired his coppery skin and dark, penetrative eyes. I saw myself reflected in them. "Mm-hmm," I murmured. He looked at me differently than in his usual coy style. I felt different in the manner he looked at me, as though nobody had ever seen me the way he saw me. I liked it a lot. "Sometimes you have to see a thing up close to realize how much."

"Do you?" His gaze lingered over my countenance, studying my features. His hands pressed tighter into my flesh, causing it to horripilate and send a quiver through my insides. I liked that too.

Lightning flashed outside. Electricity buzzed through the air and sparked along my nerve receptors. Thunder clapped. My pulse thudded with the tempo of the sleet pelting my roof. Still, his stare held me. Those ochre flecks glistening in his irises were magnets pulling me into his orbit.

I hung there, watching him struggle between wanting to save me and consume me all at once as if I was the last drop of moisture on a desert planet. He looked thirstier by the second. I yearned to fall like dew upon his parched lips, to quench his thirst and satisfy my scorching desires. The hesitation was a delicious torment. My receptors perched at full mast.

A natural instinct spurred me up toward him, elevating my heels until I poised on the balls of my feet. I balanced at the precipice of a life-changing decision. I was ready and eager to take the leap.

His pulsating spine curved beneath my palms, bringing his mouth nearer to mine. "I'm in love with you." His breathy revelation caressed my pout.

We kissed, mingling our tongues in an unspoken dialect. His short whiskers tickled my chin. His fervent, curious fingers explored my physique. Tingles emanated from my diaphragm and journeyed south. I could feel his spinal column expand as his soft tail snaked out and coiled around my ankles. He cupped my face, drinking me in. Our kiss became more passionate.

A tug on my shirt and a whoosh opened my eyes, breaking our amorous clinch. My erect wings had emerged, stretching two feet from my sides.

"Extraordinary." He moved to touch them but halted. "May I?"

I consented.

"You honor me." He stroked the smooth tissue. It kindled an exhilarating stria of hot prickles.

"Hon...honor?" my speech wavered.

"Aye. In archaic daemon testaments, before creatures learned where babies came from, our females were lauded for their magical ability to procreate." He knelt and kissed my feet. "Worshipped even."

"You don't subscribe to daemonic folklore. Besides, I'm not a daemon." I batted my pinions.

"No, you are so much more. You're perfect." He

ran his fingers up the profile of my frame. "I'd be honored to call you mine, without labels or conditions, if you'd let me." He had a master's degree in pillow talk.

"I'm not like your other conquests." I was partly presuming and partly inquiring.

"You mean the groupies?"

"I won't follow you like a lost little puppy." I retracted my wings.

"I don't want you to follow me. I want you beside me." He brushed my hair behind my ears. "I'm not the conqueror you believe me to be. I don't take from sycophants seeking to curry my favor for their ulterior motives, nor from those giving who do it solely because they think it's what I want. I'm experienced, but I'm nobody's bedpost notch." He glanced at my bedframe. "You'd be my first triumph, one I'd gladly see to the end, and the only one who matters."

I'd discovered something rarer than a human. An alpha male feminist. "I want to be yours and you to be mine."

He scooped me up and carried me to my bed. I felt like royalty, a queen revered by her king. I cozied into his buff arms and felt protruding veins furcated on their surface.

We cuddled and talked between kisses. I noticed all those things I'd overlooked before: the pentagonal contour of his jawline, the gentleness of his touch, the weight of his physique dwarfing mine. We held each other for hours—our bodies and hearts entwined in a love I'd been too naïve to recognize.

I snuggled beside him underneath the sheet and savored my first peaceful slumber in a long while, free from nightmares. I greeted the rising sun with elation instead of malaise. The dawn bathed us in warm rays of pink and violet.

"I should go before someone sees me."

I didn't want him to leave. "You'll come back later?"

"Of course. We've got a game night." He kissed me goodbye. We agreed not to mention the previous night to anyone until we figured out how to tell Mahlen and Eleleth. We were keeping so many secrets. Why not one more.

Chapter 12

Cell service still hadn't been restored in the evening. We used the spotty landline to coordinate game night. With three-eighths of our clique out of town, it was Caim's turn to host. We sat around a table in her walk-out basement playing a crossword puzzle board game with Tannin and Peth.

I couldn't concentrate on my letter tiles due to a pooch scratching on the door screen. "Caim, I think your pup is ready to come back inside."

"He isn't outside," she said, not peeping up from her tiles. "He's in his kennel."

I distinctly heard rough scrapes against a wire mesh. "Then what's scratching at the door?"

"Nice try," Agares simpered. "We're not leaving the table so you get more time on your turn."

"That's not what I'm doing. Need I remind you, I'm winning." I pointed at the scorepad. I was twenty points ahead.

"For now, 'til I get that quadruple word score."

"You mean this quadruple word which I'm about to use." I underlined the row with my index finger.

He smiled coyly and gripped my wrist. "You wouldn't dare."

"Get a room, you two." Caim tossed popcorn at us. She'd probably noticed our less than discreet footsie below the foldout card table.

He instantly released me, and we both sputtered denials.

"Listen," Peth said. "I hear it."

Everyone stopped chomping their snacks and listened. Above the sound of the humming mini fridge, a faint scraping noise came from outside the door.

"What is that?" Caim rose to investigate.

I grabbed a metal nail file from my purse, and we followed. I'd been carrying household items as weapons since the break-in.

"What're you doing with that?" Agares asked. "You gonna give 'em a bad manicure?"

"Shut it!"

Caim flicked on the switch to the exterior bulb and opened the window curtain. I expected to see a stray animal. A scrawny, familiar-looking figure materialized from the shadows.

I clutched my chest to prevent my heart from leaping out. "Crap!"

"I don't believe it!" Caim cried, ripping open the door. "Balam!"

Her frizzy mane drooped in tangled wads. She was as frightened as a wounded rabbit, jumpy and jittery. Her eyes, two enormous yellow marbles, continuously darted around for the predator who'd mauled her. "Shh. Be quiet." She stepped into the light.

I could see her complexion was a yellowish tint. She appeared jaundiced, like my grandma when her gallbladder ceased functioning. She initially thought she was sore from taking a class that taught elderly adults how to fall without breaking their hips. Turned out, her gallbladder was bloated with stones.

Balam looked like she'd been dragged across

stones. Her threadbare clothing was grimy, and her short sleeves revealed scabby track marks trailing the inside of her arm. Her elbow pits had more bruises than an overripe banana. Had she gotten herself addicted to drugs? We'd all tried vaping and smoking, but nothing stronger than tobacco or wacky weed.

Tannin dropped the popcorn bowl he held. The rest of us stood awestruck in such a dead quietude one could've heard a mosquito sneeze. We thought Balam was dead. I wasn't yet sure she wasn't an apparition or a reanimated corpse with mucky feet.

The sisters hugged and sobbed. "Where've you been?" Caim asked.

"The wuh…woods." Balam's speech was raspy.

"What? They found your car stuck in a creek. A cop told us you must've drowned and washed down the river. Why were you in the woods?"

"Hiding." Balam ushered them across the threshold. She closed and locked the door, then peeped through the curtain before switching off the exterior light. "I was taken."

"Where? And who took you?" Caim continually petted her sister like she had to keep touching her to make this unbelievable happenstance real.

"Don't know. I was attacked from behind, getting into my car after work. My head." She touched her crown. "I awoke in a medical apron strapped to an exam table in some kind of prison lab." Teardrops carved a trail through the dirt on her gaunt cheeks. "They did unspeakable acts to us. They implanted things." She cradled her belly. "I couldn't go through it again."

Tannin draped a blanket around her trembling body

and, with Caim on the other side, assisted her to the couch.

"Go through what?" Tannin asked.

I recalled the old soap opera episodes when characters hit their heads, and either suffered from amnesia or went mad. Balam could've survived her car crash, banged her head, floated onto a bank somewhere, and wandered into the forest thinking she was hiding from someone evil.

Agares looked at me and mouthed the question, *Brain injury?*

Maybe, I mouthed back.

"The torture. They tied me into stirrups." She rubbed the enflamed ligature marks circling her ankles and wrists. "I could smell alcohol and Sulphur. They pried apart my thighs. Tools clanged in a tray." She tugged her earlobes. "They were inside me, cranking the speculum, probing and prodding. It made me sick. It hurt so much." She wrenched her knees to her chest and rocked back and forth.

"You don't have to tell us anymore," Tannin said. Males got queasy at the concept of an invasive gynecological examination, let alone one forcibly performed and tantamount to sexual assault, as described in detail by the traumatized victim.

"Peth, look at her arms?" I said discreetly. "Could she have been scrounging by the loading docks all this time?" Among goods traded by the East and West during the supply exchanges were medical-grade narcotics. I had paternal cousins who were drug junkies and another who was a dealer. My father's relatives were openly trashy. My mother's folks had the decency to keep their garbage lives closeted, or at least corralled

Britt Field

within their immediate family.

"You mean like the Hypo Whores peddling their wares for dope? Nah. I would've seen her on my patrols."

"You all need to know," Balam persisted. "You need to hear how they're violating us."

Caim clasped her sister's face. "What were they implanting?"

"They didn't let me see. Just left me with the scar." She lifted her shirt.

A vicious purple cicatrix sprawled across her abdomen. I felt nauseous. Someone had sliced into her midsection. She was telling the truth.

Caim wept uncontrollably. "No, no, no,"

"Who did it?" Agares asked.

"They wore surgical masks. I don't know."

"How did you escape?"

"They thought I was unconscious, but I could hear. There was yelling from a hallway. They kept repeating, 'She's hemorrhaging!' The workers in my room left and forgot to lock the door. I ran!"

I touched her arm. "You said, 'Us.' Who else was there with you?"

"Other females, mostly daemons and hybrids like me, but some angyals too."

"Did you recognize them?" Peth asked.

"Some. I heard voices. I reckoned I was hallucinating. One sounded like my dad or my uncle." Her bloodshot eyes widened as though she'd just remembered something, "Another sounded like your sister." She glanced around. "Is Poyel here with you?"

"She went missing during the Serelia dance." He patted his pockets for his phone. "We need to call the cops."

"No, we can't!" She grabbed him. "They got me once, and they can do it again. I don't even know who they are. I can't identify them."

"We have to help the others."

"Nobody's going to believe my story. They'll poke and prod me again. They'll call me crazy." She yanked at her hair. "I can't stand anymore!"

"You're safe now." Caim wrapped her arms around her sister and pulled her back to the sofa.

"She's right," I said. "Adults don't believe teenagers, and they sure don't believe females. Remember a couple years ago when that hybrid, Charon, said she was attacked and ended up pregnant? They called her a lying slut and threatened to arrest her for filing a false police report."

"Didn't she jump off the parking garage roof of Nyettzach Hospital?" Tannin asked.

"They said it was an accidental fall. If she was shoved, we'd never know because they didn't investigate." Incompetent Nyettzach cops and a lazy medical examiner didn't prioritize cases involving dead females. One was found sitting on her couch naked, shot in the center of her forehead. They ruled it a suicide within 13 minutes. Another was gagged, hogtied, noosed, and tossed nude over a balcony railing. Manner of death: Suicide. "Just like that cop who wouldn't check on Ms. Hashmal."

"We don't know who's behind this," Agares interjected. "It could very well be dirty cops, or at best, cops who don't give a damn. We need to get Balam somewhere safe."

"And Poyel. We have to get my sister out of there."

"Peth, she was dating Daggon," I said. "During the debate, he mentioned the Incubator Farm Act, and if I were to imagine what it's like, this would be a result of it." I gestured toward Balam.

"Dang," Agares said. "I was thinking nasty sex cult, but Amitiel's right."

"You know what else?" Caim sniffled. "He worked at the pizza joint with Balam the night she closed and went missing."

We all exchanged knowing glances. Daggon had to be interrogated.

"Dad went to pick her up because her car was unreliable, and she was gone."

"Wait, your dad was there that night too?" That detail wasn't previously disclosed. In fact, Mr. Moroni said he'd been home with his wife all evening. I'd asked him myself when I requested details to add to the *MISSING* flyers I posted around town.

The stairway creaked. "Do you all need more snacks?" Mrs. Moroni walked down the steps, saw her formerly missing child, and paled. "Balam?"

"Mommy."

"Balam!" She ran crying to her daughter and showered her with hugs and kisses while simultaneously calling for her husband.

He emerged less surprised than his spouse. "What're you…what did you get yourself into?"

"Levi, wake up! It's our daughter."

"Aye, I know, but she looks like she's been doing drugs while we've been worried sick, and she's obviously unwell." He grimaced and didn't go near her as though she were contagious. "She needs to go back…she needs to go to a hospital."

"Go back?" I jabbed Agares, "Did he say—"

"'Go back'? Yup, I heard him."

"She needs to go back where, Mr. Moroni?" Peth asked.

He nervously plucked at his pajama shirt. "A hospital. I said she needs…"

"To go back." Mrs. Moroni glared at him. "You said she needs to go back. You've tried to convince me she's a drug addict. You've known where she's been this whole time? Did you sell her?"

"No. Uriel, please." He drew his palms together as if praying.

"Please, what?" She wiped her damp cheeks. "Understand? Like I understood your heavy drinking. Or forgive you? Like I forgave your gambling even after they repossessed the car."

"Yes. Because of those debts, we couldn't afford treatment for Balam's affliction, not by conventional means."

"We would've found a way to treat her lupus." She pulled the blanket tighter around her daughter. "What's wrong with you, Levi? How can you…" Realization washed over her countenance. "They took her because of your debts, didn't they?"

"Who's 'they?'" Caim asked. "Dad, you knew what they were doing to Balam?"

"It isn't lupus. Something had to be done to save her life. The doctor said if she didn't undergo the hormone therapies, she'd get sicker and die."

"Therapies?! They were carving creatures up!" Balam yelled.

"No. Your immune system generated antibodies against your newly developing cells, like when Mommy was pregnant with you and your sis and because she has a negative blood type, but you two were positives, she had to get shots to stop her body from hurting you." His voice had softened in the same manner when adults talk to diminutive children. He described the autoimmune disease's symptoms but insisted it wasn't lupus.

"Do not condescend to us, you gullible tool!" his wife shouted.

"Those new cells inside your appendages brought their own separate monocytes," he added a professor's affectation. "They normally degrade bacteria, but they reacted to your immune system like it was a pathogen. Doctors had to remove the parts before they killed the host. They were finding an antidote without causing a mass panic."

"They lied! They used us like lab rats for their experiments! They damn near killed me at their torture farm!"

"They said they were finding a cure."

"So," Peth said, "you turned a blind eye to what they did. The abductions, the assaults, the implantations."

I glimpsed Mr. Moroni's jewel-encrusted wristwatch. "How much did they pay you?"

Mrs. Moroni gasped. "You said those were simulated diamonds." She threw a full soda can at her husband's head. It smashed into his nose, and blood spurted. "You sold out your own daughter! Get out of my sight!"

An injured Mr. Moroni clenched his bleeding nostrils and hurtled into the bathroom. I wondered if he'd call whoever was bankrolling him to tell them his daughter was home.

"Tannin," Mrs. Moroni said, "go rip the kitchen phone out of the wall and throw Levi's cell into the garbage disposal right now." He did as he was told. Caim and her mother stayed to solace Balam.

"Will you be okay?" I tapped her shoulder.

"You kids should get somewhere safe."

"Come on." Agares tossed Peth his UCV keys.

We scuttled outside. Peth unlocked his truck. I climbed into the passenger seat. "Do you think Balam's dad will be arrested for what he did to her, or will the powers that be cover it up?"

"He'll be arrested for something," Agares said, "if Balam can convince cops to believe her story, and those cops aren't corrupt."

"Nah." Peth's head shook in tandem with the spinning steering wheel. "My money's on finding the entire Moroni family bobbing in the river with police saying it's a triple murder-suicide." He spoke in too cavalier a manner. "They'd say they found a note, a confession by Mr. Moroni to killing his eldest daughter because she intimated she'd declare herself, I don't know, whichever race the writer didn't think Moroni liked, or something convoluted like that." He drove us to the street near Daggon's residence and parked. We exited to creep behind a hickory tree. We saw an empty driveway and one light on inside the house.

I whispered, "I don't think his parents are home." When not working at the sewage treatment plant, they were protesting at funerals or health clinics.

"Should we go over the plan?" Peth asked.

In our haste, we hadn't formulated our strategy.

Agares cracked his knuckles. "We sneak in and beat the truth out of him."

"We're in a hurry." I held up my purse. "I have scissors to threaten to cut his testicles."

They both flinched.

"Toughen up. They're just crafting scissors. You want answers or not?"

They looked at each other and nodded.

"Okay, I'll knock on the front door, and you two sneak in the back." I waited sixty seconds before approaching the entryway. I rang the buzzer, signaling my cohorts I was in position.

A pasty-faced Daggon answered. The darkness within him materialized in the blackened crescents below his eyes. "I know why you're here."

"Do you?" I expected him to insult me and slam the door.

He stepped aside and invited me in. "You want to talk about Poyel."

"Exactly." Walking into the foyer, I kept my distance, and one hand in my purse holding the scissors.

Daggon was a serpent disguised in a pit-stained sweatshirt and raggedy shorts. "I know you hate me, and you're right to. I hate myself." He shut the door and peeked through the peephole for a moment. "Uncle Drumpf said everything would be fine. I just had to get him a few zygote chambers to prove his theory."

"Zygote chambers?" I cringed. "You mean females with healthy wombs."

"Yeah. He said he'd take care of me. He'd have scientific evidence to justify his hypothesis and his Incubator Farm Act. He'd get elected mayor, and I'd get a top spot in his administration." He touched his chest.

"So you helped him kidnap Poyel and Balam."

"Not Poyel, no." He shook his head. "She chose to go. She was a devout believer." Tears brimmed in his eyes. "She believed in me. She trusted me, and I failed her."

"How?" Other than failing at any semblance of decency. "What did you do?"

"They wouldn't help her. I begged them to." He put his palms together and looked upward. "I prayed and begged. She was bleeding too much."

The word Balam used, 'hemorrhage,' echoed in my brain. "Why was she bleeding, Daggon?"

"She was pregnant with our child. It came too soon, and the medical staff wouldn't intervene. They wouldn't save her!" He sobbed into his hands.

"She's dead?" I didn't believe him. Daggon was a proven liar. "She can't be."

"Everything they promised was a lie." He cast his swollen eyes on me. "You have to leave this town, this sector. There's going to be a coup. My uncle is in cahoots with the leadership in Omunkar, and they're agents for the Gold administration."

"You're saying the Golds are behind this?"

"Don't you know? Haven't you seen?" He gestured wildly at the windows. "When Governor Gold took power, his administration pushed for desegregating schools to show the races how different we are in attempts to stir discord. Why else wouldn't he disavow hate crimes? He used his speeches to promote violence by telling us to ignore it. He's getting his wish to make this a police state and appoint himself an autocrat."

"How?" He sounded unhinged. The door securing his insanity had blown wide open.

"Once Drumpf and his disciples institute the militia

they've formed to overthrow our government, Omunkar's police force will move in with support, then Gold will send in the Sovereign Realm Guard." He paced around, staring at his feet. "Whether or not the Incubator Bill passes, the governor is taking over and implementing his own martial law. He'll demand more than curfews for females and making it illegal for them to vote, or get a driver's license, own a business, or have bank accounts."

Agares emerged from the hall. "What are they plotting?"

"You brought a friend?"

"Friends." Peth revealed himself. Had he heard his sister's purported fate? "Answer the question."

"His militia will be going house to house seizing all fertile females—angyals, daemons, and hybrids—no matter how young, for indefinite detainment."

"Horseshit," Agares said. "You're lying."

"Are you willing to bet her life on it?" He pointed to me. "Childbirth can be a death sentence." He stooped to fetch a duffel bag off the foyer floor. Distended seams struggled to encase its contents, and wires strayed from the zipper. It projected a foreboding aura. "I'm not going to let them kill any more of us."

"What're you going to do?"

A glaze coated his reddening sclera. "I've already done it. I've rigged explosives everywhere." He tapped his bag. "Get out of this sector, this realm, as fast as you can."

We had to notify someone this fool was having a psychotic break. The three of us retrieved our cell phones hoping service was available.

"Give me some credit." Daggon scored the highest

grades in our Sci-Tech classes. If anyone could teach himself to build homemade bombs or disrupt a power grid, he could. "I disabled the towers."

My eyes pounced on the rotary telephone atop the table by the kitchen.

"And the landline network."

Dismissing him, I rushed to pick up the handset and put the receiver to my ear. No dial tone. I verified the cord was plugged in and triple-clicked the switch hook. Nothing. I slammed it into its cradle. The stakes were raised in a poker game I didn't want to play.

"The transformers and turbine generators will break momentarily. The news stations won't be capable of broadcasting either."

Agares lunged for Daggon's throat. "Bastard!"

He dodged his captor as Peth bearhugged Agares. "No! Bombs are in his bag! Are you nuts?"

He stopped struggling. I discerned the usual telltale signs of anger in his red face and throbbing temporal veins, but I saw something else too. I saw terror.

"If he doesn't off himself," Peth said, "I swear I'll come back and kill him myself. But we have to go now."

The floor rumbled underneath our feet. "It's starting." Daggon opened his front door. "You should hurry."

"Take me home!" I sprinted to the UCV. "I have to get Grandpa." He'd be afraid and bewildered with strangers knocking on his door. He might react violently and get himself hurt. Or wouldn't it be my luck that this one time he'd remember precisely where I was and who I was with and calmly give my would-be abductors the address. "Step on it, Peth!"

"Hang on." Peth opened the center console.

"What're you doing?"

He pulled out a square microphone connected to a rubber coil cable. "Calling my dad on the M.R.S. to find out what that rumble was. Probably a fracking earthquake or something."

"All the networks are down."

"This is shortwave mobile radio. It's not on the network." He pressed the side button on his transmitter and spoke, "Calling Guard Sergeant Harut, please respond." Static. "Sergeant Harut, come in." Nothing. "Soon as we're in better range, I'll retry."

Agares sat in the passenger seat, shaking his head. "Amitiel, you can't go home if what Daggon says is true about his uncle."

"He's full of it, playing a messed-up game and using Poyel like a pawn." Peth was in the denial stage.

"This isn't chess," I said. "He's a domestic terrorist, and somebody molded him into one."

"Isham told us Drumpf was up to something."

"Your cousin thinks he's hot snot since he made detective. It doesn't make him right."

"Stop bickering and park at the Wormwoods' house," I said. "There's a For Sale sign in the yard." The Wormwoods' unoccupied single-story perched on a hill overlooking my residence and had been on the market for months. Tall weeds and shrubbery had overtaken the quarter-acre property making it ideal camouflage for us to surveil my place. Peth drove beneath the covered carport.

His radio squelched. "Cadet Harut, this is the Guard Sergeant. Do you copy?"

Peth scrabbled for the microphone. "Yes.

Communications are down, but I hear you. Over."

"I need you to meet at the southern entrance for a high-low five, asap. Over."

"Copy that. Cadet Harut, out." He packed the microphone into its console.

"What does that mean?" I asked. "Is that sentry code for something?"

"It's a code, but just ours. When we were kids, Dad would tell us to meet him at the door for a farewell high five, and we'd slap palms as we left for school. If one of us stayed home sick, the other would give a high five and a low five in the other's place, like a get-well gesture."

"What does he mean now?" Agares unbuckled his lap belt.

"Not sure, but you, Amitiel, and her grandpa should pack a bag and come with me, at least until this chaos is sorted."

We egressed the vehicle and eased over to the Wormwoods' hedge line. An unfamiliar automobile was parked haphazardly in my driveway. One front wheel was on the concrete, one was in my lawn, and the other two were on the road.

"Whose car is that?" Agares asked.

"I don't know, but the dummy can't drive."

Two adult males stood in silhouette at my front entryway. One held papers. The other rang the buzzer. Josa commenced barking from inside.

"They could be peddlers selling some bullcrap appliance," Peth said. "Or maybe campaign aides soliciting for votes."

The porch light flicked on and irradiated the strangers.

"They're armed. Look at their waistbands," Agares said. "You know a lot of gunslingers who moonlight as solicitors, or are you gonna believe Isham now?"

"Zip it." I could barely hear above the heartbeats in my eardrums.

Grandpa opened the door but without unlatching the security chain or the swing bar. He spoke through less than a two-inch space. Voices were raised. "I don't know anyone by that name, and it's none of your damn business where she is!"

Whew. He was having a good night. Well, until these two gun-toting pew-jumpers interrupted it.

One stranger pulled a semiautomatic pistol from his belt and aimed his barrel at my grandfather.

My drumming heart skipped a beat. I budged to cry out a warning.

Agares grabbed me and plopped his hand over my mouth. "No, they're after you!"

"I'm gonna get my sidearm." Peth ran to his UCV.

He'd spend precious seconds typing in a fifteen-gazillion digit code, and I couldn't stand by and watch them shoot my grandpa. I wriggled in Agares' iron clinch as the stranger cocked the hammer on his gun.

"Stop!" His partner clutched his forearm. The pistol fired twice.

Grandpa slammed the door. One bullet appeared to ricochet off the metal plate surrounding the doorknob and pierced the attempted murderer in his midsection. He yelped and fell into the bushes. "I'm hit! I'm hit! He shot me!"

"Sonofabitch! You shot yourself, dumbass." His partner helped the injured shooter to their car. The driver peeled out, tires squealing around the corner.

"I'm sorry." Agares released me. "I had to stop you."

"If my grandpa's dead, I'll never forgive you!" I bewailed all those instances I doubted his conspiracy theories and pooh-poohed his ideas I thought stemmed from confused paranoia. Reality had just taken a dump all over me, and the truth stank. I sprinted down the hill.

Agares followed. "You wouldn't be alive to hate me if I hadn't stopped you!"

I bounded across the yard and up to my front door bawling, "Papa!" I turned the unlocked knob. The security chain and swing bar were still latched. "Papa, it's me, Amitiel," I said through the small slit. I could hear Josa whining and her nails tapping around the linoleum. "Open the door."

"I can't."

"Yes, you can. It's safe now. They're gone."

"I can't...stand up. The sumbitch...shot me!"

"No, no, no, no, no." It couldn't be true. In the dim lighting, I spied his bare feet and shins on the floor. I had to get inside. "I'm coming in." I rammed my shoulder against the door. The inner wooden frame bestowed one stingy little crack.

"Wait." Agares grabbed me. "Mr. Aur'ell, it's Agares. I need you to roll away from the door so I can kick it in. Can you do that?"

"I...can try. Josa, pull." We heard shuffling and dragging.

Peth jogged up, holding his pistol. "What's going on?"

"We have to bust open the door. My grandpa's been shot."

"I gotta first aid kit. Be right back." He jogged

toward his UCV atop the hill.

"O-kay," Grandpa huffed. "Kick...it."

Agares drew back his leg, swung it forward, and kicked near the doorknob with all his strength. The frame splintered. The screws holding the latches tore free and allowed us entry.

I stepped inside. My shoe skidded and squeaked to a halt. I flipped on the overhead light. It looked as though maroon paint had spilled over the ingress. Paw prints were stamped everywhere as Josa had padded around in confusion and angst. The gunshots and the door bursting open had frightened her. She cowered behind Grandpa's puffy chair.

"Papa, I'm here!" Crimson smears on the floor marked a trail to him, lying supine, his palms on his midriff. His T-shirt and boxer shorts were soaked in blood from wallowing across the floor. I couldn't immediately tell where he was shot. I looked at Agares. "Bath towels, quick!"

"Yup!" He dashed to the hall bathroom.

Josa scurried toward me, whimpering.

I patted her quivering head. "It's all right. I'm here now." I knelt at my grandfather's side. The carpet reacted like a wet sponge. I took Grandpa's right hand. "You're going to be fine. I'm sorry I wasn't here sooner."

"Better...you weren't," he labored to speak. "They said...they were...CPS."

"Child Protection Service workers who carry guns? They're liars!"

"I know. But...they...are after...you. Said...they had...court orders."

"Doesn't matter." I stroked his strained face. Josa

gave him affectionate licks. "We're leaving this realm." Agares returned with towels. He placed one beneath Grandpa's head and began wiping his skin to find a wound. I lifted his soggy shirt, seeing what appeared to be two navels, and pressed a towel over both to stymie the bleeding. One had to be a bullet hole. "Soon as we patch you up."

"You...must...go now." He endeavored to extract his knobby digits from my grasp and push me away.

I gripped him so firmly I thought I might straighten all five of them. "Not without you."

"God almighty!" Peth stepped around the blood pools. He passed Agares the first aid kit and crouched on the other side of my grandfather to inspect his anatomy. He located an entry wound on his abdomen and an exit wound on his lower back. He packed the holes with gauze and wrapped a bandage around his midsection. "Sir, can you wiggle your toes for me?"

"Who...are you?"

He knew Peth from our attending his parents' summer barbeques. Fate was an evil witch, robbing him *and me* of his cognizance in what may be his last moments. "He's my friend, Pop. He's trying to help. Can you wiggle your toes?"

"I'm wiggling...them." His toes weren't moving.

"He'll need major surgery," Peth said. "The bullet nicked his spinal column."

"Okay." I thrust my palms under his torso. "Let's put him into the UCV and get him to a hospital."

"I should drive it down here first." Peth swiped his bloody hands with a sanitized wet wipe. "And we need a board or something to stabilize his spine."

"There's a removable shelf in the hall closet that

might work."

"Let's get it," Agares said, "then we can carefully scoop him up."

"No!" Grandpa swatted at us. "Even if…doctors…could save…me, I won't live…the rest…of my life…paralyzed."

"Please, Papa." Searing tears welled in my eyes, "I'm begging you. You can't give up."

"I'm not. I'm saving…you."

"What? No!" I couldn't argue with someone out of his mind. "You'll die if we leave you. I'm getting the shelf."

"Listen." He clenched my wrist. "Jinn…was killed. Please…you don't…have time."

"He's right," Agares agreed. "Daggon warned us they were coming. He's a snake, but this time he told the truth. Drumpf's thugs will come back looking for you."

They outnumbered me two to one. Maybe Peth would convince them Grandpa could be saved, and he'd let us take him to the hospital. "Peth?" I scoured his visage for any sign of sympathetic accordance with me.

"We're not safe, Am. If we're with you when they come and we don't give you up, we're all dead."

My grandfather diverted his clouded gaze toward Agares. "Make her…pack a bag…and go."

He looked at me with his reply. "She makes her own decisions. We can board up the windows, fortify the house. I'm prepared to stay and die with both of you."

"Reverse psychology? Really? My choosing to stay kills you too?" He knew I wouldn't let him basically commit suicide.

"I'm not staying. I'm not prepared to die." Peth rinsed his hands in the kitchen sink. "I've got to go meet my dad. You've got however much time it takes me to get up the hill, get my truck, and drive by here."

"Go now," Grandpa said. "Take my...hunting rifle. It's under...my bed...with a box...of shells."

Agares ran to fetch the items.

"Amitiel...I love...you." He pushed me to go. "Mind me...please."

Everything suddenly felt numbingly cold—the air surrounding me, the blood I was kneeling in, my grandfather's hand. I had to leave, or the raw cold would consume me too. "I love you, Papa."

I spent chaotic seconds packing essentials into my backpack and saying farewell to my room. A pretty baby doll Grandpa gifted me when I was six sat proudly on a shelf. It was a token of my joyful childhood and of the life I was leaving behind. An overwhelming emptiness enveloped me. I seized the doll, held her to my chest, and wept until her Nylon hair was saturated by my teardrops.

"You ready?" Agares had my grandfather's long gun on his back, the strap slung diagonal across his chest, and the handle of a sack stocked with nonperishable food coiled around his wrist.

I wiped away the tears. "Okay, okay." I snatched the comforter off my bed on my way out. I draped it over Grandpa, told him I loved him and kissed him goodbye. Josa lay by his head. "Take care of him." I petted her.

Peth honked and revved his engine in my driveway. I couldn't leave. My feet were cemented into the floor. The numbing cold had frozen me in place.

"Go. I've…prepared…you." Grandpa's lids closed. His breaths grew shallow. Josa whined and licked his cheek.

"Come on. Let's get out of here." Agares dragged me outside and loaded us into the UCV's second-row seating.

Peth reversed into the road. He rolled forward and then hesitated. Josa had run out barking in front of us. "Move, dog!" He tried to drive around her without hitting oncoming cars and those parked on either side of the lane.

"No, pick her up!"

"I'm not taking a mut." He eased off the brake pedal.

"Stop! She trained with canine handlers. She's smart."

"Shouldn't we leave her with your grandfather?" Agares asked.

"She wouldn't have left if he was alive. She's all I have." I shook Peth's shoulder. "Let her in!"

"Fine! Gods be damned, hit the rear hatch button."

I pushed the green disc and the hatch lifted. "Come on, Josa. Jump!"

She hopped into the moving UCV, licked my chin, then lay down. I hit the button to close the hatch. We drove toward the wall's south entrance to meet Mr. Harut. We saw similar scenes of male duos knocking on doors and flashing paperwork stating they had the legal authority to take a young female from her home.

"We'll be fine in this." Peth thumped the UCV's ceiling. "It's bulletproof and can plow through a blockade of regular cars, not that I'm anticipating anyone stupid enough to test it." He clicked on the local radio stations. "Let's see if there's a broadcast."

It auto-scanned for the strongest frequency. "...Hostile takeover...assassinated Mayor Jinn...citywide lockdown..." The scanner leapfrogged through signals. "...Mayhem in the streets...martial law...Hey, you can't be in here!" Static.

"This can't be happening." Peering outside, I saw a falling star sear across the obsidian sky. I quickly made a wish. It was silly, but it was a fun thing my mom and I used to do. I wished she was alive and well and with me. A second star fell through the atmosphere, trailed by a third. An incandescent meteor shower lit up the night. Or, dependent upon your degree of intellect, the deities were irate.

Dense smoke shrouds and the scent of gunpowder permeated the muggy night air. Peth closed all the intake vents. "We don't want to inhale whatever they're spraying." He pressed the recirculate button.

Thunderous flashes boomed and flickered as though fireworks erupted in the distance and illuminated the ether. Baffled citizens gawped at the sky. Some drivers pulled over their vehicles, unsure where to go, while others whizzed by them.

An alarm blared three times. Then a faraway speaker on a megaphone commanded, "Curfew is in effect. Return to your homes. Shelter in place. The lockdown is mandated by martial law."

Drumpf had started his coup. Brutal, bloody protests would follow. I unhooked a pair of binoculars and looked through the lenses. Raging marchers picketed city hall and flung homemade bottle bombs against the pillars—now the unflinching stone monuments of oppression.

"Can you see anything?" Agares asked.

"An armed militia, wearing riot gear and masks, smothering protestors with pepper spray and tear gas." The victims scattered, screaming and crying. Machine guns fired indiscriminately. "Someone is shooting." Citizens ran for cover. They hunkered behind parked cars and garbage receptacles. Others fled to the overgrown perimeter wall and used the thick vines as ropes to climb the barricade. Soldiers carrying flamethrowers appeared. My already racing heartbeat pounded a drumroll on my temples. "Peth, we need to move faster!"

"I don't want to draw attention to us."

Agares told him to halt. "You two go ahead. Let me out. I'm staying to fight."

"Beg pardon?" Peth asked. "You can't. That's suicide!"

He held my grandpa's gun. "I can't leave my home like this. My parents…"

"Are assholes, bro! We'll come back when it's safer."

"I have to do something. Pull over!"

"Do you have a death wish?" I climbed into the middle row seating. "We're not stopping!" How could he drag me from my dying grandfather only to now refuse to leave himself? "This whole place is corrupt. Your home is with us wherever we end up." I clasped his hand. "It's with me. I love you."

He kissed my forehead. "I love you too."

"You two done arguing?" Peth glanced backward at us.

"Stop!" I screamed.

He stomped on the breaks. "Make up your minds!"

"You almost hit her!" Daevah Yanek had run in front of us. The wind whipped around her fawn tendrils. She looked like a deer trapped in our headlights.

Peth lowered the UCV beams and partially rolled down his window. "Daevah, get out of the way and go home!"

She stood paralyzed, her eyeballs glazed in an addled stupor. Her beaded bag overflowed to the drawstring top.

I scrambled to the backseat to press the hatch lift. Josa bit my shirt and tugged me as if cautioning me not to go. I patted her head. "It's ok. Stay down."

"Agares, if a Drumpfian runs up on our ass end, you shoot at 'em," Peth instructed.

I leaned around the rear of the vehicle and waved. "Daevah, it's Amitiel! You have to get off the roads!"

"Amitiel!" She sprinted toward my voice and hugged me. "Why's this happening?"

"It's a revolt. Come on, get in." I helped her inside. "Peth go!" I closed the hatch. The UCV hiccupped out of neutral and into first gear. Daeva clutched her knees to her chest.

"Are you hurt?" Agares asked.

"They shot my parents!"

I looped my arms around her. "They got my grandpa too." Josa gave my friend comforting hello licks. "Where's your little sister?"

"My grandma took her to East Realm to see the doctor." She swallowed, "Um, to uh, fix the scar from her cleft palate surgery." She surveyed the interior and its occupants. "What're we gonna do?"

"We're getting out of here. Stay low." I wrapped a blanket around her before returning to the middle seat.

Peth drove us to the southern ingress gate. "Guard Sergeant," he talked into his radio as he peered up at the tower. "Cadut Harut awaiting orders."

Mr. Harut moved to the window and replied in sign language with about three or four symbols.

"What's he saying?" I recognized the sign for the number three.

"T minus three minutes. He's opening the pylon."

"Thank the gods." Daevah huddled with Josa beneath the blanket.

As we waited for the pylon to open, a squad of Drumpf's marching militia broke from their platoon battling the civilian protestors and bore down on our UCV. Peth briefly released his death grip from the steering wheel to motion at his father high above in the guard tower. "Come on, come on."

Mr. Haruth signaled from his booth and hastily typed onto a screen. He was our only way through the wall. We couldn't burst through the steel-barred structure, even in a bulletproof vehicle. Excruciating seconds ticked by. My adrenaline surged. The rearview mirror captured the oncoming flamethrowers. They were glowing blobs hovering in the distance, moving closer and closer.

I swore I could smell the gasoline tanks. "Peth, get us out of here!"

"Just wait!"

Agares grasped my forearm with one hand and the door lever with his other as though he prepared to make a run for it and drag me along. "Is he going to let us out?"

"He will! Hold on!"

"We can't wait anymore!"

"Give it a second!"

Josa barked. "Shhh." Daevah tried to calm her. "They're getting closer."

"Drive us out of here or open the door," Agares said. "We're sitting ducks about to get torched!"

We'd be baked alive inside the metal framework. I debated how long I could stand it before shooting myself to end the pain.

"Reach under your seat and get the blaster." Peth typed in a code, and a circular portion of the ceiling opened. "I showed you how to use a similar one at the paintball range, except this one has a grenade launcher attached."

"Okay." He handed me Grandpa's gun and retrieved a magazine-fed, thick-barreled rifle from its hidden spot. He inspected the weapon before rising up to peek from the turret. We'd spent a lot of weekends playing war games with paintball guns, but the weapon he clutched wasn't firing balls of brightly colored liquid. It was designed to kill.

"Squeeze off a round at any puckered asshole you see." He pulled two pistols from below his seat and placed one on my lap. "You too. If anyone breaches that side, press the small green button twice to open the window, then aim and fire." He clicked off his safety and chambered a bullet.

I copied him, although my hands were shakier. I steeled myself to the fact that either I was going to shoot someone or burn to death with my friends.

"They're a few yards away." Agares maneuvered the slide mechanism and loaded a grenade. "Brace yourselves!"

I tucked my head and glued one palm to the inside

of the door. He fired. The explosion shuddered the UCV and my eardrums. The resulting ring, an unending crash of cymbals, perforated through my tympanic membrane. The pain was almost audible. I could no longer hear the mob chanting, "Hail, Drumpf!"

Peth shook me and mouthed a phrase I couldn't decipher. He pointed to the wall. A vertical slit materialized between the thirty-foot concrete structure. The gate was slowly opening. Relief washed over me. Once enough space formed, we could escape.

I tapped Agares on the leg to alert him. "Yeah!" he cheered.

Another few inches, and we'd be free. Peth gave his father a thumbs up. A second creature irrupted into the tower, and the gate stopped.

"What's happening?" I shouted.

Mr. Harut hit the intruder with a chair, and the gate initiated opening again. As soon as we could fit, we scraped through. The two continued fighting in the tower and the wall sealed behind us, bisecting the path of our pursuers.

"Isn't your dad coming with us?"

Mr. Harut, now the only visible figure in the booth, pasted one bloody palm against the window to steady himself as he wrote, *G-O.* Go.

"No. He isn't." A teardrop rolled down Peth's cheek.

I could hear Daevah sobbing. We were all some variant of orphan now.

Agares, with his blaster barrel still sizzling, descended from the turret to sit beside me. My head rested on his shoulder as we navigated into the Barren. The West Realm, an orange metastasizing billow, receded from view.

Peth sniveled, coughed, and wiped his runny nose on his sleeve. He was half crying and half nursing his cold. I hoped it wasn't contagious, and I fretted it might evolve into pneumonia or a pathogen requiring antibiotics. Then a new question gnawed at me. Was there a grain of truth in what Mr. Moroni said about our immune systems turning against us?

A word about the author...

Britt Field began a love affair with writing as soon as she could hold a crayon. Throughout adolescence, she enjoyed penning poems and short stories and escaping into books from every genre. She earned an academic scholarship and graduated from the University of Louisiana at Monroe with a Bachelor of Arts degree in Mass Communications and a minor in criminal justice. After college, she joined the U.S. Army where she met her husband. They now live with their young son and daughter in the Midwest.

Thank you for purchasing
this publication of The Wild Rose Press, Inc.

For questions or more information
contact us at
info@thewildrosepress.com.

The Wild Rose Press, Inc.
www.thewildrosepress.com